HER FINAL HOUR

A DETECTIVE MARK TURPIN MURDER MYSTERY

RACHEL AMPHLETT

SAXON
PUBLISHING

CHAPTER ONE

Winter wrapped its grip around the Oxfordshire countryside, feathering the bare hedgerows of the Berkshire Downs with a dusting of frost, determined to maintain its hold on the hills and valley below.

Will Brennan flexed his hands, and let the leather reins give a little in his grip.

A cold mist blanketed the landscape, creating ghost-like silhouettes of the horse chestnut trees that bordered the training yard, and obscuring the large Georgian farmhouse beyond.

He was losing circulation in the tips of his fingers, despite the weather forecaster on the radio enthusing about the mild start to winter, and despite the thin wool gloves he wore. At least his helmet, covered with a bright green and blue silk cap, stopped some of his body temperature escaping.

Grey light hinted at the approaching sunrise before a cold breeze sent a discarded plastic feed bag tumbling across the concrete. It snagged on the tendrils of an ivy bush that climbed up the side of one of the brick-built stable blocks, fluttering as if to free itself.

The other stable lads called out to each other, swearing as they prepared the horses, their voices muffled by the thick air.

Brennan murmured a greeting to one of them as he passed, a new kid whose name he couldn't remember, who had the soft facial features of someone who hadn't yet spent a winter on the Downs, exposed to all its elements. Another year or so and he'd be as ruddy as the rest of them.

Vapour escaped Brennan's lips, mixing in the air with the heat wafting from the horse's nostrils, the beast snorting and shaking its head as he led it across ice-covered puddles.

Coffee would have to wait until he returned, and after the horses had been tended to.

At a call from the back of the string, he was given a leg up into the saddle and the horses set off at a brisk pace.

Weak sunlight began to crest the horizon as the string of racing horses entered the lane from the yard, their hooves clattering across the pitted surface while their riders shivered and grumbled.

Not too loudly, though.

After all, MacKenzie Adams was known for choosing a lucky few to ride his horses in races even if, to begin with, those races were at the smaller courses around the United Kingdom.

For many it had been the start of an illustrious career, and Brennan was hungry for the same.

His stomach rumbled loudly, and he cursed the turn of thought. Keeping the weight off was a constant struggle, especially when his girlfriend's mother insisted on feeding him twice as much as everyone else whenever he was there.

He peered between the horse's ears, a tight grip on the reins, listening.

At this time of the morning it was unusual to see any traffic, but the lane was narrow with a twisting curve that had spewed out its share of speeding motorcyclists over the summer, touring the Oxfordshire countryside at high speed with little regard for their safety, or that of a horse and its rider.

Half a mile up the hill, they turned onto the gallops through a gap in the bramble hedgerow, and Brennan's heart rate edged up a notch in anticipation.

From here the view swept over an undulating field, fallow and ready for planting, abandoned hay bales spiky with thick frost. In the distance, clumps of ancient oak and birch trees huddled close within shaded copses.

The hillside swept down through the valley and past the space where the old power station cooling towers had once pierced the horizon, then onwards through the Vale to Oxford.

Years ago, before his time, these had truly been the Berkshire Downs. A flourish of ink, a handshake at local government level, and the boundary had slipped into Oxfordshire.

And on April Fool's Day, according to his grandfather.

A mud and stone track led across the field to the gallops, and when the horse paused at the bottom of the slope, Brennan loosened the reins before giving him a swift kick that sent the animal trotting towards the open gates.

The lush green grass on either side of the gallops sparkled with frost that reached out to the dirt- and sawdust-layered track, clumps of churned-up earth shadowing a racing line created by yesterday's training session.

Brennan sniffed, resisting the urge to wipe his nose with the back of his glove. He needed both hands on the reins.

The beast beneath him tended to lose his riders if given half the opportunity, and Brennan had no intention of being the horse's latest victim. He knew that the rest of the stable lads were running a sweepstake to see how long it would take.

He scowled. They may have been eager to make some money from his misfortune, but he was keener to make MacKenzie Adams sit up and take notice of him.

He glanced over his shoulder to where Adams stood next to a dark-green four-by-four vehicle at the side of the track, binoculars in his right hand, thermos coffee cup in the other, bundled up in a padded jacket and scarf against the elements.

He raised his thumb, and Adams lifted the cup in response.

Brennan turned his attention back to the course and kicked the horse, relishing the sudden power as he leapt into action.

He squinted to see through the swirling mist that cloaked the oval course, and leaned forward as the horse pushed into the first corner, recalling McKenzie's instructions to him before they had set out from the yard.

'He's racing at Newbury on Saturday, so give him a gentle workout. The last thing we want is an injury.'

The problem was, Empire of the Sun – or Onyx, as he was known in the stables – didn't understand the concept of a gentle workout.

It was why MacKenzie had sent him out ahead of the rest of the string, given it was common knowledge that any hint of another horse in front of him would send Onyx into race mode. The trainer always joked that the animal possessed two speeds – fast, and faster.

The horse's withers tensed as his shoulder muscles

trembled, and Brennan felt the power beneath the sleek black coat. The temptation teased him as they entered the first straight. It would be so easy to loosen the reins further and let the horse fly over the soft earth.

Almost as if Onyx could read his mind, the horse surged forward, straining at the bit between his teeth.

Common sense prevailed, and, with some reluctance, Brennan kept a tight grip and eased the animal back to a slower pace as they approached the next sweeping corner.

Onyx tensed, and Brennan dug his heels into the stirrups at the sudden deceleration in speed, confused.

He stood and peered between the horse's ears, and then saw what was spooking the animal.

To the left of the track, under the white metal railing that the horses followed along the gallops, was a discarded bundle of rags.

'It's nothing, you idiot. Get on with it.'

He dug his heels in and urged the horse forward.

Onyx reared up and twisted to the right without slowing down, without giving Brennan a chance to correct his position or slow his trajectory as he was catapulted into the air, the reins snapping from his grip.

He had a swirling view of green grass and grey sky tumbling over one another, and then hit the ground.

Seconds later, winded, Brennan rolled over and lay on the dirt, staring at the swirling mist. He wiggled his toes and fingers, slowly working his way along his limbs until he was sure no bones were broken, and then eased into a sitting position.

Onyx stood on the far side of the track, peering down his nose at him.

'Dickhead.' Brennan brushed off his jodhpurs and stomped across to the horse, snatching up the reins before it decided to take off without him.

The mist blanketed his position from the start of the training oval and, if he could remount, no-one would know and he'd still have a chance of a race at the weekend.

Except the horse refused to cooperate.

Onyx whinnied, then sidestepped, turning his rear to the course.

'Bloody hell. Move, will you?'

Brennan tugged at the reins, and then glanced over his shoulder.

Under the soles of his boots, the ground began to tremble a moment before the thunder of hooves reached him.

'Come on. Please.'

He used all his weight to turn the horse, pushing against his flanks in an attempt to get Onyx to do as he was told for once, and then collapsed against him, sweat pooling under his arms.

'Right now, I hate you.'

He sighed, and then raised his gaze to the horse's

head, expecting a knowing sideways look from the animal.

Instead, Onyx was staring at the bundle of rags under the railing on the inner side of the course, his ears flat, his hooves planted firmly on the turf, the whites of his eyes glaring in the winter light.

Brennan kept hold of the reins and moved in front of the horse. He opened his mouth to urge him forward, and then stopped as he drew closer to the discarded clothing and realised why the horse was so scared.

Blood had congealed in her hair, the dull red glistening as a beetle wandered across her forehead.

Her hands had been tied behind her, her pink lace knickers twisted around her left ankle, and her blank stare watched the clouds, accusation in the milky film that blurred her eyes.

Brennan let the reins fall, the horse forgotten, and dropped to his knees.

A moment later, he vomited over the lush turf.

CHAPTER TWO

Detective Sergeant Mark Turpin forced the car door shut
and cursed under his breath as a biting wind whipped at
the hem of his waterproof coat.

He squinted against the weak sunlight that bathed
the landscape with a bleached grey while Detective
Constable Jan West eased herself from the passenger
door and staggered backwards, surprise on her face.

'Bloody hell, Sarge.' She gathered her black leather
handbag from the back seat and slung it over one
shoulder, buttoned up her padded jacket, and then fell
into step beside him. 'I'd have thought the horses
would've been running backwards in this wind.'

'At least it's cleared the air so we can see what
we're doing.'

He ran his gaze over the mist that had receded from

the Downs and now clung to the streams that criss-crossed the countryside, and shivered.

Eight jockeys with their enormous horses milled about at the gate Mark had driven through, the animals stomping hooves at the ground, impatient. The sweet aroma of fresh horse dung wafted on the air, reminding him of holidays in the countryside with his daughters when they were younger.

Turning his attention to the plateau where they'd parked, he spotted an ambulance close to one of the patrol cars that had been manoeuvred onto the gallops, both vehicles blocking access to the course, the emergency vehicles' bright livery a stark contrast to the bleak countryside.

Blue and white striped tape had been stretched behind the vehicles, reiterating the restricted access now imposed.

In front of the cordon two more patrol cars had been manoeuvred off the track and onto the verge, the occupants speaking to each of the horse riders in turn, notebooks out and brows furrowed as witness statements were taken.

Mark strode across the soft turf towards the nearest police constable, a familiar face from the local station.

'Newton.'

'Morning, Sarge.'

'Everyone else here?'

PC John Newton blew on his hands, and then

pointed across the gallops to where several vehicles had been corralled in one corner.

Mark recognised the crime scene investigators' vehicles. Three white-suited figures milled about near the railing in the opposite corner, heads bowed. Next to their van, a grey panel van had been parked facing the cordon, its dark colouring almost fading into the landscape. The mortuary team wouldn't be allowed to leave until the CSIs were satisfied the victim's body could be removed. He shook his head at the forced indignity.

'What can you tell us?'

'The first jockey in the training string found her,' said Newton. 'They all got up here at seven o'clock, just as it was getting light. That's the trainer over there, MacKenzie Adams.'

'Is that his vehicle?'

'Yes. The victim is Jessica Marley, nineteen years old. Lives in Harton Wick and attends the agricultural college nearby. Has a part-time job at the Farriers Arms in the village.'

Mark frowned. 'You know who she is already?'

'One of the other lads told us her name. The one who found her wasn't coherent when we tried to speak with him. Poor bugger's in shock.'

'I'll bet he is.' Mark peered across to the CSI team. 'How long have they been here?'

'About an hour. The pathologist is over there with

them. She declared the victim deceased at 8.05 and then stayed. Said she wants to learn as much as possible here before doing the post mortem.'

The police constable tugged at his vest pocket and pulled out a notebook. 'Just as well one of the jockeys identified her. We found nothing on her – no handbag, no mobile phone, no purse. We've been helping the CSIs to check the surrounding hedgerows but have come up empty so far. We've got four people on the far side of the gallops over there continuing the search.'

'Good. Where's the lad who found her?'

Newton jerked his thumb over his shoulder. 'William Brennan. He's in the back of the ambulance. He was hoping to race at Newbury this weekend. Can't see how he's going to manage it now.'

'What did the other lad say – the one who recognised her – when you interviewed him?'

'Paul Hitchens. He said he last saw Jessica at the Farriers at eight o'clock last night. He said it was unusual for him to stay that late the night before a training ride but William was catching up with friends he hadn't seen for a while and they lost track of time. Jessica and another girl, Cheryl, were working on the bar with the owner, Noah Collins, so she wasn't due to leave until they'd cleared up after closing.'

'Have the parents been notified?'

Newton's mouth twisted. 'Yes, about half an hour

ago. There's a patrol car there now, and a Family Liaison Officer has been arranged.'

'All right, thanks. Jan – let's go and have a look, shall we?'

'Excuse me?'

He turned to see the horse trainer striding towards him, his expression determined.

'Yes?'

'MacKenzie Adams. You are?'

'Detective Sergeant Mark Turpin.'

'I need to get these horses back to the yard,' said Adams. 'They have to be fed, and standing around like this is doing them no good at all, especially the one that was spooked by the girl's body.'

Mark looked towards the horse to which Adams gestured, a large black beast whose ears twitched back and forth and who seemed more interested in the goings on around it than nervous.

He turned back to Adams and narrowed his eyes at him. 'You can move your horses once my team have finished taking statements from the riders, not before. We're dealing with the death of a young woman, and that takes precedence over the horses. They can eat the grass, can't they?'

'Detective, these horses were supposed to run three furlongs this morning. Four of them have races at the weekend, and I have owners to report to. When will the gallops be reopened?'

'When I say so.' He tapped West on the arm. 'Let's go and hear what Gillian has to say.'

He stomped ahead and tried to ignore the biting wind that assaulted his ears, wishing he had a hat to ward off the chill. He settled for shoving his hands in his coat pockets.

'What the hell is a furlong, Jan?'

'About a third of a mile.'

'Got it. Keen on horse racing, are you?'

'Can't stand it, but my grandfather used to watch the racing on television on Saturday afternoons and have a bit of a flutter, so I suppose I picked up the jargon.'

They reached the taped-off cordon and scrawled their names across a page clamped to a clipboard guarded by a uniformed constable, and then, once they'd donned protective bootees to cover their own footwear, Mark led the way towards the vehicles parked at the far end of the course.

He glanced over at her as she shivered, smiling at the calf-length boots she wore and envious of the thick woollen scarf she'd tucked into her collar.

His own leather boots sank into the soft layers of dirt comprising the exercise route for the horses, the plastic coverings making progress slippery and every step kicking up a thin layer of mud that stuck to the hems of his trousers.

'Bet you're glad you moved out of the boat before the winter now,' said West, as she pushed her hair from her face. 'It would have been bloody freezing in this weather.'

'It was too small, anyway. At least renting a house I could get the rest of my stuff out of storage.'

His estranged wife had been more amenable than he thought he'd deserved, even storing the last of his belongings in the single garage at the house he'd once shared with her while he organised the move, but a sense of melancholy seized him at the finality of renting his own place.

They passed the ambulance, its back doors open and the two crew members speaking with another police constable.

Mark noticed the lonely figure sitting on one of the stretchers, the man's shoulders hunched as he stared blankly at the floor.

'We'll try to talk to the jockey on the way back,' he said.

They fell silent, Jan easily keeping up with his pace.

As they drew closer to the far end of the gallops, he could see two figures idling next to one of the vans while several others milled about, and recognised the plain paintwork of the vehicle that would be used to convey the victim to the mortuary once the crime scene had been processed.

Approaching the end of the straight line, Mark moved closer to the rail and checked the position of the crouched figure in protective clothing at the apex of the curve ahead.

'So, the jockey must've lined up here to take the corner,' he said. 'The grass is long on the inside of the railing, so even with the extra height being on the back of the horse, he wouldn't have seen her.'

Jan paused next to him, following his line of sight. 'Why there, I wonder?'

Mark didn't reply, but began walking towards the bulkier member of the CSI team, and raised his hand.

'Got a minute, Jasper?'

'Detective.' Jasper Smith lowered his mask and scuffed his way through the grass to join them, his breath clouding in front of a short dark beard. 'We wondered when we might see you. Do you want a word with Gillian too, while she's still here?'

'If you don't mind.'

'Follow me.' The technician led them across a demarcated path that avoided a number of coloured markers set out on the ground.

As they moved past, Mark ran his gaze over the team as they worked. Their movements were meticulous, each and every suspect item bagged and recorded in the event of being required for future evidence purposes.

'Any sign of drag marks?'

'Nothing, no.' Jasper sighed. 'And no tyre marks over this side. Anything that we could've taken a sample from near the gate was obliterated by the horses and the trainer's four-by-four. You've seen the mud over there – it's a quagmire.'

The CSI technician paused a few metres from where the body lay.

Mark could make out a shock of blonde hair matted with a dark thick substance that glistened in the morning sun, the young woman's face a mottled blue, her lips parted as if in surprise or shock.

She wore a long woollen skirt, thick jumper, and leather jacket, her legs bare. Flat black shoes covered her feet, and Mark's lip curled at the pink knickers that hung down around one of her ankles.

'What about footprints?'

'Hers, obviously, and perhaps a second set. We've taken what samples we can from the area but don't hold your breath. That long grass softened the tread.'

Mark peered at the prone figure. 'Heavier than her?'

'Hard to say. If you don't mind, I'll get back to my team. We need to get as much as we can before the weather turns again,' said Jasper. 'You'll get our report by the end of the week.'

Mark nodded his thanks, then turned his attention to the Home Office pathologist, who was striding across the churned dirt and pulling the paper mask from her face as the two mortuary workers carrying a stretcher followed in her wake.

'Morning, Gillian.'

Grey eyes flashed, and then she exhaled as a weariness crossed her features. 'Before you ask, there's a blunt trauma wound to the back of the head. I'll confirm once I've had a chance to do the post mortem in the morning whether that was what killed her.'

Mark watched as the two mortuary workers carefully placed the young woman's body into a large plastic bag.

'Any sign of sexual interference, given the knickers?'

'Hard to say at this point. I'll let you know after the post mortem.'

Mark ran his gaze over the length of the gallops to the gate that led through to the field beyond, and then back to the pathetic bundle that was now being gently lifted into the back of the van.

West's voice cut through his thoughts.

'What are you thinking, Sarge?'

'No sign of any tyre treads. If she walked here, then maybe she knew her killer.'

CHAPTER THREE

Jan West hunkered into the thick scarf she'd tucked around her neck and picked her way across the grass, her gaze sweeping back and forth in an attempt to spot any rabbit holes before her foot disappeared down one.

Turpin walked behind her, talking into his mobile phone and updating Detective Inspector Ewan Kennedy with their findings to date.

Which, Jan mused, didn't amount to much at present.

She tucked a straggle of unruly hair behind one ear, hitched the strap of her handbag up her shoulder and dipped beneath the blue and white police tape cordon that a constable held up for her, thanking him as she passed.

'Jan.'

She waited for Turpin to catch up, tucking the

mobile phone into the inside pocket of his coat as he jogged across the turf.

'What's up, Sarge?'

'The guv wants us to report back to the incident room when we're done here. Uniform are out collating statements from the regulars at the pub and the family's neighbours. They'll go to the agricultural college where Jessica was studying as well. Her teachers have been informed.'

'Okay.'

Jan stalked across to the ambulance, catching the eye of the driver as they approached, who wound down his window and leaned out.

'All right if we have a word with the jockey who found her?' she said.

'Derek's got him in the back.' The driver of the ambulance jerked his thumb over his shoulder. 'Makes a change to pick up one of these lads in one piece.'

Jan rolled her eyes, then walked the length of the vehicle to the open back door to where the other paramedic was speaking with the jockey.

'Excuse me?' She held up her warrant card and introduced herself and Turpin. 'William Brennan?'

'That's me. Will.'

The jockey's complexion was stark against the navy padded jacket he wore, and he shivered as he hugged his arms around his slight body. His corn-coloured hair stuck up in clumps, his riding hat upside down on the stretcher beside him.

'We need to ask you a few questions,' said Jan.

She thanked the paramedic, who moved away with a knowing nod before climbing through to the front cab to sit with his colleague, and then turned her attention to Brennan.

'Are you all right? No injuries?'

'I'm all right. I… I can't get her face out of my mind.'

'We understand that you knew her?'

A single tear tracked down the man's face, and he nodded. 'She's – was – my girlfriend, Jessica.'

'I'm sorry to hear that, Will.' Jan sat on the stretcher next to him, and gave him a moment to collect his thoughts before proceeding with her questions. 'When did you last see her?'

'Last night. At the pub in the village.'

'What time did you leave?'

'Eight. We have to be up early to exercise the horses but I got carried away chatting.'

'Who with?'

'Just a couple of the locals. They're usually a good laugh, and I hadn't seen them for a while.'

'Where do you live?'

'Near the yard. I rent one of the houses on the estate with two other blokes who work for MacKenzie.'

'Who?'

'Paul Hitchens and Nigel White.'

'Did you contact Jessica at all after leaving the pub?'

'We texted each other at eleven.'

'Can I see your phone?'

Brennan reached into an inside pocket of his jacket and extracted a smartphone, then began to flick though the messages.

'Hang on. I'll take that.'

Jan swiped the phone from the jockey's hand, ignoring the surprised "o" his mouth formed, and scrolled through the messages until she found a string of texts from someone he'd saved into the phone as "Jess xx".

'Is this her?'

'Yes. Look, do you have to do this?'

Jan moved to the back door of the ambulance so that Turpin could read the messages over her shoulder. Once she was satisfied the exchange between Brennan and Jessica showed no signs of the woman being threatened by the jockey, she checked the recent calls list.

There were three calls between the two, all prior to the time Brennan said he'd been at the pub.

'Is that the only phone you own?'

'Yes.'

'All right. We're going to have to take this with us.' Jan pulled a plastic evidence bag from her handbag and dropped the phone into it before removing her gloves.

'What time did you get back home after you left the pub?'

'Just before eight-thirty. It's only a short drive, and Paul reckons he's a Formula One driver anyway.'

'Paul?'

'Hitchens. One of the lads that rents the house with me. That's him, over there on the grey horse.'

Jan leaned past the back door of the ambulance until she could see the group of jockeys. The only grey horse was ridden by a man wearing a bright-red cap and green rain jacket. She couldn't make out his features, but from the way he was hunched in the saddle, he was as impatient as the horse he rode to be back at the yard.

'You said you rented a house near the yard. Where?'

'We rent one of the cottages that backs onto the land behind it. MacKenzie owns them. It's cheaper than renting in the village, and better for the early starts.'

'Do you own a car?'

Brennan snorted. 'Can't afford one. Got a motorbike – only a cheap one, mind. Bought it before I went up north.'

'Did you go straight home from the pub, or did you stop anywhere on the way back?'

'We went straight back to the yard. MacKenzie gets irate if anyone gets back after midnight. Says it disturbs the horses.'

'Did you have much to drink?' said Turpin.

'Two or three pints. Maybe a chaser.'

'Seems rather a lot for a Monday night.'

Brennan's face began to form a sneer, and then he seemed to think better of it. 'Yeah, well, I've been away for a while. Last night was the first time I'd had a chance to catch up with people.'

'Where've you been?' said Jan.

'Up north.' He sat up straighter, a hint of pride entering his voice. 'I've wanted to be a jockey as long as I can remember. There were no jobs down here for me, so I applied everywhere I could. I took the first offer that came my way.'

'Whereabouts was that?'

'Near Ripon, in Yorkshire.'

'What brought you back here?'

He sagged against the side of the ambulance, crestfallen. 'Jessica. We kept in touch, you see. Tried to catch up every few weeks. It was because of her that I came back.'

'Not the racing?' said Turpin.

Brennan scowled. 'That, too. Although I'll be lucky to ever ride for MacKenzie again after today.'

'Why?' said Jan.

'All this, it'll mess with his reputation. You watch. It'll be all over the news, and then everyone at the races at the weekend will be talking about it. I'll be out of a job by Monday.'

'Seems a bit harsh.'

'Yeah, well. There you have it.' He broke off as his stomach rumbled.

Jan frowned. 'When did you last eat?'

'I dunno. Lunchtime yesterday, I guess.'

Jan sighed, reached into her handbag, and pulled out a cereal bar. 'Have this.'

'I don't feel like—'

'Eat. You'll thank me afterwards, trust me.'

She climbed down from the ambulance, and at Turpin's signal moved away from the vehicle until they were out of earshot.

'We'll need to check his movements with everyone at the pub and the other jockeys he rents with,' he said. 'What do you reckon?'

She peered over her shoulder at the jockey, who had unwrapped the snack and was nibbling at a corner of it, staring with a wistful expression at the string of horses that were now being led away from the gallops.

'There are no missed calls to Jessica, so he didn't try phoning her after she left the pub. There's nothing on the phone to suggest they'd argued, but maybe that's deliberate,' she said. 'He could've deleted anything incriminating.'

'Well, we'll get the phone to digital forensics to see what they can tell us.' Turpin shielded his eyes with his hand and looked back to where the CSIs were still working. 'He knows the area well. Could've brought her out here after ditching his friends back at the yard.'

'On a motorbike?' Jan shook her head. 'Can't see it myself. It was bloody freezing last night, and if he did, why not ride it all the way over to where her body was found? There were no tyre tread marks, remember.'

'It seems too bloody convenient that he was the first on scene to find her body, Jan.'

She had no answer to that, and glumly followed him back to the car.

CHAPTER FOUR

By the time Mark had held open the door to the incident room for Jan and followed her through the maze of desks, the place was teeming with uniformed officers and plainclothes detectives.

Two administrative support staff crossed the room between the desks, distributing tasks with ears deaf to complaints in an attempt to organise the growing number of actions required for the new murder investigation.

Mark craned his neck until he could see across the low-ceilinged room to where Detective Inspector Ewan Kennedy paced in front of a whiteboard, his shirt sleeves rolled up over his elbows and his back turned to the room.

Weaving his way across worn carpet tiles and past two junior uniformed officers who were attempting to untangle a years-old photocopier, Mark approached the DI and cleared his throat.

The lanky figure swung around at the sound, then jerked his chin in greeting. 'Just got back, did you?'

'Guv.' Mark glanced over his shoulder as Jan joined him. He held out his mobile phone. 'I've already emailed these to Tracy so she can put them on the system and print out a couple of copies to go on the board.'

As DI Ewan Kennedy flicked through the photos with a grimace, Mark ran his eyes over the content of the whiteboard, his gaze falling on a photograph of Jessica that appeared to have been taken during the summer.

A halo of light shone around her blonde hair, giving her fair features a natural radiance that was amplified by her wide smile. She wore a white vest top with blue cornflowers that accentuated her eyes, and someone out of frame had an arm draped around her shoulders.

'Poor angel,' Jan murmured next to him. 'She didn't deserve to die like that.'

Mark swallowed, battening down the thought of what he'd do to anyone who harmed either of his daughters, and tried to concentrate instead on studying the young woman's features, committing them to memory and resolving to find her killer.

'Her parents provided that this morning.'

Kennedy's words interrupted his thoughts, and he took a step back from the board.

'Did a Family Liaison Officer go over there?'

'About an hour ago.' Kennedy's pale-blue eyes peered over Jan's head and swept the room. 'All right, I think that's everyone. Let's get this briefing underway.'

Mark wandered across the room and sat next to Jan at the side of the gathering investigative team. He took a sheet of paper that DC Caroline Roberts handed to him with a nod of thanks.

Running his gaze down the list of tasks that had been entered into the HOLMES2 national enquiry database and then assigned to each member of the team, he noted he and Jan would be paired up for the duration of the investigation. He turned his attention to the front of the room as Kennedy began the briefing, and flipped to a new page of his notebook, pen poised.

'Right, ladies and gentlemen. Our victim is Jessica Marley, nineteen years old and from Harton Wick. Her parents tell me she was a busy girl – studied part-time at the local agricultural college and worked two part-time jobs, one at the Farriers Arms pub in the village and then two afternoon shifts at the local supermarket. On top of that, she recently started to help out on an ad hoc basis at MacKenzie Adams' racing stables.'

Mark raised an eyebrow at Jan.

'No-one mentioned that,' she said under her breath.

Kennedy paused while Tracy passed him the

photographs Mark had taken at the crime scene, then held each one up before pinning it to the board.

'Thanks to Mark and Jan who attended the crime scene this morning, the pathologist currently has a theory that Jessica was killed by a single blow to the head, although that will have to be confirmed after the post mortem. Any sign of a weapon, Mark?'

'No, guv,' he said. 'There were no vehicle markings near her body, and it's unlikely any footprints will be found in the long grass. The CSIs will have to confirm what prints they collect from the gallops – the dirt was churned up by the horse and its jockey, as well as the riders who were next around the corner of the course, so it's going to take them a while to sort it all out.'

'Okay. Caroline – make a note to keep on top of that report, please. As soon as it's in, get it distributed.'

'Yes, guv.'

'According to Jessica's parents, she had no enemies and only a handful of close friends. Despite working at the pub, she didn't socialise much, and was considered an introvert. Happier studying than going to nightclubs, is what her mum said.'

'Any problems at work?' said DC Alex McClellan. 'Difficult customers, that sort of thing?'

'That's what I'd like you and Caroline to find out,' said Kennedy. 'Speak to Jessica's manager at the supermarket. When you've done that, head over to the college and speak with her lecturers there as well. Mark

– I want you and Jan to go and see the parents this morning. They were too distraught to give much of a statement earlier but we need to learn more about her movements this week, and leading up to her shift at the pub last night. After that, have a chat with the landlord of the Farriers Arms. Like Alex said, find out if there were any problems with the patrons there.'

'Do you want us to re-interview MacKenzie Adams as well?' said Mark. 'Jan just pointed out to me that neither Adams nor Brennan mentioned to us that Jessica was working at the stables when we spoke to them on the gallops earlier. Bit of an omission, isn't it?'

'Agreed. If Adams gives you any trouble, let me know. He's got a reputation for being difficult at the best of times.'

Kennedy completed the briefing by working his way around the assembled officers, ensuring any new team members were introduced, and then made his way back to the whiteboard and rapped his knuckles on the surface next to the photograph of Jessica taken that summer.

'Nineteen years old, hard-working and with her whole life ahead of her,' he said. 'Let's find the bastard that did this to her.'

CHAPTER FIVE

Jan exhaled and then rang the doorbell for number six Ashton Close, going over the questions she wanted to ask Jessica's parents.

She stepped back off the doorstep, nearly colliding with Turpin who was standing with his hands in his pockets staring at the ornamental path that led back to the street, and then ran her eyes over the picture-perfect front garden.

Jessica's mother was evidently a keen gardener – a window box of primroses and crocuses clung to the front windowsill of the house, offset by colourful displays in pots placed on the tiles underneath. A large magnolia set off a lush lawn bordered by flowerbeds, the first green shoots of daffodils poking through the soil.

The whole effect was one of homeliness, comfort,

and safety.

She couldn't imagine what they were going through. If either of her boys were harmed, she reckoned that rage would drive her to find justice, tempered by a grief that would never leave her. Her jaw clenched.

A blurred figure appeared behind the frosted glass at the top of the UPVC front door, and then it swung open and PC Grant Wickes peered out.

'Come in,' he said, gesturing to a door on their left. 'Mr and Mrs Marley are through there.'

Turpin held up his hand. 'Before we go in, is there anything we need to be aware of? Updates to their statements?'

'They haven't mentioned anything in the past two hours,' said Wickes, his green eyes troubled. 'They were formally interviewed at nine o'clock after they were informed of Jessica's death – I arrived here half an hour after that. Obviously, they're both in a state of shock, but Mr Marley has already provided us with photographs of Jessica to help with the media campaign and wants to do anything he can to help us find who did this to his daughter. You'll find him very forthright.'

Jan pulled her mobile phone from her bag and turned it to silent, wondering if Jessica's father was as stoical as Wickes thought. No doubt his attempts at helping were a coping mechanism for his grief, and she was grateful the experienced Family Liaison Officer was on hand. At some point, Mr Marley would need him.

'What about the wife?' said Turpin.

'Quiet, as you'd expect in the circumstances,' said Wickes. He brushed an imaginary piece of lint from his jacket sleeve. 'Distraught by what's happened but trying to hold it together.'

'Thanks, Grant,' said Jan. 'Could you lead the way?'

She followed the FLO into the living room, quickly running her eyes over the photographs that lined a mantelpiece above a wood-burning stove. The fire within pushed out warmth into the room, an orange glow spilling out over a rug from which a small wiry dog rose to its feet and sniffed at Turpin's shoes as he introduced them to Jessica's parents.

Mr Marley pushed himself out of his armchair and held out his hand, taking Jan's in a firm grip. 'Call me Trevor. This is my wife, Wendy. Have a seat.'

Jan perched on the end of a three-seater sofa while Turpin took the other end and leaned forward, his elbows on his knees as he addressed the couple.

'We'd like to extend our condolences to you both,' he said. 'We know this is a very difficult time for you, and we will do all we can to manage our investigation to find out who did this to Jessica.'

'What can you tell us?' said Wendy, dabbing at her eyes with a ragged paper handkerchief before dropping her hands to her lap.

'We want to know everything,' said Trevor, his voice gruff. 'I want to know what that bastard did to my daughter.'

Jan opened her notebook. 'Before we do, please can you tell us about Jessica? What were her interests, hobbies, that sort of thing?'

'How's that going to help?' Trevor demanded.

'I'd like to know her as a person,' said Jan. 'Not as a victim. And, it may be that something you tell us helps to form a picture of what happened to her. It's important we learn every detail, no matter how small you think it is.'

Turpin nodded. 'It's true what Detective West says. At the moment, we understand Jessica studied part-time at the local agricultural college and worked at the Farriers Arms pub in the village two or three nights a week as well as having a job at the supermarket. How did she travel around?'

'By bus, mostly,' said Trevor. 'To college, at least. Then she'd do Tuesdays and Thursdays at the supermarket nearby and get the bus back from there.'

'Sometimes I'd pick her up on my way home if I'd been working late,' said Wendy. 'I work as a bookkeeper at a food distribution company about five miles away.'

'Did Jessica drive?' said Jan.

'A bit,' said Trevor, 'but she didn't have her own car. After she passed her test, she decided to save her money for a while. She was talking about taking a year out to travel before making any permanent plans after her course finished.'

'What was she studying?'

'Agricultural management,' said Wendy. She straightened, her expression proud. 'She wanted to work with minority groups in Asia, with a charity.'

'Did she ever report any problems at work or college?' said Turpin.

Trevor frowned. 'You mean harassment?'

'Anything, really. Did she ever raise any concerns with either of you?'

Both parents shook their heads.

'Jessica was one of the most easy-going people you'd ever meet,' said Wendy. 'She was one of life's helpers.'

'Tell me about her relationship with Will Brennan,' said Jan.

'He found her, didn't he?'

'Yes, that's right.'

'The poor lad must be inconsolable. He has no immediate family down this way, did you know that?'

'No, we didn't. Where's he from?'

'Gloucestershire, originally,' said Trevor. 'His parents live outside Cheltenham, and he's got a younger sister at secondary school. Lovely lad, he is.'

'When did Jessica start working at MacKenzie Adams' yard?' said Turpin.

A tic began under Trevor's left eye, and Jan held her breath.

'I wish she'd never got involved with him,' he said. 'She had enough to do, what with college work and two jobs. She didn't need to go and work for him as well.'

'She wanted the experience, love,' said Wendy, her tone conciliatory. 'You know that.'

Trevor scowled. 'She could've done anything with her life. She didn't need him.'

'Will didn't mention it to us when we interviewed him this morning,' said Jan.

'They had a falling out about it,' said Wendy. 'Nothing too serious, but I don't think Will wanted her there.'

'Any ideas why not?' said Turpin.

'Adams has a reputation for eyeing up the girls,' said Trevor. 'Not underage, nothing like that, but I know from gossip at the Farriers that he's broken a few hearts over the years.'

'Goodness knows what he put his poor wife through when she was alive,' said Wendy, shaking her head. 'Terrible.'

'Were you worried he and Jessica—'

'No, not at all,' said Trevor. 'We had a chat about it when he offered her the occasional Saturday morning up there, and she said most of her friends thought he was too old for them. I told her she could always come and speak to us if anything did make her uncomfortable but she never did.'

'But you were still unhappy she worked there?' said Turpin.

Trevor's eyes flashed. 'It was the gossip,' he said. 'Doesn't matter whether anything happened or not, people can be bastards. They might've seen it as harmless teasing to wonder if anything was going on between them, but it upset Jessica. She was just trying to get ahead in life.'

'And she was head over heels about Will,' said Wendy. 'She'd never cheat on him for a start.'

'How did Jessica get to work last night?' said Jan.

'I dropped her off,' said Trevor. 'It's my local so I stayed for a couple of drinks – low alcohol, mind. I left at about nine o'clock.'

'Did you see Will Brennan there?'

'Briefly. He left about an hour before me – I suppose he was up early this morning with the horses.'

'And what were Jessica's plans for getting home?'

'She said she'd walk back once she'd finished helping Noah clean up afterwards. Sometimes she stays late and gives them a hand preparing for the next day, you see.'

'I'm surprised she'd walk home this time of year,' said Turpin, 'especially given the narrow lane.'

Trevor wiped at his eyes. 'I know, but she wouldn't

listen. She always said she liked the walk – she said it gave her time to think and wind down after a shift.'

Jan dropped her notebook back into her handbag and rose from her seat. 'Thank you for speaking with us. We'll leave you now – Grant here will continue to act as your liaison, so if you have any questions about what's happening with the investigation, he'll be able to assist.'

She and Turpin shook hands with the Marleys and then made their way back to the car.

Jan tossed her handbag onto the back seat, then rested her hand on the roof and peered across at Turpin. 'So, if she didn't own a car, and she didn't borrow her mum's that night, she must've got a lift with her killer or was picked up while she was walking home.'

'Time to have a word with the landlord of the Farriers Arms, I think,' he said. 'Find out who was the last person there to see her alive.'

CHAPTER SIX

The Farriers Arms public house wore its history with tired reluctance.

At the front and leading down to the road, a wide garden laid to lawn had been covered with picnic bench tables in strategic places so that in the summer months patrons could make the most of the warmer weather. The benches lay bare now, the bright umbrellas used for sun shade stored away, and the grass beneath them overgrown.

Mark ran a practised eye over the pub's exterior, taking in the chipped burgundy paintwork surrounding the four windows that faced the cracked and potted asphalt of the car park, which had fared little better over the preceding winters than the quiet country lane that led to it.

The thatched roof of the pub had been replaced at least, although the fresh reeds reminded him of a new haircut that hadn't yet worn in. Smoke rose from two of the four red-brick chimneys, and the faint aroma of burning logs filled the air as he drew closer.

Originally a fifteenth-century forge, the building had a chimney breast that thrust its way skywards from a dark thatched roof and bore a chiselled inscription of 1922 for its conversion into a public house, the finality of a dying trade stamped upon its brick bones.

Mark followed a crazy-paved path towards the front door of the whitewashed building, the outer walls on each side of the entrance bearing the metal tools of the old farriers' trade.

He pushed against the dark oak front door, the rough surface scarred and scratched, its centuries-old iron hinges creaking theatrically under his touch as he held it open for Jan.

A silence greeted him – an eeriness he hadn't expected, which was exacerbated by the lack of music or conversation.

As he crossed the worn flagstones, he peered around at the uneven windowsills lined with bric-à-brac that had seen better days; pewter jugs with dull surfaces, and hardback books whose torn spines only hinted at titles and writers' names.

A figure stood behind the bar with his back to them,

a broad man with a receding hairline who shuffled along to the till and switched it on, oblivious to their arrival.

'Excuse me,' said Mark.

The man turned, surprise etched on his round features. 'Sorry – I was in a world of my own there. Didn't see you come in.'

Jan held up her warrant card. 'Are you the licensee?'

The man moved from behind the bar, dropped a yellow duster beside an aerosol can of furniture polish on the table next to them and wiped his hands on the back of his jeans. 'That's right. Noah Collins.'

'We wondered if we could have a word about Jessica Marley,' said Mark. 'Got a minute?'

'Of course. Come on over and sit down.' Collins jerked his thumb towards the oak bar that swept the length of the room. 'Do you want a coffee?'

'No, we're fine, thanks.'

Mark waited until Jan had settled on a bar stool then took a seat next to her and cast his eyes over the back wall.

Bottles of liquor were arranged into varieties of gin, vodka, whisky and brandy alongside displays of photographs and more knick-knacks associated with the pub's history.

Collins caught him staring, and leaned against a glass-doored refrigerator under the till. 'Are you the ones investigating Jessica's death?'

'How did you find out about it?'

'The driver who brought this morning's oil delivery. I reckon he heard it from someone up at the stables – they're not on mains gas, either.'

'How long had Jessica worked here?'

'Since she was seventeen – she started in the kitchen, and then moved to help on the bar after she had her eighteenth birthday,' said Collins. 'She used to work here full-time until she started at college. She was doing two to three days a week these days in between other commitments.'

'What was she like as an employee?' said Jan.

'Dependable. Honest. The sort of person you could leave to run the pub on her own of an evening without worrying. She was going to look after the place for us when we go on holiday in May.' A sadness washed across his face. 'I don't know what we'll do without her. The regulars will miss her, that's for sure. Always had a smile for everyone, and gave as good as she got when it came to banter.'

'Well liked, then?' said Mark.

'Absolutely.'

'Any idea why someone would attack her?'

'No, and it's been something that's been going around in my head since I heard she was found,' said Collins. 'Jess didn't make enemies. I think it helped that she only worked here part-time. When she was here, people were so intent on catching up with her, they didn't think to argue.'

'No arguments over the past few weeks?'

Collins shook his head. 'If there were, I've never been told about them.'

'Do you get much trouble here?'

'It's a quiet pub. It's mostly locals who come here, although we do get people dropping by for lunch or dinner. My wife, Sonia, is the chef.' A sense of pride filled his voice. 'We've won a few pub awards and she's been featured in a couple of local magazines.'

Mark made the appropriate approving noises, and then cast his eyes around the pub.

'Is she here at the moment?'

'She went out about half an hour ago – she wanted to get some plastic containers. She's planning to make some meals for Jessica's parents. Things they can put in the freezer to keep them going, stews and things, you know?'

'That's good of her.'

'We didn't know what else to do. I can't imagine what they're going through.'

'No children of your own?'

'No.' Collins managed a smile. 'This environment isn't exactly conducive to bringing up kids, although I know some publicans who do.'

'How many staff do you have working here?'

'Six part-time bar staff and three part-timers in the kitchen.'

'Any problems amongst them? Any personality clashes?'

'None that I know of. We can all get stressed when it's heaving with people out here, and the kitchen is smaller than our needs, so that doesn't help, but nothing that isn't put to rights by the time we're done for the day.' Collins gestured to where they sat. 'I always encourage them to have a last drink with me – coffee or a soft drink, if they prefer – once the doors are closed for the night. It helps to wind down and talk through any issues before they become a real problem.'

'And she seemed happy enough?'

'Yes, same old Jessica really.'

'What time did she leave here last night?'

Collins ran a hand over his chin. 'Doesn't seem possible we're talking about her like this. I can't believe it's only a few hours ago since she was here. I suppose it must've been about half past eleven by the time we got everything cleared away.'

'Did she leave with anyone?'

'No, she said she was going to walk. Her parents' place is only a mile up the road and it's well lit. Not much traffic that time of night. She's done it plenty times before.'

'It was cold last night.'

'She always said she warmed up by the time she was

nearly home.' His voice broke, and he gave a slight shake of his head before blinking. 'Sorry.'

'None of the regulars offered her a lift?'

'There was no-one here by the time we finished packing up.'

'Would she get a lift from any regulars who drank here in the past?'

'From time to time, yes, if she wasn't leaving with a friend.'

'We'll need a note of the names of other staff members, and the regulars if you've got them.'

'No problem.' He took Jan's notebook from her and began to write on a clean page, scrolling through his mobile phone for numbers and adding those where he could.

'Was there anyone else working in the bar or kitchen that could have driven her home?' said Mark.

Collins shook his head and passed back the notebook. 'Not last night. Martin, who helps in the kitchen, rides his push bike here – he lost his licence six months ago – and he was out of here as soon as he and Sonia had finished cleaning up. That was about nine-thirty. Cheryl lives in the opposite direction, towards Hazelthorpe. She left an hour before Jessica, because she'd started earlier.'

'Why didn't you give Jessica a lift?'

A sheepish look crossed the man's face. 'I'd been drinking, and couldn't risk it. So had Sonia. We tend to share a bottle of wine sometimes if the pub is a bit on the quiet side.'

'And what did you do after Jessica left the pub?'

'Went to bed,' said Collins. 'We had to be up at eight o'clock this morning to take delivery of half a ton of logs for the fire, and the oil tank resupply.'

'Hard work,' said Jan.

'Yes, and it makes you wonder why so many people say they'll retire and run a pub.' Collins pushed himself away from the till and wrapped his fingers around the nearest beer pump. 'Look, if there was anything else I could tell you, I would, but after Jessica left here, me and the missus were out like a light.'

Mark rose from the bar stool and slid across a business card. 'All right. We'll let you get on. Call me if you remember anything that might help us – or if you overhear anything.'

Collins tucked the card into the breast pocket of his shirt. 'I will.'

Outside, Mark waited until Jan had closed the door and then strode back towards the car. He paused at the roadside and peered up the uneven camber of the lane in the direction of the Marleys' house.

'Narrow, isn't it?' said Jan. 'No pavement, and a blind corner.'

Mark cocked his head, but no vehicles sounded in the distance, only a tractor that rumbled across a field behind the pub.

'Do you think she knew her attacker, Sarge?'

Mark shoved his hands in his pockets and glared at the white clouds that scudded across a greying sky.

'From what we're hearing about her, she was a smart young woman,' he said. 'I can't see her accepting a lift home from a stranger, can you?'

CHAPTER SEVEN

Noah Collins watched the detectives' car turn into the lane before removing the tea towel from his shoulder and rubbing at the bar where they had been sitting.

Smudges removed, he returned to the bar, picked up his pen and crossed off the day of the week on the calendar below the clock on the wall, wondering if he would ever forget the date.

The day Jessica Marley was found murdered.

He glanced over his shoulder at the sound of a car entering the car park beyond the front windows, and then a flash of blue passed by.

Noah picked the last of the clean pint glasses out of the washer under the bar, gave each a polish and then slapped the tea towel over his shoulder once more. He wandered through to the kitchen, opened the back door and smiled as his wife handed him a laden tote bag.

'Did you get them?'

'There's seven in there that I can use for Jessica's mum and dad, and I bought some extra for us as well. I thought perhaps we could experiment and offer a takeaway service over the winter.'

Dark-haired, shorter than her husband, Sonia had green eyes that flashed with excitement.

'I love the idea,' he said. 'What are you going to put on the menu?'

'The simplest meals possible. That way, if we're busy out here with orders from the bar, it won't cause too much disruption.' She followed him into the kitchen and closed the back door. 'Any more news?'

'The police were here just now.'

'Again?'

'Two detectives this time.'

Sonia blew her fringe out of her eyes and placed two more tote bags on the stainless-steel worktop. 'What did they want?'

'Not much. Just asking the same questions the two coppers asked us this morning. Do you want a coffee?'

'Sounds good. I'll get the fryers and everything switched on, and then I'll come and join you.'

Noah returned to the bar and busied himself with the state-of-the-art coffee machine he had purchased in the summer. He swallowed, his thoughts turning to the shift he and Jessica had spent together trying to learn how to work the damn thing.

She had known more about the business than most, and her absence was going to be hard to bear.

The rich aroma of ground coffee beans filled the air and he shook his head to clear the memories before filling two cups and wandering over to the table near the window.

Sonia sat in a chair that was nearest to the weak beam of sunlight that shone through, the warmth accentuated by the central heating.

'They wanted a list of who was in last night,' he said, placing one of the hot drinks in front of her.

Her eyes widened. 'Do they think one of the regulars killed her?'

'I don't know. They're not saying much. They can't, I suppose.'

Sonia brought her hand to her mouth as he sat opposite her. 'What do we do?'

'Carry on as normal, I suppose. Nothing else we can do.'

'But if they think a murderer comes in here to drink?' She dropped her hand. 'Think what that'll do to the business, after everything we've worked for.'

'There's not a lot we can do about it, love. Let's just hope it turns out to be nothing. After all, she was found up on the gallops, wasn't she? It could be someone around there that did this.'

'I suppose you're right.' She pulled her cardigan around her shoulders, her mouth twisting. 'Still—'

'They asked me if we had kids,' he said, his gaze on the milk froth bubbles that popped as the coffee cooled. 'I didn't try to explain to them that Jessica and the others are like our family. Jess more so. We've been so dependent on her. What are we going to do without her?'

Sonia looked at him over the rim of her cup, then placed it on the table. 'I don't know. I was thinking on the way back here that we're going to have to advertise for a replacement at some point but it seems so crass, doesn't it? We're going to have to wait.'

He nodded. 'We'll manage. I don't want to upset anyone.'

Peering out of the window, she wrinkled her nose at the inclement weather. 'Should we open today?'

'I think so, yes. I'd imagine people will want to talk about what's happened. It's how some people cope, isn't it? I think it'd look odd if we didn't, but—'

'Maybe stay closed at lunchtime and open this evening for a few hours. We only get passing traffic anyway this time of year during the week, but chances are the locals will come in tonight. Some of them have nowhere else to go and no family at home.'

'If you're sure?'

She reached out and placed her hand over his. 'It'll give me time to cook those meals for her parents and take them up there. I'm still trying to come to terms with all of this, to be honest. I haven't a clue what I'm going to say to them. When we started this business, I knew we'd get trouble from time to time but nothing like this.'

'I know.' Noah sighed. 'Nigel phoned from the stables.'

'Did he? Did he say how Will is?'

'Not good. In shock, I'd imagine, after finding her this morning.'

His wife bit her lip and shook her head, her eyes filled with sadness. 'I can imagine he is.'

CHAPTER EIGHT

Mark twisted the key in the deadlock and pushed open the front door, seconds before a brown mottled ball of fur barrelled down the stairs and launched itself at his ankles.

The dog's feet scraped against his trousers as he crouched to pick up the letters deposited on the door mat, before an excited snuffling accompanied by a wet lick across his nose made him step back and wipe his face.

'Enough, Hamish. I'm home now. Good boy.'

Satisfied he was telling the truth, the scruffy mongrel tore into the living room, the sound of a toy being squeaked to death reaching his ears.

Mark shrugged off his coat, tweaked the thermostat on the wall, and held his breath until he heard the boiler start up.

He ignored the faded decor that covered the walls. If it were his house he'd strip back the decade-old wallpaper and use a couple of cans of white paint to cover the plaster before hanging the prints that were currently covered in plastic wrap and stored in the garage that abutted the property on one side.

He'd finally left the rented narrowboat on the Thames two months ago but was reluctant to unpack his life. The boxes that had previously covered much of the seating in his water-based home had simply been scooped up, thrust into the back of his car and dumped in the garage together with the paintings and everything else from the storage unit he'd been using.

The neighbours kept to themselves but seemed friendly enough when he'd arrived, offering help if he needed it, and relieved to find out he was a serving police detective. Part of him relished the solitude; part of him kept an open ear for the doorbell. He'd discovered when he had first joined the police force in Wiltshire that some neighbours would rather knock on his door than dial triple nine. It could make for an exasperating time if he was trying to get his head down after a late shift.

However, the middle-aged couple next door had so far respected his privacy.

Despite his best attempts to pack up his belongings from the boat, he still couldn't fathom where he'd stored some of the day-to-day things he needed. On his first night in the house, he'd had to eat his fish and chip supper with the aid of a pocketknife. It took him another three days to locate the box with the cutlery inside.

The semi-detached house suited his purposes for now. With three bedrooms and a separate living and dining area, it provided him with a chance to spread out, especially after the cramped living conditions on the boat. For all that though, this, another roof over his head that didn't belong to him, felt like a temporary reprieve.

Flicking through the day's post, he tossed aside the marketing leaflets from a local curry house and a pizza delivery service, then frowned as he ran his fingers over a plain brown envelope with a Swindon postmark on the label.

He hadn't heard from Debbie for a few weeks. His last scheduled turn to have his daughters stay the weekend had been postponed so that they could go with their mother to the south of France for a last-minute cheap holiday. Instead, he had followed their exploits – mostly larking around by the hotel's swimming pool – on social media and tried to ignore the churning in his stomach as he did so.

Mark tore open the envelope and pulled out the contents, his brow furrowing while he ran his gaze across the logo at the top of the page and unfolded the attachments.

'What the hell?'

A sickness tore through him, and he pulled out his

mobile phone with a shaking hand while stomping towards the kitchen, switching on lights as he went. He paced the floor, his jaw clenched.

'Come on. Pick up. Pick up.'

'Mark?'

'A divorce petition? Are you kidding me?'

'They– they've sent it to you already?'

He stopped in the middle of the tiles.

Debbie sounded confused, and then—

'Shit. I'm so sorry. They were meant to hang on until the end of the week to send it. To give me time to speak to you first.'

Mark staggered, then reached out for the edge of the sink and leaned against it, heart racing.

'A divorce?'

'Hang on.'

He heard her move, then call out to Anna and Louise to make sure they were doing their homework before she returned.

'I just had to shut the door.'

'Do they know?'

'What? Of course not – I wanted to discuss it with you first.'

'It's a bit late for that, by the looks of it. I mean, why not talk to me before you spoke with the solicitors?'

'Mark, we've been living apart for over six months. You've moved on—'

'It was meant to be a temporary move, you know that.'

'If it was only temporary, why did you transfer to Thames Valley Police?'

'You know why. I was planning to move back, Debs. In time. I just needed to get away for a while after everything that happened, you know that.' He pushed himself away from the sink and headed towards the living room, warming to his theme. 'What about the girls? What are they going to think?'

'I-I don't know. This won't change anything, Mark – they'll still come and stay with you every month. I won't stop you seeing them or anything stupid like that. I just need to move on. I—'

'Are you seeing someone else?'

'What? No, I—'

'What, then? What's brought this on?'

He heard the scrape of one of the chairs being pulled out from under the kitchen table, a rustle of paper, and then a deep sigh as Debbie sat.

'Mark, we've been drifting apart ever since you were stabbed. You know your job always worried me. It's got worse the more you took on – it was bad enough when you were in uniform, but this— Ever since you were promoted to DS, it's become an obsession. We hardly saw you before the attack, and when that happened I thought I was going to lose you for good…

Now look at us. We haven't even lived in the same house for months.'

Mark ran his gaze over the documentation once more, his throat aching with emotion. His legs unsteady, he paced the living room in a daze, the silence at the end of the phone increasing his dread.

She had nothing more to say.

Collapsing onto the sofa, he blinked back the sting at the corners of his eyes. 'I can make it better, really I can. I could move back. I can tell Kennedy I've made a mistake. I can—'

'It's too late, Mark,' she whispered. 'I can't do this.'

'Debbie, please—'

'I'm sorry, Mark.' She sniffed. 'I've got to go. The girls will want their dinner.'

'Wait, Deb—'

He swore as the call ended and sat for a moment, his hands clasped between his knees as he tried to process what had happened.

That was it.

His old life was over.

Everything he had hoped for, everything he had worked for.

Gone.

Hamish whined, then jumped on the sofa beside him and tried to lick the salty tears that covered his cheeks.

Mark exhaled, then leaned back into the cushions and closed his eyes, groaning under his breath.

Had he been fooling himself all this time? Did he really think he could ever return to what he had walked away from?

All this time, he had tried to convince himself he was doing the right thing for his family. Protecting them, giving them some time to heal, playing at happy families while an undercurrent of hopelessness ebbed at the edges of his fractured marriage.

Perhaps Debbie was right.

Perhaps it was too late.

Perhaps she was simply braver than him.

Maybe he had been holding on to a false hope since he had arrived in the Vale of the White Horse.

Opening his eyes, Mark wiped at the tears and ruffled Hamish between the ears.

'Don't worry. I'll be all right, boy. Honest.'

He chose to ignore the tremor in his voice.

CHAPTER NINE

The next morning, Jan took the stairs up to the incident room two at a time, brushing past an older uniformed sergeant carrying a cardboard archiving box before she weaved in front of a pair of administrative assistants, their heads bowed as they gossiped in low voices.

At the top of the stairs she turned right and hurried along the dimly lit corridor, checking her watch.

She was twenty minutes early, adrenalin buzzing after an early morning spin class, and determined to get a head start on her emails before DI Kennedy began the morning briefing.

Turpin was already at his desk and held up his hand in greeting, his other clutching the phone pressed to his ear.

His eyes were bloodshot, exhaustion etched across

his features, and she wondered if he had slept at all that night.

Frowning, Jan turned away before he caught her staring.

She swung her handbag onto the floor next to her chair, signed into her computer and then glanced across the screen at Turpin as he finished his call and swore under his breath.

'What's up, Sarge?'

'I was trying to get hold of MacKenzie Adams so we could interview him today. Turns out he's gone to Ascot – won't be back until after nine tonight.'

Jan frowned. 'After what happened yesterday?'

'I know. You'd think he'd show a bit of decorum in the circumstances.'

'I suppose he's still got to make a living.'

Turpin's top lip curled. 'I don't think there was ever a risk of him losing money over this, Jan. I can't help feeling he'll be revelling in the extra attention. Just you wait – I'll bet his face is all over the news tonight.'

Jan sighed. He was right. Her first impressions of the racehorse trainer had been that he was self-serving, reinforced by Brennan's comments regarding his future job prospects at the yard.

'Do you think he killed her? I mean, after all, Jessica's parents said he has a reputation for being a womaniser, and he didn't tell us about Jessica working for him.'

'I'm not ruling it out,' said Turpin. 'By the way, have you seen the email from Gillian? She's scheduled the post mortem for Friday morning. I said to Kennedy that we'd go if he was up to his eyeballs – that all right?'

'Sure.' Jan hit "send" on another email in her mailbox and then glanced over her shoulder as Kennedy wrenched open his office door and stalked across to the whiteboard at the end of the room.

She pushed back her chair and followed Turpin over to the detective inspector, who moved to a nearby desk and leaned against it while he waited for his team to assemble.

'Thanks, everyone,' he said. 'Let's begin with an update from Caroline and Alex. How did you get on at the supermarket where Jessica worked?'

Alex cleared his throat, then tugged a notebook from the breast pocket of his jacket and flipped it open. 'We spoke to her manager, Annie Hartman, and a full-time member of staff called Isaac Fisher who supervises Jessica on a day-to-day basis. They confirmed Jessica worked two afternoon shifts. She worked the checkout register in the delicatessen area on Mondays and then often helped out in the petrol station on Thursday afternoons.'

'Any problems with other members of staff?' said Kennedy.

'None whatsoever,' said Caroline. 'And there are no

complaints from customers on record, either. When we spoke with Isaac Fisher about her shift last Thursday in the petrol station, we asked if there were any problems in case there was anything that warranted a closer look, but he said it was a quiet afternoon; just the usual commuters and shoppers. He and Jessica spent time restocking the shelves in between serving customers, and she left on time at four o'clock that afternoon and travelled by bus to her home in Harton Wick in time for her shift at the Farriers Arms.'

'They were all shocked to hear about her death,' said Alex.

Kennedy wrote a précis of Jessica's supermarket shifts on the board before re-capping the pen and turning back to the two detectives. 'What about the college?'

'We've left a message with her form tutor to give us a call. He wasn't there, and isn't due back in until Monday. He only teaches part-time. We tried phoning him, but there's no answer on his mobile and when we phoned his wife she said he's visiting his father in Wales and won't be back until later tonight.'

'Keep on top of that,' said Kennedy. 'Liaise with Mark and Jan if you need help.'

'Will do,' said Caroline.

'Mark, Jan? How did you get on speaking with the landlord of the Farriers Arms?'

'It sounds like Jessica was the model employee there

as well,' said Jan. 'Nothing to report by way of altercations. Noah Collins – the licensee – said that Jessica left the pub after work Monday night at eleven-thirty. The other staff member lives in the opposite direction at Hazelthorpe and had finished earlier, so Jessica said she'd walk home – one of the regulars offered her a lift an hour before, but she couldn't leave early because they were still clearing up. According to Collins, the road is well-lit between the pub and the Marleys' house and she'd often walked home in the past. It's a little over a mile, though, and there's no pavement in parts.'

'Okay, get yourselves over to Harton Wick stables this afternoon and speak with the jockey, Will Brennan, again. Go over his initial statement, see if there are any discrepancies or additional information he can give us to work with. Interview MacKenzie Adams while you're there, too.'

'Can't, guv. Apparently he's at the races today.'

'Arsehole. All right. Just make sure you get to him as quickly as possible.' Kennedy ran his gaze over the assembled officers. 'I don't need to tell you, but we're now approaching thirty-six hours since Jessica was murdered. We need to speak to people while their memories are still fresh, so I want to begin before lunchtime today. We'll reconvene here at six o'clock tonight. Dismissed.'

The team began to disperse from the area beside the

whiteboard and then assembled around Caroline, who called out team leaders for the enquiries and coordinated with the administrative support staff.

Jan set her shoulders before crossing to her desk in Turpin's wake.

He swiped a set of car keys from on top of a motorbike magazine and then tossed them to her. 'Can you drive? I want to read through the statements Caroline and Alex put together while we're on the way over to Harton Wick.'

'No problem.'

CHAPTER TEN

Jan swore under her breath as the car lurched forward, keeping a tight grip on the steering wheel while she followed the stony track from the lane.

The potholed surface was covered in deep puddles and ruts that shook the car's suspension and spat out stones from the tyres as she tried to pick her way along the quarter-mile route.

Rain lashed the car, and a moment later a harsh wind buffeted against Turpin's door, rocking the vehicle from side to side.

He seemed oblivious to the movement of the car and stared out of the window across the barren landscape, lost in thought.

'Everything all right, Sarge?'

His head jerked around. 'Sorry, what? Miles away.'

'Is something the matter?' she said. 'You didn't look

too good this morning. I wondered if you were coming down with the flu or something. It's going through the boys' school like wildfire at the—'

'Debbie wants a divorce.'

Hitting the brakes, she turned to face him. 'Bloody hell. Sorry.'

He shrugged, glancing at her, and she saw a sadness in his eyes that she hadn't seen before. 'It is what it is.'

'If you need anything, if Scott and I can help out—'

He managed a smile. 'Thanks. Do me a favour? Keep it to yourself for now.'

'No problem. My lips are sealed. What are you going to do?'

'I'm not going to make it difficult for her. She's right – we've drifted apart since I was attacked, and it's not fair on the girls, not this limbo we're living in. I suppose it just took one of us to be sensible about it all, and Debbie was always the sensible one.'

'Are you going to be okay?'

'Yes. Shall we?'

Jan nodded. She could take a hint.

As she accelerated away, she glanced at the low hedgerow that separated the track from a fallow field, the brambles and nettles doing little to protect them from the onslaught passing through the countryside.

Stunted trees bore evidence to the windswept terrain, their branches leaning away from the track as if trying to escape. Twigs broke away, striking the bodywork before tumbling into the thin weeds on either side.

She braked for a gentle curve, worried she might encounter a vehicle coming the other way, and then relaxed as the track widened out in front of a two-storey house.

Jan applied the handbrake and drummed her fingers on the steering wheel, peering through the windscreen at the ramshackle cottage.

Tendrils of ivy clung to the brickwork, the dark green a stark contrast to the washed-out paintwork that peeled from the window frames and front door. A cascade of water plummeted from a broken gutter under shattered roof tiles and slopped onto the threadbare garden below, splashing the side of the house with mud.

'I hope to hell they've got heating,' she said, and flicked off the wipers.

The whole property exuded an air of something temporary, its residents only passing through on their way to chasing their dreams of fame on the racing circuit.

'How many of them live here?' said Turpin. 'Just Brennan and the other jockey – what's his name?'

'Paul Hitchens. There's a third bloke, too – older. Nigel White. I think he helps out with exercising the horses but doesn't race anymore.'

'All right. Let's see if Will's in.'

Turpin buttoned his coat and then shoved the door open

before dashing towards the front porch, water splashing under his feet and coating the hems of his trousers.

Jan pulled up the hood of her waterproof coat and launched herself from the driver's seat, aiming the key fob over her shoulder as she dodged between puddles to join him.

She shoved her hands in her pockets while Turpin banged his fist against the door, then turned her back to the field as a fresh blast of wind and rain smacked against her face.

Thankfully, the door opened within seconds and Will Brennan peered out.

'Oh, it's you.'

'Can we come in?' said Turpin.

'Sure.'

Jan closed the door and wrinkled her nose.

Dampness clung to the plasterwork walls, and it was evident the jockeys' priorities didn't stretch to cleaning the place on a regular basis. A stack of *Racing Post* newspapers filled a corner behind the door, the pages browning with age. Thick dust covered the staircase balustrades, while the carpet suffered from scuff marks, cigarette burns and ages-old muddy boot prints.

Will hovered next to the stairs, his arms wrapped around his stomach and his mouth downturned. 'I'd offer you a cuppa, but the milk's off. Paul's meant to be buying some on his way back later.'

'Not a problem,' said Turpin. 'Is there somewhere we can sit and have a chat?'

'In here.'

Will gestured to a doorway opposite the staircase.

As she stepped inside, Jan tried to imagine what the living room had looked like when the cottage was first built, and failed.

Yellow damp patches clung to a ceiling that had once been slathered in layers of white paint and decorated with swirling patterns. Wallpaper hung in strips from darkened corners of the room, and a blue-grey fog of old cigarette smoke lingered in the box-like space.

She glanced over her shoulder at Turpin and raised an eyebrow.

He shook his head; evidently the stench wasn't enough to aggravate his damaged throat – yet.

She turned back to Will, who was gathering up discarded magazines, a laptop computer and various items of clothing from the dilapidated sofa before dumping everything onto an armchair tucked into the far corner of the room beside a chimney breast.

A wood-burning stove emitted a faint orange glow within the hearth, and as Jan ran her gaze around the rest of the room she realised there were no radiators.

'No central heating?'

'No, and it's fucking freezing here this time of year,'

said Will. He moved away from the sofa, pointing at it. 'Make yourselves comfortable.'

He moved to a large wicker basket to the left of the hearth and pulled out two logs before opening the cast-iron doors to the stove and shoving the fuel inside. After stoking the flames and coaxing another blast of heat to escape into the room, he slammed the doors shut and turned his back to it, his red-rimmed eyes accentuating his grief-stricken features.

'Please. Have a seat,' he said.

Jan eyed the sagging cushions, and then perched herself on the edge of the armchair nearest the fireplace. Turpin elected to sit on the arm of the sofa, his hands clasped loosely in his lap.

'How are you holding up, Will? Have you got anyone you can talk to?'

The jockey shook his head, lowering his eyes to a brown and red rug that partially covered the wooden floorboards. 'All my family are back in Gloucestershire. Not that I'd really want to talk to them about this anyway.'

'We need to ask you some more questions, Will. Do you want to sit down?'

'No. I'll stand, thanks.' A faint smile crossed his face. 'It's warmer here. Can't you feel the draught coming off the window behind you?'

'Who owns this place?' said Jan.

'MacKenzie. He owns this one, and two others near here.'

'Is it safe?'

'It's solid. Nothing's falling off it, yet. Like I said to you before, it's cheaper than renting anywhere else around here anyway.'

'Will,' said Turpin, 'when we spoke to you yesterday, you stated you'd met Jessica on Monday night while she was working. What time did you get there?'

'Early. About six o'clock, or thereabouts. Paul and me didn't want to be out late because we were due to be up early the next day to exercise the horses.'

'That's Paul Hitchens?'

'Yes – he drove there and back.'

'Who else lives here with you?'

'Nigel. Nigel White.'

'Where are they now?' said Jan.

'Nigel will be over at the yard – he's got a cushy seven-to-five job with MacKenzie now he's retired from racing. Helps out rehabilitating any horses with injuries, overseeing the stable lads, that sort of thing. Paul's got a race this afternoon so he won't be back until late.'

'When you saw Jessica on Monday night, what happened?' said Turpin. 'Did you argue?'

'What? No!'

'What did you talk about then?'

'Just the usual stuff, I suppose.' He ran a hand down

one arm, and shivered. 'I wish I could remember it word for word, I really do. We were making plans for the weekend – I was due to race on Saturday, but I had Sunday off. If the weather was good, we were going to go for a ride on the motorbike. Maybe over to Uffington or Waylands Smithy, take a picnic, that sort of thing. She couldn't talk much, though – I mean, obviously she was working and they were busy on Monday.'

'Unusual for a pub to be busy that time of the week, I'd have thought,' said Jan.

'Yeah, I think it caught them all off guard. Just one of those things, I suppose when everyone orders their meals at the same time.'

'What time did you leave?'

'Eight, like I told you. I remember that, because there's a sodding big clock behind the bar, next to the bell for last orders.'

'Did you talk to Jessica before you left?'

Will tugged his sleeve over his fist before wiping at his eyes. 'Only quickly – Paul was keen to get moving.'

'Why?'

'I don't know, he just was. He's like that – couple of pints do for him, and like I said, he was driving. He gets bored if he has to sit around watching everyone else drink and he can't.'

'Did Paul ever argue with Jessica?'

'Not that I know of.' Will sniffed. 'Why would he?'

'That's what we're trying to establish, because

somebody knew Jessica was going to be walking along that lane on Monday night after leaving the pub. Somebody who was familiar with her shift patterns.'

'Did you come straight back here when you left the pub?' said Jan.

'Yeah. MacKenzie keeps a couple of horses in the field on the other side of the car park out there and says we're to keep the noise down after midnight. I'm usually out like a light by eleven o'clock, anyway.'

'What did you do when you came back?'

Will shrugged. 'Cooked some beans on toast, then read my book for a bit. Like I said – early night.'

Turpin rose to his feet and peered out of the dirt-smeared window. 'And you didn't leave the house again after that?'

'No.'

'Did you speak to Jessica after coming back here?'

'No, I just sent her a text to let her know I'd call her in the morning about the weekend. The one I showed you. I sent that at eleven before I put my light out.'

Turpin turned back to Will. 'Did you harm Jessica?'

The jockey paled. 'Why would I kill her? I loved her. I was going to propose to her this weekend.'

CHAPTER ELEVEN

'Guv, got a minute?'

Mark stuck his head around Kennedy's office door and eyed the paperwork strewn across the detective inspector's desk.

He ran his gaze over the framed certificates, commendations and photographs depicting the DI with various dignitaries and senior officers. A newspaper article took pride of place in the middle of the display; a report about the bravery award the DI had received whilst a probationary constable. Mark had heard the story while settling into the station six months ago, and knew the senior officer kept in contact with the man he'd rescued by jumping into an icy river to haul him to safety.

Kennedy looked up from his computer and beckoned. 'I'd rather have an update from you two than deal with these budget figures. At least you'll be talking sense.'

He gathered up the documentation and shoved it into his filing tray as Mark and Jan dropped into the seats opposite his desk.

'How did you get on with Will Brennan, then? I presume that's what this is about?'

'Apparently he was going to propose to Jessica Marley at the weekend,' said Mark. 'Had it all planned out – motorbike trip over to Uffington, picnic at Waylands Smithy, the lot. Sodding great engagement ring, as well – he showed it to us before we left.'

'It must've taken him months to save for it on his wages,' said Jan. 'Trainee jockeys don't earn that much, do they?'

Kennedy reached out for a pen and scrawled a note on a pad next to his keyboard. 'I'll get the finance team to take a look into Brennan's income and expenditure in case there's something amiss. Mind you, he said he'd moved down here to be with her, didn't he? He could've been saving for some time.'

'I think it's worth having them check anyway,' said Mark. 'At least to rule out anything dodgy.'

'He's probably managing to save more by staying at the cottage,' said Jan, wrinkling her nose. 'The place was a hovel.'

'Oh?' Kennedy dropped his pen. 'Any health and safety concerns?'

'I don't think so, guv. It could do with a bloody good clean, though. Looks like it's been left to go to rack and ruin.'

'I suppose if Brennan and the others rent it cheap, and Adams is happy to let them do so, it works well for everyone involved. I'll flag the rental arrangements to finance when I speak to them and ask them to make sure it's all above board. Back to the engagement – did anyone else know?'

'A friend of Jessica's, Bethany Myers,' said Mark. 'Apparently Brennan roped her in to help spring the surprise at the weekend to make sure Jessica was free on the Sunday. Myers occasionally works at the Farriers Arms on a Sunday if they need extra cover.'

'Was she on the list Noah Collins provided?'

'Yes. I spoke with uniform – she's been away since Friday and out of mobile range. We'll try to speak to her as soon as she gets back.'

'The poor woman's going to get a shock when she finds out about Jessica,' said Jan.

'What was your impression of Brennan now that you've had another chance to speak with him?'

'He came across as genuinely shocked,' said Mark. 'I mean, he's only a young lad, he's just found his girlfriend dead and I didn't see anything resembling a temper or anything while we were interviewing him.'

'He looks like he'd blow away on a wisp of wind,' said Jan. 'I realise he's got a lot of upper body strength from riding those bloody huge horses, but I'm not sure he'd have the stamina to carry Jessica's body a long way if he killed her. And, as for motive—'

'Might've got cold feet?' said Mark. 'Or, he's lying about their perfect relationship.'

'Having cold feet's a bit of a stretch, isn't it, Sarge? Anyway, we're stuck until we get to speak to Myers. Maybe she can shed some light on his state of mind when she last saw him.'

'I've left a message on her voicemail asking her to call me the moment she picks it up,' said Mark. 'I don't want her talking to Brennan before we've interviewed her.'

'Maybe we're looking at this the wrong way,' said Kennedy. He pushed his chair back and led the way out of the office and across the incident room to the whiteboard. He clasped his hands behind his back. 'Perhaps she was struck by a car when she was walking home from the pub, and whoever hit her dumped her body,' he said, and then wrote the thought on the board next to the other avenues of enquiry. 'I'll speak with Tom Wilcox in the morning while you're interviewing MacKenzie Adams and task him with expediting the house-to-house enquiries along the route Jessica should have taken home from the pub on Monday night. We'll get a second group to do the same for one mile from the Farriers Arms towards Hazelthorpe in case anyone saw her that side of the village. As soon as you're finished with Adams, get yourselves over there to coordinate any findings with Tom.'

'Will do, guv.'

'While you're doing that, I'll get someone to speak with the bus company that runs the route through Harton Wick. Apparently, the council has been running a late service trial for the past two months to test demand. Find out who the driver was on the last shift and the one who took the first shift the morning after, and see if we can get the camera footage from the vehicles as well.'

'What about Jessica's parents, guv?' said Jan. 'What do we tell them about Brennan's intended proposal?'

Kennedy's lips thinned. 'Nothing. Not until we've interviewed Bethany Myers. We'll take another look at the situation then. I don't want to cause them more pain than they're already suffering.'

CHAPTER TWELVE

Frustration swept through Mark as he closed his front door.

To date, there was little by way of progress or breakthrough into their enquiries about Jessica's death, and the teenager's brutal murder plagued his thoughts.

Until they found evidence to the contrary, Will Brennan would remain on his list of suspects. During his career he had seen similarly grieving spouses turn out to be cold-blooded killers, and all too often in domestic violence cases.

The racehorse trainer, MacKenzie Adams, had seemed more upset by the inconvenience of interruption to his routine than having a dead girl's body on the gallops, and Mark ground his teeth at the memory of the man's officious attitude at the crime scene.

And what of Brennan's two housemates? Had

jealousy driven Paul Hitchens or Nigel White to murder?

Mark sighed and ran a hand through his hair as he kicked off his boots.

He made a fuss of Hamish, let him out of the back door into the garden, and then fetched the dog's food bowl and filled it while the mongrel ran back and forth across the darkened lawn, chasing imaginary foes.

At the sound of the can opener he tore back inside, tongue lolling while Mark refilled his water bowl and then ruffled his fur.

'Get stuck in.'

Mark made his way upstairs, tugging at his shirt and tie. Changing into jeans and a sweatshirt, he finally felt his shoulders start to sag a little.

He wouldn't relax until Jessica's murderer had been charged, but a seeping tiredness crawled through his body. He pulled out his mobile phone, rang the local takeaway to place an order for one, then wandered down to the kitchen.

He popped the metal cap off a bottle of Bishop's Finger ale, closed the refrigerator door with his foot, and padded along the narrow hallway to the living room.

As he picked up the television remote control, Hamish raised his chin from the bed next to the radiator under the window, his eyes quizzical.

'Chinese takeaway tonight, m' boy. And if you're

lucky, there's half a vegetable spring roll with your name on it when it gets here.'

The dog licked its lips.

Mark grinned, leaned down and scratched him between his ears.

The familiar opening theme for the late evening news finished, and he sank into a worn black leather armchair with a sigh before taking a long swig of beer as the newscaster began to run through the day's headlines.

He had missed the local news earlier. Alex McClellan had phoned to say MacKenzie Adams had featured prominently, and Mark wanted to get the measure of the man before interviewing him in the morning.

He closed his eyes and rubbed the back of his neck as the newsreader turned her attention to the main news story of the day – a meeting of global leaders being held somewhere exotic, expensive, and paid for by taxpayers – and ran through the events following the house-to-house enquiry.

His eyes snapped open at the sound of a familiar name, and he refocused on the television screen as the scene changed from the newsroom to an interview that had been recorded earlier that day.

The male reporter stood with a notebook in one hand and a microphone in the other, and repeated the words Mark had already seen in the latest press release issued that morning. In the background, Mark noticed the white railings and tall hedges of a racecourse. A steady stream of people passed behind the reporter, casting curious stares at the outside broadcast.

'One man who does know more about this murder and who has been personally affected by Jessica Marley's death is MacKenzie Adams. MacKenzie, what can you tell us about what happened yesterday with the discovery of Jessica's body on your training gallops?'

Mark leaned forward, clutching the beer bottle between his hands, and gritted his teeth as the camera swung to the right, bringing Adams into shot.

'Well, obviously it is a terrible shock for everyone,' said the racehorse trainer. 'I can't imagine what the poor girl's family are going through right now.'

'We understand that it was one of your jockeys who discovered her body?'

'Yes, yes – that's right. He was riding what we hope will be the favourite to win on Monday.'

'What's the current state of people's minds in the area?' said the reporter. 'Are the police any closer to finding out who was responsible for Jessica's murder?'

Adams' chest broadened, and he cleared his throat. 'No, the police don't appear to have any good leads. As you can imagine, with so many young people living in the area, it's a worry for us locals. Nothing like this has ever happened to us, so we're all very concerned.'

'And moving on to your plans for the weekend, can

you give us any indication as to which of your horses will be racing in the Cup?'

MacKenzie chuckled, then launched into a blatant self-promotion spiel about his winning chances.

Mark lowered his gaze as his mobile phone began to ring, and saw Kennedy's number displayed.

'Guv?'

'Are you watching the news?'

'Yeah. Adams is revelling in the attention, isn't he?'

'Callous bastard.'

'Some people know no bounds, guv.'

'Well, make sure when you talk to him tomorrow you make it quite clear from me that I'm not impressed. And, if he gives you any grief or you've got any reason to suspect him of anything more serious than stupidity, bring him in and we'll formally interview him.'

'Understood.'

'Enjoy your evening.'

Kennedy hung up as the doorbell went, and Mark drained the dregs from the bottle.

'Stay,' he said to Hamish, who had jumped to his feet and was pointing his nose towards the hallway.

Mark greeted the takeaway driver, handed him a tip and then hurried to the kitchen as his stomach rumbled.

Helping himself to another beer from the refrigerator, he popped open the cardboard lids, placed the foil containers on a tray and grabbed a fork before wandering back to the living room.

Hamish sat with his back to the television, his tail a blur.

'No good looking at me like that. You're not getting anything until I've finished.'

Mark dived in, ravenous. He was taking a sip from the beer when his phone began to ring once more, but this time the caller ID made him smile.

'Lucy.'

'Hello. Got any more of those boxes unpacked since I last saw you?'

'I have. And I found the vacuum cleaner. There's hope for me yet.'

A husky laugh reached his ear. 'You'll be fine. You're a landlubber. You would've frozen your arse off if you'd stayed on the boat. It's no wonder O'Reilly can't get a tenant over the winters. He never will if he doesn't put in a wood-burning stove, or something like what I've got.'

'Who's looking after the boat while it's empty?' he said, and took another sip.

'No-one. He took it out of the water earlier this month to get the hull checked and it's been in his yard ever since. I don't know whether he's going to rent it out again in the spring. You were one of his better tenants – I don't know whether he'll want anyone else there now; you've softened him up. Anyway, you're eating your dinner and it's getting cold. What've you got?'

'Szechuan chicken.'

'Oh, spicy. Just the way I like it.' That laugh again.

Mark put his fork down, and took a deep breath.

Should I?

Then: *why not?*

Debbie had made it clear that there was no going back, and he was tired of being alone.

'Look, do you fancy coming over to dinner one night soon?'

'I'd love to.'

'Really?' He exhaled.

'Yes, I would. I miss our chats in the evenings.'

'So do I. How about next Thursday? I've got some late nights coming up, but—'

'Thursday would be perfect. I'll bring the wine.'

A shiver of excitement, anticipation and nervousness flittered across his shoulders. 'We're in the middle of an investigation at the moment, so if anything crops up that means I'll have to change the day—'

'Don't worry about it. The wine won't go off.'

He smiled. 'Fantastic. See you about seven o'clock? I'll pick you up on the way home to save you walking.'

'Sounds good. See you soon.'

Mark ended the call and tossed the spring roll to Hamish.

'Date night, dog. You'd better be on your best behaviour.'

CHAPTER THIRTEEN

Early the next morning, Jan waited for the security barrier to rise, and then steered the pool car out into the road and pointed it in the direction of the Berkshire Downs.

Soon, the urban sprawl faded into narrow lanes and bare hedgerows, the traffic reducing to the occasional tractor or bus heading in the opposite direction, and Jan turned her attention to the impending interview.

'How do you want to approach it?' she said.

Turpin turned away from the window and dropped his mobile into his coat pocket. 'I was thinking about that. I reckon it'd be a good idea for you to lead the questions. I spent some time watching old interviews of his on the internet after dinner last night. He's interesting – he has a different way of answering questions if there's a woman involved. With male reporters, he's jocular, one of the lads. I'd like to gauge how he responds to a woman being in control of the situation – to see if there's any indication he has the reputation we've been led to believe by Jessica's mother.'

'Okay. How does he react to women in the interviews you watched?'

'He's a flirt. He deflected awkward questions by complimenting them on what they were wearing. If that didn't work and they pushed him, he became defensive. But he definitely comes across as if he thinks he's a ladies' man – do you know what I mean?'

'Ugh, yes. A dinosaur, then?'

'Exactly.'

'Right.' Jan flexed her hands on the steering wheel. 'I'm going to enjoy this.'

'Thought you might.'

Half an hour later, she turned the car between a pair of moss-covered gate posts and into a wide yard. Parking next to a large shed, its open doors displaying row upon row of saddles and bridles, she climbed out and pocketed the keys.

A magpie cawed as it ducked and swooped overhead before landing on the roof of the Victorian farmhouse.

Jan bundled her scarf around her neck and cast her gaze around the yard.

The first of the stable blocks began a discreet distance away from the main house. A low-slung building with timber cladding and a tile roof, the building housed six stables. Three horses peered out from open doors, their ears twitching as they eyed the newcomers.

The sweet scent of horse dung and fresh hay lingered in the air.

The second of the stable blocks appeared deserted. All of the doors were open, and at the far end a young lad raked dirty straw bedding towards a wheelbarrow.

Beyond the stable blocks, an exercise ring was in use, a horse tethered to the frame as it walked in a circle. A lone man in woollen hat and padded jacket stood on a metal viewing platform, his arms resting on the top of the railing.

Jan held up her hand. 'We're looking for MacKenzie Adams.'

'In the main house,' the man called.

Turpin met her on the doorstep and rang the bell.

Jan huddled into her jacket as they waited. A cold wind from the hillside above the property swept through the yard, blowing strands of hay into the drainage gullies around the concrete hardstanding.

After a while, she heard footsteps, and the door was hauled open.

MacKenzie Adams peered at her over reading glasses, his dark-grey hair tousled as if he'd been running his fingers through it. He rested one hand on the doorframe, the other clutching a tablet computer. 'Detectives. What do you want?'

'Just a few routine questions please, Mr Adams.'

'Oh, do they let the girls out to do that?'

'I'd advise you to treat my colleague with courtesy,' said Turpin, taking a step forward. 'Otherwise, we'll continue this interview formally under caution at the station. It's up to you.'

Adams raised an eyebrow, but moved back. 'No need to be like that, detective. We'll use the study. Less chance of being interrupted.'

Jan caught Turpin's wink as she brushed past him and followed Adams along the hallway. She squared her shoulders, and ran through the questions she wanted to ask the racehorse trainer as he stopped and held open a door.

A large wooden desk faced the room, the window behind it providing a view of the busy stables and yard beyond. Framed photographs covered the wall to her right; a mixture of horses racing past winning posts, and their trainer shaking hands with various dignitaries and owners.

A cluster of four leather armchairs faced the desk, and it was to these that Adams gestured to before placing the tablet computer on a leather-bound desk planner. 'I'm a very busy man, Detective West. I hope this won't take long.'

'It'll take as long as it takes, Mr Adams.' Jan took

the chair to which he directed her. 'Please clarify where you were on Monday night between half past eleven and seven o'clock Tuesday morning.'

His face flushed. 'I beg your pardon? Am I a suspect?'

'Answer the question, please.'

'You—' His jaw worked, and then he shrugged. 'All right. Have it your way. I was here. In here, to be precise.'

'All night?'

'No – until about midnight. There's a lot of paperwork to do in a successful business like mine.'

'And from midnight until seven o'clock?'

'Asleep, what do you think? I got up at six and drove up to the gallops to wait for the horses.'

'What sort of car do you drive?' said Turpin.

'What's that—'

'Please, answer the question.'

'The silver estate car out the front there. You passed it on the way in.'

'Any others?'

'The four-by-four you saw me using up at the gallops. That's it.'

'Is the gate between the field and the gallops kept locked at all times?' said Jan.

'No – never seen any reason to before now.'

'Do any other trainers use the gallops?'

'One of the smaller yards, from time to time.'

'Which one?'

'Millar's, over at West Barcross.'

'We'll need contact details.'

Adams wrenched open the top drawer of his desk, rummaged inside and then tossed a business card across the desk to her.

'How many people work here?'

'Eight stable lads are employed permanently. I've got a housekeeper here in the main house, and then there are six part-time temporary staff.' He winced. 'Make that *five* part-time temporary staff.'

'When did Jessica Marley start working for you?'

'About three weeks ago.'

'And yet you failed to mention that to us on Tuesday morning when we spoke at the gallops.'

'I was in shock. I forgot.'

'But you didn't tell the uniformed officers who took your statement later that day, either. Why not?'

Adams visibly squirmed. 'I'm sorry. I forgot. As I said, she'd only been here a little while, unlike my other employees.'

'How did she get the job?'

'She emailed me.'

'Had you ever spoken to her before that?'

'Once or twice, just to say good morning when she dropped by to visit Brennan.'

'Did she give you any indication then that she was interested in working here?'

'No. None at all. But she seemed keen – she was certainly qualified. I could only offer the occasional Saturday, on the basis that if one of the others quit, she could have their shifts.'

'Any problems?'

'Not that I can think of. She'd only done three shifts.'

'Were you aware that Will was planning to propose to Jessica this weekend?'

'What? Was he?' Adams drummed his fingers on his desk. 'I had no idea. The press is going to bloody love that, aren't they?'

'He never mentioned anything to you?'

'No. Nothing. If he had, I would've said something.'

'Such as?'

'Well, they're a bit bloody young to be settling down, don't you think? He's got a whole career ahead of him. Before you'd know it, she'd want kids and that'd be the end of it. Not many jockeys can afford to support a family when they're just starting out, Detective West.'

'Who supervised Jessica while she was here?'

'Nigel White. He's the head stable lad and manages everything that goes on out there for me.'

'We're going to need to speak to him and everyone else who works here.'

Adams sighed. 'Thought you might. There are only three of the lads here at the moment, though.'

'Where are the rest?' said Turpin.

'Out on the gallops, training.'

'You're using the gallops already?'

'Nothing wrong with the turf, detective – your lot have finished with it, haven't they? Besides, I've got horses racing this weekend. They need to be exercised.'

'I'd like a full list of your staff and contact numbers for them,' said Jan. 'And obviously, you'll tell them to make themselves available for interview when our colleagues from uniform get in touch later today.'

Turpin moved to the bay window that overlooked the yard, and then turned back to Adams.

'Why aren't those horses in the stable block over there out with the others?' said Turpin.

'Because those are racing on Saturday, detective. It would do them no good at all to exercise them today. They need to rest so they have a better chance of winning.'

'Is Will around today?'

'Doctor's appointment in town. Left about half an hour before you got here. He didn't say what for, and I didn't ask, although I can guess. I presume he's dealing with Jessica's death in his own way.'

'What will happen to him?' said Jan. '

'Hopefully he'll stay. Between you and me, I couldn't buy this sort of publicity. And Will? Look at him, would you? I mean he looks like a bloody pop star compared to the other jockeys on the circuit. The media will love him.' He shook his head. 'No, believe me –

that young man is going to be back on a horse as soon as I can convince him to get over his loss. I need him out there, earning money for me before this whole story goes cold.'

Adams checked his watch. 'Speaking of which, I've got an interview with the BBC in a little under an hour. Was there anything else you needed from me?'

'Yes. You'll need to report your travel plans to us in order that we know where you are at all times, Mr Adams. Don't forget. It could be detrimental for you.'

His eyes widened. 'What? That's preposterous! Am I a suspect now?'

'You always were.' Jan pushed her chair back. 'We'll see ourselves out.'

CHAPTER FOURTEEN

Mark blew on his hands and flipped up the collar on his coat as he and Jan stood in the middle of the car park of the Farriers Arms.

A chill breeze snatched a white puff of smoke away from the chimney, leaving a waft of burning wood on the air.

Three patrol cars lined up against the privet hedge that bordered the property, the occupants conversing at the kerb outside a 1930s terrace of four cottages opposite.

Mark watched as they split up in different directions – two working their way towards Hazelthorpe, while the other four took a side of the road each and began to knock on doors.

The owner of the first dwelling in the terrace peered out over a brass chain, her brow furrowed as she listened to the uniformed constable. Apparently satisfied he was a genuine police officer, not impersonating one, she reached up to loosen the chain and then the door opened wider before she leaned against the frame, her arms crossed over her chest as she spoke.

'Calmed down a bit?' he said to Jan as she joined him. 'I thought you were going to take MacKenzie Adams' head off back there.'

'Sorry, Sarge. I tried to be professional, but in the circumstances…'

'Nothing to apologise for. The man's full of hot air. I enjoyed seeing you take him down a peg or two.'

She smiled, then inclined her head towards the uniformed officers who progressed slowly from one property to the next. 'It's a fine line, isn't it? I mean, people around here will either take the opportunity to gossip about what's happened, or genuinely have some information that'll help us.'

'It's got to be done.' He checked his watch. 'We'll give them a few minutes then wander up the road to see how they're getting on. Sound good?'

'No problem. Do you think we're going to find out anything?'

He shrugged. 'Hard to say. It'd be nice if someone along here has security cameras outside their house, given that there's no CCTV.'

'Did Caroline have any idea how long it'd take to get the camera footage from the bus company?'

'She didn't say anything to me. I've had to request it in the past though – it could take anything from two days to a week; it depends who you're dealing with.' He peered up at one of the windows on the top floor of the pub as a curtain dropped back into place. 'Hopefully Noah Collins will keep his ears open for us as well, in case anyone's tongue gets too loose over a few pints. Let's take a wander. I'm freezing standing around here.'

Mark kept his hands in his pockets and fell into step beside Jan as she walked out of the car park and turned left into the lane.

Tree roots split the narrow pavement in several places, and he kept his eyes to the ground to avoid tripping over them before letting Jan take the lead.

She removed a folded piece of paper from her handbag and straightened out the creases before passing it back to him. 'That's a copy of the map Caroline drew up based on what we know about Jessica's usual route from the pub. Apart from the terrace across the road, the houses are big along here, with quite a lot of land. There are only twenty properties between here and the Marleys' home.'

Mark peered at the map, checked the progress of the two enquiry teams going from door to door, and then handed it back. 'It won't take too long to do this, then.'

'Depends who's home, I suppose.' She stepped off the last of the pavement and into the gutter of the lane.

They passed a post box mounted on a wooden stake

beside the hedgerow and Mark watched as two of the uniformed constables ducked beneath a weeping willow that hung over a gate, before negotiating their way up a crazy-paving path leading to a whitewashed cottage with a thatched roof.

'Come on,' he said. 'Leave them to it. They can catch up with us.'

He set a brisk pace, his eyes sweeping the lane as they progressed towards the Marleys' house, and crossed to the other side before walking along the curve that narrowed the lane at its apex.

'I don't think I'd have been happy about one of my daughters walking along here at night,' he said. 'Bloody dangerous this time of year.'

'I suppose she and her parents thought she was safe,' said Jan. 'I mean, at night she'd hear any cars approaching and could step up onto the verge in plenty of time. I don't think it would've ever crossed their minds that she'd be attacked. It seems to be a friendly community, so they'd never imagine the worse could happen. It's naïve, but that's what people are like until something like this takes place in their neighbourhood—'

She collided with Mark and stopped in her tracks as he held up his hand.

'What's up?'

'I'm not sure. Stay there.'

He ignored the frown that flickered across her face

and stepped sideways to crane his neck towards the grass verge, then upwards.

Jan's eyes were troubled when he looked back at her.

'Don't come any closer. We'll need to get this area taped off.'

'What have you found?' she said, an edge to her voice. 'Blood?'

'No.' Mark pointed to a series of pot holes that clogged the gutter. 'Plastic and glass. There are shards everywhere here.'

'Could be from a car headlight. Do you think the guv was right about a hit-and-run driver? He could've collided with Jessica here, and then moved her body.'

In reply, Mark gestured for her to join him, and she stepped towards the middle of the road, avoiding the area he indicated.

'Look,' he said.

Jan followed his hand as he pointed upwards.

The streetlight had been broken, the plastic lamp cover half missing, with jagged remnants of the filament hanging from the fixture.

Mark lowered his gaze to the pieces scattered across the road and gutter, his mouth dry. 'I don't think she was hit by a car. Whoever killed her could have broken the streetlight and waited here for her. If so, then it wasn't an accident. Jessica's death was planned.'

CHAPTER FIFTEEN

Mark glanced up at the sound of his name to see DI Kennedy hurrying towards him, his mobile phone in his hand.

The DI paused at the blue and white tape that now separated Mark from the verge and watched as three crime scene investigators made their way meticulously through the undergrowth at the side of the lane.

Traffic crawled past.

As soon as Mark had realised the significance of his find, he'd arranged for one of the patrol cars to be parked close to the broken street light. Two constables directed vehicles and an inquisitive dog walker past the CSIs using the far side of the lane, while a white barrier was erected to shield their work from onlookers.

'I've spoken with the Traffic division,' said Kennedy. 'They've got two cars at the end of the lane creating a diversion so you shouldn't get many more vehicles coming through here.'

'That's good, thanks, guv.'

Kennedy ran an appraising eye over the CSIs and then craned his neck to see down the road. 'What about neighbouring properties? Anything?'

'The couple who live in that cottage on the opposite side reckon this light was working a few days ago.'

'So, there's a possibility it was damaged on purpose.'

'Yes.'

Kennedy dropped his phone into his pocket. 'Anyone along here have security cameras?'

'No, nothing guv. Uniform have finished speaking with residents further up the lane towards the Marleys' house. The problem is that most of the houses are set back from the road here and at this time of year, once the sun goes down, they're cocooned behind curtains and sitting in front of the television. No-one saw or heard anything.'

'Shit.' Kennedy jerked his thumb at the white-suited figures beyond the tape. 'Have they found anything else?'

'Not yet, guv.' Mark pointed up the lane. 'The next light is up there, on the curve. This whole stretch would be dark and give anyone an opportunity to attack Jessica when she walked by. It's why we taped it off – they'll work their way up from here to that next light, and back down the lane as well.'

'Bloody lucky find.'

'I thought it was from a car headlight at first.'

'So, we can discount the hit-and-run theory?'

'I think so, yes. Unless they find anything around here to support that. I'm of the belief that this light was destroyed on purpose. A large stone could have been thrown against the bulb up there before Jessica finished her shift.' He pointed to a stunted tree a few metres away, its thick gnarled truck covered with ivy. 'Jessica's killer could've waited there for her.'

'He would've then had to transport her up to the gallops, though. Why not dump her here?' Kennedy wrinkled his nose. 'She might not have been found for a couple of days if no-one walked past. It would've been easier to roll her into the verge than get her into a vehicle, wouldn't it?'

'It would.' Mark exhaled, his eyes finding Jan who was talking with a uniformed sergeant further down the lane towards the pub. 'I'm beginning to wonder if Jessica's body was dumped on the gallops for a reason.'

'Symbolic, you mean?'

'Yes.'

'Hmm.' Kennedy tugged his earlobe. 'All right. We'll work through that back at the station. It's a hell of a risk, though. At that time of night, there might've been another car coming this way.'

'According to the residents along here, it's not that busy after eleven o'clock.' Mark craned his neck and peered up and down the lane. 'But there's nowhere to park a car, either. So maybe Jessica wasn't killed here. Maybe the killer simply extinguished the light so it was harder for her to see? Disorientate her, and then come to her rescue perhaps?'

'That would make more sense.' Kennedy shoved his hand in his pocket as his phone began to trill, and then groaned as he looked at the screen. 'I'm being summoned. Got to go. Get yourself and Jan back to the station in time for the afternoon briefing, will you? I want to take a closer look at your symbolism theory. Have a think about who it could be aimed at while you're waiting here, all right?'

'Will do, guv.'

Mark watched as Kennedy hurried back towards the pub, his car exiting the car park moments later, and then turned his attention to Jan as she approached.

'Okay, that's the last of the statements taken from the house-to-house enquiries. Nothing to report, unfortunately. It's what we suspected – by that time of night, everyone around here was either in bed asleep or sitting in front of the TV.' She peered over the tape. 'Anything yet?'

'No. The guv wants us back at the station in time for the briefing.'

'Did you tell him about your theory about her body being left up at the gallops on purpose?'

'Yes.'

'What did he say?'

'He wants to work through it when we get back.' Mark turned his back on the CSIs and squinted as a cold breeze pushed up the lane towards them. 'If Jessica's killer was trying to make a statement by leaving her there, I'm thinking that there could've only been two people whose attention he was seeking.'

'MacKenzie Adams or Will Brennan.'

'Right. So, why?'

Jan frowned. 'We'll need to look into previous boyfriends Jessica's had in the past. Maybe someone took umbrage at her impending engagement. Perhaps her killer figured if he couldn't have her, nor should Brennan.'

'According to Brennan, not that many people knew about the engagement. Jessica's parents certainly didn't.'

'People gossip all the time, Sarge.' Jan pulled out her notebook and a pen. 'Perhaps by killing one of his jockey's girlfriends and leaving her there, our killer was sending a message to Adams for some reason.'

'Sarge!'

They turned at a shout from one of the CSIs, who then beckoned them closer to the tape.

'What have you got?'

The technician held up a gloved hand. 'Mobile phone, Sarge.'

Mark raised an eyebrow at Jan. 'What make was the one Jessica's parents said she had?'

'That one,' said Jan. 'Great work, Gareth.'

CHAPTER SIXTEEN

Jan held open the door for Turpin before hurrying across to Tracy, who sat at a desk strewn with objects garnered from Jessica Marley's bedroom.

'Could you log this into evidence?' she said, handing over a plastic bag containing the mobile phone. 'And then let Alex have a look to see what he can find in relation to the calls and text messages. It's flat at the moment, so you'll need to charge it.'

'Will do. I'll correlate the calls and texts between this and Brennan's phone as well, to make sure he hasn't deleted anything.'

'Great, thanks.'

Jan shrugged her coat off her shoulders as she made her way over to her desk. She ran a critical eye over the emails that had accumulated in her absence.

The incident room echoed a cacophony of noise

from the team that had been corralled to work on the investigation, but Jan revelled in it. The door swung open as another uniformed constable hurried across to Tracy with an armful of brightly coloured manila folders, and a second later rushed by Jan's desk on another errand, dropping three of the folders into her top tray.

She looked up from her work as Kennedy stalked past, grateful that he had been assigned to the murder inquiry as Senior Investigating Officer. He had a no-nonsense reputation, as well as a track record that included mentoring several younger members of the murder investigation team. He didn't so much demand respect as command it – he led by example.

She glanced over her shoulder. Kennedy had reached his office, loosened his tie and already had the desk phone to his ear, barking instructions to some unfortunate sod at headquarters.

She smiled, turning her attention back to the folders that had been left for her. The first contained a copy of the witness statements from Jessica's manager and supervisor at the supermarket, and, as she read through the typed-up notes, a wistfulness gripped her.

Annie Hartman's statement confirmed that the young woman had been hard-working, attentive to detail and had never once turned up late. The manager had been distraught upon learning about Jessica's murder and, according to Caroline, had already put up posters in the windows with the Crimestoppers number, asking customers to get in touch if they had any information.

Isaac Fisher, the man with whom Jessica had worked in the petrol station on Thursday afternoons, was similarly upset; Jessica was the same age as his oldest granddaughter, and, like Annie, he hadn't a bad word to say about her.

Jan closed the file and tossed it to one side, then flipped open the next one, pulling out a wedge of paperwork and casting her gaze over the words. To her relief, it related to another case that she and Turpin had closed out last month and all that was required was her signature on two of the pages.

She scrawled her initials where indicated and dropped it back into her top tray and then peered at her computer screen. Fighting back the urge to groan, she replied to as many of the new messages as she could, delegated the rest and then glanced up as Kennedy moved to the front of the room and cleared his throat.

'Let's get a move on, people. Briefing, now please.'

'Here.' Turpin appeared at her side and passed a takeout coffee cup to her. 'Thought you might need this.'

'You're a legend, thanks – I was starting to struggle after all that fresh air today. I couldn't sleep last night. I kept thinking about Jessica, walking up that road on her own.' She shivered. 'These days, you'd think it'd be the last thing a woman would do.'

'I suppose it's a tight-knit community where everyone knows everyone,' he said, as they stood at the back of the assembled group of police officers. 'And that's the problem, isn't it? She must've thought she was safe. All the times she'd walked that lane before with no problem—'

'Are you saying she was complacent?'

'No. I'm saying she should have been safe. It's just that there are some evil bastards out there.'

Jan murmured her agreement, and turned her attention to Kennedy as he started the briefing.

'My thanks to the team who facilitated the house-to-house enquiries today in Harton Wick,' he began. 'As some of you will be aware, during that time Mark found evidence to suggest that a streetlight had been deliberately smashed so that Jessica Marley would've had to walk a length of the lane back to her parents' house in darkness. We've checked with the local council and, because of the current late night bus trial, the lights along there don't switch off until one o'clock in the morning at the moment. They switch on again at six a.m. for a couple of hours.'

He held up his hand for silence as murmurs swept through the room. 'Alex and Caroline, I want you to chase up the CCTV camera footage from the buses that drove along that route on Monday night. Arrange to have the drivers brought in for questioning – I'd like to observe.'

Kennedy turned back to the whiteboard and tapped the photograph taken at the murder scene on the gallops. 'Why was Jessica's body dumped here? And, where was she killed?'

'Jasper and his team confirm there were no traces of blood on the road itself or the verge,' said Turpin. 'There are no blood traces on her mobile phone, either. As for where her body was found, perhaps it serves as a message to either Will Brennan or MacKenzie Adams.'

'Both of whom remain suspects until ruled out otherwise,' said Kennedy. 'How did you get on interviewing MacKenzie Adams this morning? Can you provide an update for everyone while we're here? I take it from your mood that he lived up to expectations?'

'The man's an arsehole,' said Turpin. 'A misogynist for starters, and all he cares about is how much publicity he can get out of Jessica's death.'

'Feel better now?' said Kennedy to a ripple of laughter.

'Yes, guv. Sorry – he got to us.'

'Well, you've got a fair point about him being an arsehole. It's been noted in other circles, according to the background research Caroline's been doing. How'd you get on with the questioning?'

'He confirmed the gate through to the gallops isn't kept locked, even though he has a key,' said Jan. 'There's a second racing yard run by someone called Dominic Millar who uses it to train his horses from time to time. We checked on the way back – his is a much smaller yard, perhaps only eight horses at the moment.'

'His website states that he's been training for about eighteen months,' said Mark. 'He had a bad fall three years ago, and that put paid to his riding career.'

'Was he any good?'

'No big wins, but it appears he was making a decent living out of it.'

'Enough to set himself up as a trainer?'

'We plan to look into that, guv,' said Jan. 'There wasn't much online.'

'All right. Get PC Newton to help if you need to.'

'Will do.'

'What did he have to say about Jessica working for him?'

'He said she'd only started there three weeks ago and had worked three shifts. He said he forgot to tell us about her previously because he was in shock.'

'Bollocks.'

'That's what we thought, guv. We'll check her work arrangements with the other staff at the stables once uniform have all the interviews complete, plus we'll get someone to look into his finances to make sure the payroll records are up to date. That'll at least confirm the dates for us.'

'Thanks, you two.' Kennedy turned his attention to Police Sergeant Wilcox. 'Tom – I want you and your team coordinating the witness statements from the regulars in the pub. I realise we've got some based on the list of names Noah Collins provided, but we need to make sure no-one's been overlooked. Take a look at the ATM in the pub as well, and get onto the bank Collins uses for his card machine. I want records of everyone spending money in that place on Monday night. Once we have those, we can find out from them who else was in there. I want everyone interviewed as soon as possible.'

'Guv.'

'Mark – make sure you follow up with Jasper to get a note of their findings from this afternoon's search, even if it's not a full report. I want regular updates from him and his team so we can keep this investigation moving forward.'

'Will do, guv.'

'All right, that'll do. Thank you, everyone, for your hard work so far. We've got a long way to go, but we will find who murdered this young woman. Dismissed.'

CHAPTER SEVENTEEN

Mark clutched the collar of his jacket tight around his neck as he led the way towards the double doors of the building that housed Oxford City Council's mortuary.

Grey and foreboding clouds tumbled overhead, a portent for the heavy downpour that had been forecast for the morning, as well as the task that lay ahead.

As the last of the weak sunlight disappeared from view, it transformed the red brick of the single-storey building to a dull hue and sucked the colour from the shrubs that had been planted either side of the entrance.

His phone beeped in his pocket, and his mood improved as his eyes skimmed the text from Lucy.

Thanks again for the dinner invitation. Looking forward to it xx.

'Not that I'm in a hurry to get in there,' said Jan, 'but open the door, Sarge. We're about to get soaked.'

He pocketed the phone and wrenched open the door, standing to one side to let her pass before following her across the tiled floor to a reception desk.

Clive Moore looked up from the computer he was working on, then pushed a clipboard across the desk to them. 'Morning, detectives. Sign in, please.'

Mark pointed at the computer. 'New kit? About time.'

'Our illustrious leaders decided to grant us a smidgen of funds to embark upon a humble spending spree,' said the pathologist's assistant, peering down his nose as he handed a pen to Mark. 'A shame the rest of the pleas we've made for additional money have gone unheeded.'

Mark bit back a smile and signed the visitor log before passing it to Jan.

Clive's dreary demeanour was accentuated by the grey sweater he wore. Lanky, in his late twenties, he almost aged another two decades in front of them when he took the clipboard from Jan with a sigh, as if the weight of the world was on his shoulders.

'Busy?' said Mark.

'Always. Especially with Gillian having to be in court this week. We could've done without that. We're going to be working over the weekend now to try and catch up. Oh, here she is.'

Mark turned at the sound of footsteps to see Gillian

hurrying towards them, a mask pulled down around her throat.

'Morning,' she said. 'Can you get ready as soon as possible? I want to make a start straight away.'

'No problem,' said Mark. 'Clive was just telling us you're having to work this weekend.'

Gillian's eyes steeled. 'It's worth it. Did he have a chance to tell you my evidence helped get a conviction yesterday? Six years for a domestic abuse case. The poor woman was unrecognisable by the time he'd finished with her. At least he won't see the light of day for a while.'

'Well done.'

He meant it, too. Despite their past animosity, he and the pathologist had a mutual respect these days, and her role within the court system was well renowned. She would have been a formidable asset to the prosecution's case.

'Thanks. See you in there in five minutes.'

She nodded to Jan, then spun around and headed back to the examination room, the steel door slamming in her wake.

'You know where the changing rooms are,' said Clive as he left the desk and hurried after her. 'I'd better go and help her get ready.'

Mark left Jan to get changed and stepped into the men's locker room. Pulling apart a plastic sealed gown that had been left in a pile on a nearby wooden bench, he shrugged it over his shoulders and then added the matching bootees to his feet.

Squaring his shoulders, he moved out into the corridor and saw Jan waiting by the doors.

'All set?'

'As I'll ever be,' she said. 'Let's get it over with.'

Gillian peered over her mask at them as they entered the examination room. 'I figured I'd make a start while I was waiting – you don't mind?'

'Not at all,' said Mark. In fact, he was glad he hadn't had to watch the pathologist brandishing the saw she had used to open the girl's skull, and noted relief in Jan's eyes as they moved closer to the table.

He listened while Gillian dictated her findings into a microphone clipped to her lapel as she worked, her movements methodical and steady.

Clive passed various instruments to her as she requested them, the two of them working in tandem, a fluidity to the way they progressed through the brutal reality of a post mortem.

Finally it was done and, while Clive began to sew Jessica's broken body back together, Gillian beckoned them away from the table and across to a stainless-steel sink where she scrubbed her hands.

'Okay, well, you probably got the gist of all that but I can confirm she was killed with a single blow to the back of her head, just above her ear. I believe she would've been rendered unconscious with that – any hope of survival was lost when her attacker decided to dump her body on the gallops instead of seeking medical attention.'

'So, she might've survived if she hadn't been dumped?' said Jan.

Gillian lowered her mask and grimaced. 'I wouldn't want to hazard a guess as to her quality of life after a blow like that, but it is a possibility, yes.'

'Was she assaulted?'

'No – I haven't found any indication of sexual assault.'

'What about the fact that she was found with her knickers around her ankle, then?'

'Maybe her killer was interrupted.'

'There were a couple of theories we were progressing in the incident room,' said Mark. 'One was the possibility of it being a hit-and-run accident—'

'No,' said Gillian. 'There are no signs of lesions to her skin that you'd typically see in a hit-and-run. If that was the case, we would've seen abrasions where she'd been hit and dragged along the road. What else were you thinking?'

'The possibility that it might've been an accident. That she might've been injured by a horse – if she'd been thrown off, or kicked.'

The pathologist shook her head. 'You can rule that out as well. The angle of the strike to her skull is all wrong for a kick from a horse – and I've seen plenty of those in my time working here. Again, if she had fallen, then I would've expected to see evidence of grass stains, bruising to her limbs or breakages in fingers or wrists where she tried to slow her fall. There's nothing here to support that theory.'

Mark sighed and cast his gaze back to the pitiful figure on the table, her face now covered with a sheet while Clive began to clean the floor.

'Then it's definitely murder,' he said.

CHAPTER EIGHTEEN

Jan paused at the garden gate to the Marleys' home, a sickness twisting at her stomach.

Turpin joined her, pocketing his mobile phone. 'Kennedy says once we're done here, that's us for the day. We're due over at MacKenzie's stables tomorrow to oversee the remaining interviews there.'

'Okay. He's sure about this?'

'Better they find out from us than local gossip. It's not going to be long before someone finds out and lets it slip.'

'All right.'

Four days of grief had taken their toll on Jessica's father. When he opened the door, Jan was taken aback by the pallor of his face and the dull ache in his eyes.

The family dog barked once from behind the living room door, its claws scratching at the wooden surface before Jan heard Jessica's mother berating the animal. The scratching stopped, followed by the sound of the latch being turned.

Jessica's father shuffled backwards to let them in, and then glanced over his shoulder as PC Wickes emerged from the kitchen.

'Grant said you were on your way over. Have you caught anyone yet?'

'It's very early days, Mr Marley, but we're doing everything we can. We've got a lot of new information coming in,' said Turpin. 'Would it be all right to give you and your wife an update?'

Trevor Marley nodded, his eyes downcast. Pointing towards the living room door, he let Turpin lead the way, Jan following the two men.

Jessica's mother sat in the same armchair as last time, the small dog in her lap. Wendy Marley's eyes had the same redness about them as her husband's, and she twisted a paper tissue between her hands as she watched Turpin and Jan take a seat on the sofa.

'They say they want to update us,' said Trevor. He ran a hand across the brightly patterned throw on the back of his armchair, and then sat with a sigh. 'Go on, then.'

'The Home Office pathologist concluded her post mortem this morning,' said Jan, her gaze moving between the two parents. 'She has told us that Jessica died as a result of a single blow to the back of her head.

The pathologist has ruled out a hit-and-run accident or any possibility that Jessica might have fallen from a horse.'

Trevor ran a hand across his face, then stood and moved across to where Wendy sat, wrapping his arm around her as he lowered himself to the arm of her chair. 'Did she die straight away, or did she suffer?'

Jan swallowed. 'The pathologist confirms that the knock to her head was enough to render her unconscious immediately.'

'Oh my God,' said Wendy, and leaned into her husband. 'She was still alive when he left her out there?'

'I'm sorry, yes. That is what the pathologist believes.'

'Who would do such a thing?' said Trevor, wiping at his eyes with the sleeve of his shirt. 'Our beautiful girl. She never hurt anyone in her whole life. Never had a bad word to say about anyone. Why?'

Jan glanced across at Turpin, who gave a slight nod. She turned back to the Marleys. 'I'm sorry to ask you this, but were you aware that Will was planning to propose to Jessica at the weekend?'

Wendy began to cry once more, and shook her head as her husband turned pale.

'Was he?' he managed.

'He informed us when we interviewed him,' said Jan. 'You had no idea?'

Trevor plucked a paper tissue from a box on a side table next to his wife and blew his nose. 'No.'

Jan paused while Wendy wiped fresh tears away. Conscious of his owner's distress, the small dog nudged at Wendy's elbow, whimpering.

Trevor stared at the carpet, his Adam's apple bobbing in his throat. 'He would have made her so happy.'

'You wouldn't have a problem with her planning to settle down so young?' said Jan.

'As long as she was happy, that's all that would've mattered to us.'

Wendy pressed her handkerchief to her lips.

'Were you aware of Will and Jessica arguing at all lately? Did she seem on edge about anything?'

'Not on edge, no,' Wendy managed. 'I do think all the work she was doing on top of her college studies was starting to take its toll, though.'

'Oh? In what way?'

'I got the impression things weren't going as well there as she tried to make out sometimes. When I tried to ask her about it, she told me she had more important things to worry about than her grades.'

'When was this?'

'About three weeks ago.' Wendy looked up at her husband. 'I didn't say anything to you because I didn't want you to worry.'

'It's all right, love,' said Trevor. He squeezed her

shoulder, then turned to Jan. 'Jessica would've told us if there was something bothering her, I know she would have.'

Turpin rose from his seat. 'We'll leave you in Grant's capable hands, but if you do think of anything – anything at all that might help us – then please phone, won't you? It doesn't matter if you think it's not important. It helps us to understand your daughter and what might have happened.'

'Of course,' said Trevor.

Five minutes later, Jan took a deep gulp of fresh air as they walked towards the car. 'Talking to the parents is always the hardest part, isn't it?'

'I know.'

She slid behind the wheel, then waited while Turpin buckled his seatbelt. 'Have you got anything planned after work, Sarge?'

'No – quiet one for me. Why?'

She jerked her head in the direction of the house. 'I'm going to need a drink after that and the post mortem this morning.'

'What about the twins?'

'Scott's taking them to brass band practice this evening.'

'So, you get away with not having to listen to them?'

'You've got me there, Sarge.'

'All right. First round's on me, though.'

CHAPTER NINETEEN

Mark weaved through the after-work crowd gathered around the bar of the Journeyman's Tavern.

He kept his elbows out to carve a path between a group of men who lurched as one towards the space he'd left behind, and tried not to spill the two pints of copper-coloured ale he clutched.

The place was heaving, and as he made his way back to their table, he spotted the tell-tale ID cards of different companies based at the nearby science park clipped to belts and jacket lapels.

At half past six, it was already dark beyond the window next to where Jan sat, the inside of the pub reflected in the panes of glass.

The detective constable had her chin in her hand, her gaze unfocused while she traced an indeterminate pattern across the table with her forefinger.

Mark had chosen the pub for its position on the river that wrapped its way around the spit of land on which the seventeenth-century building stood, and for the fact that, as far as he was aware, none of their colleagues frequented the place given its distance from the police station.

'Here you go.'

Jan jerked her head up at the sound of his voice. 'Sorry. I was miles away.'

'I thought you were.'

They clinked glasses, and Mark took a long sip before setting down his drink on the table with a sigh. 'I needed that.'

'Me too. How did you find this place?'

'I stumbled across it when I was out for a walk with Hamish. There's a huge garden behind the building – it slopes down to the river and there's a sort of beach there that's lower downstream than the weirs. Back in September, it was full of kids and dogs playing – it was still warm enough. You and Scott should bring the boys here in the summer. They'd love it.'

'I will, and you're right – they would. I've lived this way for years, and I can't believe I haven't been here before.'

They fell into a companionable silence for a moment, and Mark cast his gaze around the pub.

A group of regulars clustered at one end of the oak-panelled bar, an elderly man on a stool holding court while he balanced a small terrier on his lap. The dog's eyes watched the men gathered around, and he snapped greedily at the crisps and savoury biscuits that were broken up and handed to him as they talked.

'How are you holding up, Sarge?' said Jan, breaking into his thoughts.

He took a sip of his drink first.

'All right, under the circumstances.'

'Have you had a chance to speak to your girls about it?'

Mark grimaced at the memory.

Debbie had phoned the night before and he had spoken with his youngest, Anna, first.

The twelve-year-old had been tearful, argumentative – and it hurt to hear her pain. She had calmed down after a little while, after he and Debbie had made sure she understood that she would still see him on a regular basis and that he and his ex-wife were still friends, and then Louise had taken the phone from her sister.

At fourteen, the girl had a way with words and left him under no illusion as to what she thought of her parents' divorce.

He managed a small smile at the memory. His older daughter was growing into a formidable character, and he had no doubt that she would hold him accountable if he let them down.

'They're all right,' he said to Jan. 'Or they will be, at least.'

'Did Louise kick your arse?'

He laughed. 'She did.'

'I'm sure they'll be okay, Sarge. I get the impression from the way you talk about them that they're mature for their ages.'

'Thanks, and call me Mark while we're out, okay?'

'Cheers. It was interesting what Wendy Marley said about Jessica's grades.'

'And her comment that she had more important things on her mind. Do you think she'd found out about Will's proposal?'

'Perhaps. From what everyone's told us about her, she sounds as if she was quite canny.'

'Would that affect her college work, though?'

Jan leaned back against the wooden pew that served as a bench seat, her gaze falling to the pitted surface of the table.

'It's hard to say. I mean, I look at the amount of homework my two get every week, and they're not even at grammar school yet. Maybe Jessica's grades had been slipping because she'd simply taken on too much.'

'And perhaps she didn't want to acknowledge that.' Mark shrugged. 'I don't know.'

Jan raised her glass to her lips, then paused. 'Do you think she would've survived if someone had found her out there on the gallops?'

'Don't.' Mark held up his hand. 'Don't do that to yourself. Jessica died because some bastard whacked her across the head with a blunt instrument. That's what we focus on. That's what we investigate. If you start thinking about what could've been, it won't do you any good at all.'

Her face fell. 'I know.'

'It's okay. It's all right to feel like this. I know if anyone harmed Anna or Louise, I'd want answers. We'll get there.'

She managed a smile, and clinked her glass against his. 'I'll drink to that.'

CHAPTER TWENTY

Leaving Jan in the car with her phone to her ear as she received an update from the incident room, Mark cast his gaze around the walls of the brick stable block and whistled under his breath.

The whole building had been converted from a bay of six stalls into an open breakout area for the jockeys and stable lads who worked for MacKenzie Adams.

Central to the space were eight long tables, bench seats alongside in various states of disarray, as if the occupants had left in a hurry and couldn't be bothered to tidy up after themselves.

Near the door, next to where he stood, a cheap kitchen had been installed with two microwaves, a dishwasher, hob, and a sink cluttered with piles of crockery. A waft of stale coffee emanated from one of the percolators plugged in on a worktop that ran the length of the wall to the first of four windows.

Beyond the panes of glass, Mark could see the sweeping brow of the Berkshire Downs poking through a curling mist that enveloped the surrounding countryside, and then shivered.

It seemed Adams' attempts at providing a canteen for his staff didn't extend to proper insulation or heating.

'Budge over, I'm dying for a cuppa.'

Mark stepped aside at the sound of the voice, then looked down as a compact man in his twenties pushed past and hurried over to the electric kettle.

The man reached into a cupboard, then held up a chipped china mug.

'Want one?'

'No, thanks.'

'Are you a copper?'

'One of them, yes.'

'Saw a bunch of uniforms turn up fifteen minutes ago. This about Jessica, then?'

'Yes.'

The kettle started to rumble on its stand, and the man flicked the switch before it had boiled. 'Wastes electricity otherwise,' he said, then shrugged. 'That's what my old man always told me, anyway.'

He bent down and opened the refrigerator next to

Mark, sniffed an open carton of milk, then shrugged again. 'It'll have to do, I suppose.'

He stirred it into his tea, tossed the spoon into the sink with a clatter, and then held out his hand. 'Paul Hitchens. You must be Turpin. She said I'd find you in here.'

Mark wondered what Jan had made of Brennan's housemate, and pulled out his warrant card. 'Detective Sergeant Mark Turpin.'

Hitchens jerked his thumb over his shoulder at a long table near the window, weak sunlight stretching across the pine surface. 'Do you mind if we sit over there? It's warmer.'

'After you.'

Hitchens sat on a bench with his back to the window and rubbed a hand across the back of his neck as Mark sat opposite. 'That's better. I reckon I must've been a lizard in a past life. I can't feel my fingers and toes until I get some sunshine on them, especially this time of year.'

'Doesn't Adams turn the heating on in here?'

Hitchens choked out a bitter laugh. 'No point, not with that door opening and closing all the time. Besides, look at the state of the place. It's not like we spend a lot of time in here. He doesn't pay us to sit on our arses unless we're on the back of a horse.'

Mark peered across at the clutter and mess that covered most of the tables. 'Who cleans up?'

'I don't know.' Hitchens frowned, and then took a sip of tea. He scowled. 'Fuck. Milk's off.'

Pulling out his notebook and a pen, Mark flipped to a clean page and cleared his throat. 'Did you know Jessica Marley?'

'Only in passing. Will never brought her back to the cottage. You've seen it, right? Can't blame him.' Hitchens shoved the mug of tea to one side. 'I only ever saw her down the pub.'

'The Farriers Arms?'

'Yes. Mind you, I didn't know they were boyfriend-girlfriend. Not until he came back down from Yorkshire.'

'You saw her in the pub before Will worked for MacKenzie?'

'Well, it is my local. I suppose I didn't really notice her. I mean, we go there to drink and have a laugh. She weren't my type, so I suppose I—' He broke off and scratched at his ear. 'Seems strange, talking about her like this.'

'We understand that she worked here before she was killed.'

'Only recently.'

'But you just said you only saw her down the pub.'

Hitchens crossed his arms and leaned on the table. 'That's right. By the time she turned up for work, I was already out on the gallops, exercising the horses. She were only here part-time. Shovelling shit and stuff.

Christ knows why – Will says she had two other jobs on top of her college course. Talk about being overambitious.'

'Do you think she took the job to spend more time with Will?'

Hitchens snorted. 'Doubt it. Like I said, by the time she turned up for work we were up there on the Downs. And she'd be gone before we got back. I think she was doing two or three hours at a time. I mean, she might've got some more hours given to her in time. I mean, if she hadn't… Christ.'

He leaned back in his seat and cast his gaze to the ceiling, before his eyes found Mark's once more. 'Do you know who did it?'

'It's an ongoing enquiry.'

'Which means you don't.'

'Where were you between six o'clock Monday night and seven o'clock Tuesday morning?'

Hitchens threw up his hands. 'Oh, great. Here we go.'

'Answer the question, Paul.'

'I went to the Farriers on Monday night. Will and Nigel were with me. I left with Will at about eight 'cause we were riding out early the next day.'

'Who drove?'

'I did. I don't like drinking much. Makes me sick.'

'Did you come straight back?'

'Yes. Back to the cottage.'

'Then what happened?'

'Nothing. I was sat watching one of them real-life cooking programmes or whatever. Stupid, really. They always make me hungry and I'm on a diet at the moment. I tend to put on too much weight between races otherwise.'

'Where was Will?'

'Upstairs. In bed, I suppose. He went up more or less as soon as he'd had something to eat. Said he was tired. Occupational hazard.'

'And where were you between Monday night and seven o'clock Tuesday morning?'

'Asleep. My alarm went off at four-thirty and I put the kettle on. Me and Will had a cuppa and then headed off to the yard. We got there at five-thirty, and started getting ready to ride up to the Downs.'

'What happened up there, on Tuesday morning?'

Hitchens swallowed. 'Of all the people to find her—'

'Why did Will go first?'

'Because MacKenzie had him riding that nutter Onyx. He has to go before everyone else, otherwise the dumb animal takes off after everything and anything in front of him.'

'What happened when Will found Jessica?'

'I don't know. I wasn't there when he found her. Like I said, Onyx needs to be out there in front to blow off some steam before the rest of us start. One of the older lads, Stephen, was the one who found Will. Said he looked like he'd seen a ghost. 'Course, after that, all hell broke loose.'

'Did you see her?'

'No, thank God. As soon as Stephen came riding back, we could see something was wrong. MacKenzie told us all to wait by the gate to the gallops while he phoned the police. Then your lot turned up.'

Mark drew two straight lines under his notes, and then pushed the bench seat back so it resembled the other castaways.

He handed Hitchens a business card. 'Let me know if you think of anything else, Paul. Anything at all.'

The jockey turned the card between his fingers and then lifted his chin. 'You find the bastard who did that to her, Detective Turpin. She didn't deserve to die like that. No-one does.'

CHAPTER TWENTY-ONE

Nigel White glared at Jan as she crossed the stable yard towards him, Turpin at her side.

A woollen hat covered White's head, and he had bundled himself up in a thick padded coat and scarf, his jeans partially hidden in a pair of well-worn black riding boots. He peered down at her with piercing blue eyes as she approached.

'Mr White?' Jan flipped open her warrant card and held it up. 'We need to have a few minutes of your time. Routine questions.'

'I've already spoken to the police,' he said. He turned back to the exercise machine at a loud bang on the side of the galvanised metal panelling. 'Easy, boy.'

'Mr White, we can do this here or down at the police station. It's up to you.'

He ran a hand across the grey stubble covering his

jaw, then turned back to her. 'You'll have to get up here, then. I need to watch this one.'

Jan took the proffered hand, and climbed onto the viewing platform next to him while Turpin wandered around the circular structure to another platform on the opposite side. His head and shoulders appeared a moment later, and he rested his arms along the top of the barrier as he watched the horse inside.

She followed the animal's anti-clockwise progression for a moment, and then turned to White. 'What's wrong with him?'

'Pulled a tendon at Newmarket the other week. He's on the mend, but this allows us to exercise him without aggravating that injury. If we tried to put a rider on him and send him up to the gallops, there's no knowing what he'll do. It's all about patience with these creatures.'

'So how does this help?'

'It keeps the exercise consistent.' He gestured to a set of controls to his right. 'We can adjust the speed and direction from here, and it gives me a proper look at how he's moving and whether there are any other issues we need to be mindful of during his recovery. Plus, it's cheaper than having several of the lads out here walking him around.'

Jan frowned. 'What if he trips?'

'He's not tethered. That's why those gates are hinged. There's a padded blanket under each as well, and no sharp edges. If he takes a tumble, he'll get up again and carry on. It happens.' He shrugged, then turned to her. 'All right. What do you want to ask me?'

'Where were you between the times of ten o'clock on Monday night and seven o'clock on Tuesday morning?'

'I was at the Farriers Arms until ten-thirty Monday night.'

'Did you speak to Jessica Marley?'

'Only to ask her to refill my glass.'

'What were you drinking?'

'Just the local beer.'

'What did you do when you left the pub?'

'Came straight back here. I'm in charge of the lads and the yard. They were out early Tuesday to exercise some of the horses – as you know.'

'When you say "here"—'

'The cottage. Up the hill. The one I share with Will and Paul.'

'Were they both in when you got in?'

'In, and in bed by the time I got in. Like I said, they were up early on Tuesday, and I wasn't far behind them.'

'What time did you get up on Tuesday?'

'Same as always. About five-thirty. Fucking freezing, it was. Thankfully, I don't have to be out with the training string anymore. I start in the yard at seven.'

He turned away and hawked into the mud and straw to the side of the platform.

Jan wrinkled her nose and looked across the exercise machine to where Turpin stood. He raised an eyebrow, and she shook her head.

'What did you do when you got down here?' she said.

'Sorted out the tack. Saddles, bridles. Checked everything was all right. Some of the lads can cut corners if you don't keep an eye on them. Last thing I want is someone taking a fall because equipment hasn't been checked. I'd never hear the end of it.'

'How long have you worked for MacKenzie Adams?'

'About ten years. Started off as a lad, did some riding, then when I retired from that, he offered me this job, managing the yard for him.'

'Did you race professionally?'

'For a while, yes.'

'And you didn't fancy setting up as a trainer like Dominic Millar did?'

He spat out a bitter laugh. 'No. I didn't have his sort of money for a start.'

'Who managed MacKenzie's yard before you?'

'No-one. He did it all himself. Had to, starting out. It's like that. You keep your costs down as much as possible – even when you're winning.'

'Hence this exercise machine?'

'Exactly.'

He winked, and Jan looked away.

'Why did he give Jessica Marley a job?'

White snorted. 'Bloody good question.'

'You've no idea?'

'No.'

'He didn't ask you about it?'

'Why would he?' White lowered his gaze to the horse as it passed before them once more, and muttered under his breath.

'I didn't catch that, sorry?'

'I said, he doesn't ask for my opinion about anything that goes on around here. I just work here, all right? I keep my head down, and I get on with what I'm told to do.'

'What did Jessica do around here?'

'To be honest, she was a pain in the backside. She probably only got the job because she was pretty, and MacKenzie's always had a soft spot for the pretty ones.'

'So, what did she do?'

'He said he was employing her to help out in the yard, and to learn a bit about the racing industry to help with her college studies. I gave her the same jobs as the younger lads – things she couldn't mess up, mind. I didn't have time to be keeping an eye on her and running this place. She polished tack, cleaned out the stables, that sort of thing.'

'Ever get the chance to ride one of the horses?'

He sneered. 'This isn't some bloody pony trekking place, detective. No – she was never allowed near any of the horses. No-one is until they've had some experience. Too bloody dangerous.'

As if to emphasise his point, the beast in the training enclosure kicked the side of the galvanised barrier with such force that the whole structure shook.

'You can imagine what would happen if he did that to someone,' said White. 'More than my bloody job's worth.'

'Did she ever work in the house?'

'Jess? No. No need for her to go in there.'

'Did she have anything to do with MacKenzie once she got the job?'

'No.' White pressed a button on the panel next to him and climbed down from the platform. He beckoned to Jan to do the same.

She was grateful that he had at least offered her a hand down, and as Turpin rounded the corner she paused, her notebook halfway to her handbag.

'One more question, Mr White. Does Dominic Millar ever visit the yard?'

'Dom? No – he uses the gallops from time to time, but he'd never set foot here.'

'Oh? Why is that?'

White brushed past her and began to slide back the bolts on the side of the training ring. He rested his hand on the gate and peered back over his shoulder at her.

'Best you ask Dominic that when you see him.'

CHAPTER TWENTY-TWO

The first peals from the bells at St Nicholas's church reached Mark as he locked his front door the next morning.

Hamish peered through the front window, his paws on the back of the sofa and his tongue lolling.

'Get off of there,' said Mark, and rapped his knuckles on the glass.

The dog barked once, then disappeared.

Mark set a brisk pace towards the centre of town, and tugged a woollen hat over his head to ward off the damp breeze coming from the river.

Sunday, and the traffic was light at this time of the day, the town bleary-eyed from a late Saturday night of drinking and partying. Litter blew across the pavement in front of his boots as he entered the town square, and he glared at the clouds forming overhead.

He didn't want to drive; he wanted to walk.

He needed to clear his head before arriving at the incident room.

Sleep had proved impossible. The death of a young woman always troubled him, especially now that he was so far away from his daughters. He always coached his junior colleagues about the stresses and strains of the job, but kept his own thoughts to himself.

After he'd been stabbed, after the slow recovery and then the move from Swindon to the smaller Oxfordshire market town, he'd tried to put all of it behind him.

Bury it.

Sometimes it worked; sometimes it didn't.

Deep in thought, he nearly collided with a man in his fifties leaving a newsagent's. He sidestepped, apologised, and then recognised his DI.

'Sorry, guv. Lost in thought.'

'No problem, Mark.' Kennedy fell into step beside him, easily keeping pace with Mark's long stride. 'How did you get on yesterday at Adams' stables? Anything interesting?'

Mark paused while he waited for a taxi to drive past, then led the way across the road. 'Hitchens seems genuine. Career jockey, by the sound of it, lives for the work. He confirmed he and Will Brennan got back to the cottage just before eight-thirty. Nigel White left the pub at ten-thirty. Both Paul and Will had already gone up to bed by the time he got back home. They were both up early for the training ride the next morning.'

Kennedy harrumphed under his breath. 'How far is the cottage from the training gallops?'

'About three miles, I reckon.'

'Too far to walk, then.'

Mark didn't answer, and instead reached out to press the button for the pedestrian crossing.

'Present investigation aside, how're you settling in?' said Kennedy, the wind lifting his thin hair before he ran a hand over it. 'We haven't had much time to catch up since the last case we worked on together.'

'All right, guv.'

'I heard you'd moved off the boat?'

'Too cold for this time of year. I'm renting around the corner from the Abbey Gardens at the moment.'

The traffic braked to a halt, and they crossed the busy junction.

'Thinking of buying somewhere more permanent?'

'I thought I might have a look around when it gets warmer.'

'Good,' said Kennedy. 'It'd be a shame to lose you. Wiltshire's loss is our gain.'

'Thanks, guv.' He fell to silence, wondering whether his boss had heard about his imminent divorce.

It wouldn't take long to reach his ears given station gossip, even if Jan said nothing.

It was the way it was.

'Heard anything else about that incident in Swindon and the chap who stabbed you?'

Mark stumbled, and cursed under his breath as he righted himself and kept going, trying to ignore the heat that rose to his cheeks. 'Nothing, guv.'

They had reached the police station, and Kennedy waved his security card at the grey panel next to the reception desk, then led the way up the stairs.

'Well, keep up the good work, Mark. We'll find who did this to Jessica.'

'Guv.'

Kennedy shoved open the door to the incident room, and Mark waited for a moment at the threshold, gathering his thoughts.

His walk into work often served as a way to sort through the jumble of information he'd listened to over the course of an investigation, but meeting Kennedy had interrupted his usual pattern. After a few seconds, he moved across to his desk, ready to face whatever the HOLMES2 database had thrown his way by way of algorithms and data output while he'd been away from his computer overnight.

'Sarge!'

Jan burst through the door, holding up her mobile phone.

'What's up?'

'Noah Collins at the Farriers Arms just called. Says we need to get over there straight away.'

Five minutes later, he slammed the car door shut and buckled his seatbelt.

'What did he say?'

Jan stomped on the accelerator and sped from the car park. 'He sounded out of breath. Said there was someone there who wanted to speak to us. He hung up before I could ask who.'

'Bloody hell.'

The last thing Mark wanted was for Jessica's acquaintances to turn vigilante in their haste to find the young woman's killer. Tensions were already high amongst MacKenzie Adams' employees following the interviews at the racing stables yesterday, and he could only imagine the conversations that had taken place around the bar of the Farriers Arms since he and Jan had spoken with Noah Collins on Tuesday.

He held on to the handle above the window as Jan took a corner and then accelerated across a narrow bridge, her face determined as she powered the car through the narrow lanes.

Within twenty minutes, they'd reached the outskirts of Harton Wick.

The village appeared deserted, and Mark checked his watch. It seemed that at eleven o'clock in the morning, none of the residents had yet ventured out. As the car travelled along the lane towards the pub, he was struck by how spread out the village was compared with others in the area.

'No wonder no-one heard anything,' he said. 'You need a car to get anywhere around here really, don't you?'

'I know. Jessica was unusual in that she walked between her house and the pub,' said Jan. 'I noticed that when we were doing the house-to-house enquiries during the week.'

She pulled into the pub car park and braked hard, sending up a flurry of grit that had accumulated next to the entranceway.

'All right. Let's go.'

Mark led the way across the asphalt towards the front door of the pub, then took a deep breath. For all they knew, they could be walking into an emotionally charged situation, and he had no wish to be the recipient of an ill-judged assault by surprising someone on the other side.

He knocked twice, and then as he pushed against the heavy oak door into the pub, he blinked to ward off the sudden lack of light, and peered into the gloom.

Before he'd taken a step further, a slight figure barrelled across the room towards them, her dark hair flying.

'Is it true? Is she dead?'

'Sorry.' Noah Collins' voice boomed across the room before Mark saw the landlord appear through a doorway behind the bar, drying his hands on a towel. 'I didn't hear you come in.'

'What's going on? Where is she?' The young woman hugged her arms around her middle, turning from Mark to Noah, then back, her red-rimmed eyes wide in her pale face. 'What happened to her?'

Jan moved forward, her voice calm. 'Who are you?'

In response, the woman burst into tears.

'Bethany Myers. I work with her. You left a message on my phone, right? We're – we were best friends. I was going to be her bridesmaid.'

CHAPTER TWENTY-THREE

'Noah, could you make Bethany a cup of tea? Lots of sugar,' said Jan.

She steered the woman towards a large round table that had been placed in an alcove at the back of the pub's seating area, away from the windows and any prying eyes.

Compared to the wall painted a deep russet and the array of cushions that lined the old church pew Bethany sat on, her face appeared even paler than Jan had first realised. The effect was almost ethereal.

Blue eyes peered out from under a dark fringe, and the woman twisted an intricate silver ring on her right hand, watching as Jan and Turpin pulled out seats opposite.

'When did you get back?' said Turpin.

'Last night. Late – about ten-thirty,' said Bethany. 'I

got your message when I got to Chepstow – the mobile coverage was shit where we were staying.'

'Where was that?'

'At a friend's house outside Tintern. Just a bit of a break, that's all. I go up there maybe two or three times a year.'

'Have you spoken to anyone else since you got DS Turpin's message?'

Bethany bit her lip. 'I was driving so I only got that when I'd stopped for petrol and a sandwich to keep me going on the way back here. I didn't want to phone Will when I got home because I knew he was usually asleep by then, and, of course, by the time I tried to phone him this morning he was already out with the horses. I came here at eleven o'clock when I knew Noah and Sonia would be getting ready to open. Is it true? Is she dead?'

'I'm very sorry to tell you this, Bethany, but yes. Jessica's body was found on the gallops on the Downs above MacKenzie Adams' yard on Tuesday morning.'

Bethany let out an anguished shriek, then brought her hand to her mouth. 'Why would someone do that to her?'

'We believe she was attacked on her way home from work here on Monday night.' Jan leaned forward. 'Do you have any idea who might have had reason to harm Jessica?'

'No. She was lovely, she really was. Everyone liked her. She—'

Bethany broke off as a shadow fell over the table.

Jan peered over her shoulder as Noah Collins approached, a steaming mug in his hand.

'Tea,' he said. 'Plenty of sugar, and a splash of cold water so you can drink it straight away.'

Bethany grimaced at the first mouthful, but murmured her thanks while the burly landlord hovered a few steps away, his face full of concern.

'How did you know Jessica?' said Jan.

'From secondary school. I didn't know her well back then, just in passing. Then I applied for a job here about two years ago in the kitchen, and Jessica was already here. I learned loads off her.' A wistful smile crossed Bethany's face. 'We used to have such a laugh.'

'Good times,' said Collins, and nodded. 'It won't be the same without her.'

Jan glanced at the landlord, then back to Bethany. 'Did you always work with Jessica?'

'No, only on the occasional Friday night when it got busy. Noah called her and asked her to come in to help out at short notice. A lot of the lads from the stables around here get paid that day, same as a lot of the tradespeople who live nearby so everyone's out having a drink and letting off steam. I work Fridays and Wednesdays.'

'How do you get to work?'

'I've got a moped.' Bethany's gaze fell to her hands. 'I never liked walking, not like Jess. I rent a room in a house too far from here to walk anyway. Anyway, I don't think I'll ever risk walking anywhere after this. Not now.'

Jan reached into her bag and extracted a packet of paper tissues, plucked out one and passed it to Bethany.

She gave the young woman a moment to gather her thoughts, and then said, 'When we first came in, you said you were going to be Jessica's bridesmaid. Can you tell us about that?'

Bethany let out a shuddering sigh, and nodded. 'Will had it all planned out. Did he tell you?'

'Why don't you tell me what you know?' said Jan, and gestured for her to continue.

'He wanted to surprise her. Make it something special. They really were a nice couple. Of course, she'd found it hard when he went up north for a while but I think she realised he needed to do it, to give his racing career a shot.' She smiled. 'She was over the moon when he came back, though.'

'Did you ever see them arguing?'

'God, no. Not proper arguing. They'd disagree about stuff, same as any couple would. But they never had a full-blown argument. Not in front of me, anyway.'

'When did you last see Will Brennan?'

'On the Friday, when I was working here.'

'And how was Will when you last saw him?'

'Excited. Looking forward to this weekend. And

nervous, too. He really loved her, you know. I could tell.'

'Did you know Will prior to Jessica going out with him?'

Bethany's mouth quirked into a sardonic smile. 'I dated him for six months before they got together.'

'Oh?'

'I'd split up with him about four months before he met Jess, so it was nothing like that.' Bethany waved her hand as if dismissing a bad smell. 'Obviously, it took a bit of getting used to, but like I said – I was the one he asked for help in planning the engagement, and he said she'd probably ask me to be a bridesmaid because we were such good friends.'

'And you didn't find that strange?'

'No, why would I? Me and Will hadn't been going out with each other for ages by then.'

'When you last worked with Jessica, did she seem concerned about anything?'

'Not that I can remember.'

'Was she worried about anyone, or did she mention being intimidated by anyone in the pub?'

'I can assure you, my regulars aren't the sort of people to go around attacking young women,' said Collins. He dropped his hands to his sides as he approached the table. 'And if Jessica was having any issues, she'd have come and talked to me.'

Bethany smiled up at him, then turned to Jan and

Turpin. 'Noah keeps a look out for all of us, don't you? No, I don't remember her saying anything about any trouble here, but—'

Her face fell.

'What is it?' said Turpin, straightening in his chair.

'It could be nothing.' The young woman shrugged. 'But Jess did mention that when she was working at the petrol station a couple of weeks ago she saw someone hovering about near the cold drinks cabinet while she and the bloke she works with there were serving other customers. I got the impression it worried her.'

'Did she say who it was, Bethany?'

'No – it got busy then, and when I started to ask her, she said it didn't matter and that she probably shouldn't have said anything.'

'Bethany, when was that? Can you remember the day she said she saw this man?'

'It was the Thursday before I went to Wales. Like I said, we were working together the Friday night here before I left, because it was busy.'

Jan swivelled in her seat to face Turpin, who wore a determined expression. He gestured to her to put away her notebook, then turned to Bethany and handed her a business card.

'Thank you, you've been very helpful. Please call me if you think of anything else that could help us.'

CHAPTER TWENTY-FOUR

'Who do you think he was?' said Jan as they hurried back to the car.

Mark waited until she'd started the engine, then ran his eyes over her notes from the interview. 'I don't know, but he obviously made some sort of impression on Jessica because she felt the need to tell Bethany about it. It's like when you're trying to process a thought, isn't it, and the only way you can do that is to talk about it to someone else.'

He pulled out his mobile phone and scrolled through his contacts list, then hit the call button.

It was answered after the second ring.

'Caroline? Can you let me have the phone number for Isaac Fisher, Jessica's supervisor from the petrol station?' He scrawled the number on a clean page. 'Does he work Sundays? No? All right, no problem. Got an address for him? I'll call him on our way.'

He ended the call after thanking the detective constable, and then dialled the number she'd given him.

Jan slowed the car as they approached the junction to the main road and pulled over, waiting as the dial tone began.

Mark stuck his thumb up as the call went through. 'Mr Fisher? Detective Sergeant Mark Turpin with Thames Valley Police. You spoke with two of my colleagues last week regarding Jessica Marley... Yes, that's right. We have some further questions that I'd like to discuss with you, and I wondered if we could drop by your house... Now would be perfect. Thank you.'

'Where?' said Jan, her hand on the gearstick.

'North of Abingdon. Cut around the ring road and head for Oxford. He's expecting us.'

Half an hour later, Jan slowed the car to a standstill outside a modest semi-detached house that had been rendered off-white and extended to the right of the front door.

The driveway looked new, and as Mark led the way to the door, he noticed a pile of empty cement bags pegged under four house bricks, the edges flapping in the wind that tugged at Jan's hair.

She fastened it into a bun, then stabbed the doorbell with her forefinger.

When the door opened, Mark was surprised by the size of the man who stood on the threshold.

In his late forties, with a rotund protruding stomach and spiky greying brown hair, Isaac Fisher wore a harried expression that did nothing for the frown lines that criss-crossed his forehead.

'Are you Detective Turpin?' he said.

'Yes, and this is my colleague, Detective Constable Jan West. Is it okay if we come in?'

'Sure. We'll use the kitchen – the wife's catching up with her soap operas at the moment.'

Mark followed Fisher past an open door through which a cascade of broad Australian accents bemoaned their latest lot in life, and then stepped into a bright kitchen that wrapped around the back of the house.

Skylights had been punctured into the ceiling at the far end, and Fisher led them into a space that Mark realised took up the back half of the new extension. Three sofas surrounded a low square table, and patio doors faced an expertly terraced garden.

'You've been busy. I saw the cement bags outside,' he said.

Fisher straightened, his smile broad. 'Finally got it finished three weeks ago. Julie – that's my wife – loves it. I can't wait until the summer when we can have those open. We've finally got the perfect space to have parties.'

His expression softened as he gestured to them to

take a seat. 'I couldn't believe it when I heard about Jess. Have you caught anyone yet?'

'I'm sorry,' said Mark. 'We can't comment about an ongoing investigation. Do you have a moment to answer a few more questions about Jessica and her work at the petrol station?'

'Of course.' Fisher lowered his considerable weight onto the sofa opposite and rested his elbows on his knees. 'What do you need to know?'

'We have reason to believe that Jessica might have been concerned about a customer who came into the petrol station on Thursday afternoon – the week before her death. She told a friend that a man came in and hovered by the cold drinks cabinet while you both worked, as if he was watching her. She was uncomfortable about it enough to tell her friend that evening. Did she mention anything to you?'

Fisher leaned back on the sofa and rubbed his chin, the frame groaning. 'She never said anything. I always thought she knew she could talk to me about anything.'

'Are your customers mostly regulars?'

'Pretty much. We see the same faces each week – probably because we're part of the supermarket chain and right next door to it. People do their shopping and then fill up on the way out. We're not near a main road – it's what Annie calls a "destination shop" – but we do get a few people each day dropping by to top up the tank if the price is cheaper than the bigger petrol station up near the dual carriageway.'

'And you didn't notice anything peculiar about anyone that Thursday?'

'Can't say I do. We had a regular stream of customers coming by, but it wasn't overly busy. We had time to restock the shelves in between serving everyone. The only time it got congested on the forecourt was just after three o'clock – we always get a flurry of customers once the school pick-up's been done and the parents are driving home. Jess left at four o'clock so she could get home in time to do her shift over at the Farriers.'

'How did she get there?' said Jan.

'By bus, same as she always did, unless her mum or dad happened to be passing by.'

Mark peered across at the notes Jan had taken, and then rose to his feet. 'Thanks for your time, Mr Fisher. We'll need to see CCTV film from the petrol station for that week. What's the best way to get it?'

Fisher pulled a mobile phone from his back pocket. 'I'll phone Annie now. She'll have to clear it with head office, but if we do that today, then she might be able to let you have it by, say, Tuesday. Would that be all right?'

'That'd be perfect, thank you.'

CHAPTER TWENTY-FIVE

Kennedy wasted no time in calling a briefing the following morning, corralling his bleary-eyed team around the whiteboard as soon as the last person walked into the incident room.

'For those of you who worked the weekend, thank you. We're a lot further forward than we were a week ago, so let's get on with it. Tom – what's happening about the camera footage from the bus company and the list of drivers?'

The police sergeant stepped forward, his tall frame towering over his colleagues. 'I spoke with the depot again on Saturday afternoon but according to the woman who answered the phone, there were no supervisors available. They can't hand over the recordings until they've had the paperwork signed off by two managers. I'm going to give them another call after this briefing.'

'Put them onto me if you don't get any joy,' said Kennedy. 'Someone needs to light a firework under their arses. What about the drivers?'

'I've been given two names,' said Tom. 'Leonard Smith and Michael Brockman. The HR manager I spoke to on Friday afternoon says they can't attend without a union representative so he was going to phone me back today to confirm when they can be here. I'm pushing to get them both in tomorrow morning.'

'Good man. Keep on top of that. Alex – what has Jasper and his team of CSIs managed to glean from the lane where the broken streetlight was found?'

'We've had a breakthrough with that,' said the detective constable. He flipped the cover from a report he held in his right hand. 'Jasper found a minuscule amount of blood spatter on some stones that were found on the grass verge a couple of metres away from the streetlight. A crisp packet had blown over the top of them, protecting them from the rain shower we had last week.'

An excited murmur filled the room.

Kennedy held up his hand for silence. 'Is it confirmed as Jessica's?'

'Not yet, guv. He's sent samples over to the specialist laboratory for a comparative analysis. Hopefully it won't turn out to be from a rabbit instead, so we can definitely place Jessica at that location when she was attacked.'

'Any sign of the murder weapon?'

'Sorry, guv. No.'

'Never mind. We keep looking then.' Kennedy rapped his knuckles on two photographs on the board. 'Paul Hitchens and Nigel White were interviewed on Saturday and each confirms their movements and Brennan's on Monday night and Tuesday morning. So far, we still have no motive for Jessica's murder, though, so I'm leaving them up here until we find out otherwise. Jan – when are you two planning to interview Dominic Millar?'

'Tomorrow, guv.'

'Bring that forward to today. I want everyone who has access to the gallops where Jessica's body was discovered interviewed by close of business. If Millar's setup is as small as MacKenzie Adams would have us believe, then you and Mark should be able to do that with the help of uniform this afternoon.'

'Yes, guv.'

'All right, next. Mark and Jan interviewed Bethany Myers yesterday – she's the lass who Jessica was helping out because it was a busy shift the Friday before she died. Bethany's informed us that Jessica was worried about a customer she'd seen the previous day while working at the petrol station with Isaac Fisher who might have been monitoring her movements. Mark

– how are the CCTV images from the garage coming along?'

'I spoke with Fisher this morning,' he said. 'Annie Hartman, his manager, has requested the relevant permissions from their head office to access the files in order to get them sent across to our digital forensics team. I've asked Fisher to make sure we get all the footage from the forecourt and the shop for the week leading up to Jessica's death.'

'Good, thank you. Caroline – speaking of digital forensics, how are you and Tracy getting on with the two mobile phones?'

Caroline pushed forward until she stood near the front of the room and raised her voice so everyone could hear her. 'Brennan's phone checks out, with calls to Jessica exactly as he said in his statement when Mark and Jan interviewed him. There are no calls or texts from his phone to Jessica or anyone else after eleven oh-five on Monday night.'

Kennedy paced in front of the whiteboard as he listened. 'And Jessica's?'

'This is where it gets interesting, guv. We got lucky and managed to guess Jessica's passcode – it's Brennan's date of birth. We checked her phone and at twelve thirty-five last Monday night she made two phone calls. Each only lasted for a few seconds, so at the moment I'm guessing that whoever she called didn't answer and it went through to voicemail both times.

Given the timeframe, she couldn't have had time to leave a message. She must've dialled one, got no answer then hung up and tried the other. Again, the second call only lasted a few seconds.'

'So, she was on the phone while she was walking home from the pub?' said Kennedy.

'Looks that way, guv.'

'And neither of those calls were made to Will Brennan?'

'No.'

The detective inspector wrote an update on the board, and then turned back to the team, tapping the end of the pen against the back of his hand. 'If Jessica had the phone to her ear while she was walking up the lane, then she might not have heard her attacker approaching.'

Jan hissed through her teeth as the fine hairs on the back of her neck stood on end. 'And if either of those calls had been answered, she might've been able to get help.'

The room fell silent.

'Bloody hell,' said Alex. 'There but for the grace…'

Kennedy pointed at Caroline. 'Try to find out who those numbers belong to—'

'I've already done that, guv,' she said. 'I ran the first one through HOLMES2 just before the briefing. It's Bethany Myers' number.'

'She said she didn't have a mobile phone signal where she was staying in Wales,' said Jan.

'Hence why Jessica hung up and tried someone else,' said Kennedy. 'Any luck with that one?'

'Yes,' said Caroline. 'We've traced it to Wayne Brooks. Jessica's tutor at college.'

'Hang on,' said Jan. 'When you tried to speak to him last week, where was he?'

'According to his wife, he was visiting his father in the Wye Valley,' said Alex.

Jan twisted in her seat until she could see Turpin towards the back of the group.

He raised an eyebrow in response. 'Are you thinking what I'm thinking?'

CHAPTER TWENTY-SIX

Jan flicked through the social media profile for Jessica Marley as Mark drove them towards the agricultural college, her thumb tapping the screen to scroll through the photographs the young woman had uploaded over the past year.

'Anything?' he said.

'Not yet.'

After the briefing had ended, Kennedy had tasked them with interviewing Wayne Brooks.

'And find out what the hell he was up to last week,' he'd said as they'd hurried from his office. 'I want some bloody answers.'

After fighting his way through rush-hour traffic for twenty minutes, Mark turned into the car park for the college, driving into a space that gave them a clear view of the campus.

He peered through the windscreen as a group of students hurried across the concrete apron of the college carrying an array of backpacks and sports bags.

By the way they shouldered their loads, he estimated each bag weighed several kilos, bringing back memories of his own commute to school and then university.

Jan put away her phone and reached into her bag for two cereal bars, handing one to him.

'Thanks. How are your two getting on at school?' he said.

'All good,' she said between mouthfuls. 'They're actually playing in tune these days. There's hope yet.'

He coughed, spluttering into the napkin before glaring at her.

'Serves you right,' she said, and winked. 'We put in the application for the boys' school yesterday.'

'With a year to go?'

'There's a waiting list. Better to get it in early.'

Mark swallowed the last of the cereal bar and wiped his fingers, then sat up straighter as a man in his late thirties jogged up the three steps leading into the college and disappeared through the double doors.

'That's our man. Come on. With any luck, we'll catch him before class starts.'

They walked across the car park, Jan brushing crumbs from her suit trousers before tucking a strand of hair behind her ear.

Entering the building, Mark was struck by the dated

decor. Although he knew from the college's website that construction had been completed in the late 1970s, he was surprised to see many of the original fittings in situ, including a wide wooden stair bannister that guided them from the reception hall up towards a room signposted for the administration department.

'Takes me back to my secondary school days,' said Jan. She tapped him on the arm as she peered past his shoulder.

Turning, he met the harried stare of an older woman with greying blonde hair who was glaring at them from behind a desk.

'Can I help you?' she said as she rose from a battered chair.

They pulled out their warrant cards, which were inspected in turn and handed back.

'Is this about Jessica Marley?'

'Yes – and you are?'

'Angela Spetcroft.' The woman tugged at the hem of her grey jacket before fastening the two buttons. 'You'll be wanting to speak to her form tutor, then?'

'Wayne Brooks? Yes, please,' said Mark.

Spetcroft turned her wrist outwards and looked down her nose at her watch. 'He's due to begin class in fifteen minutes.'

'Well,' said Jan, 'if you could point us in the right direction, he might make it on time.'

The woman huffed, then waved them away. 'Next floor up, third door on the right.'

'Thanks.'

'Bloody hell,' said Mark, as he followed Jan up the stairs to the next level, 'she reminded me exactly of my old headmistress from primary school.'

Jan slowed her pace until they were side by side. 'How old do you think she was?'

'I don't know. Forty, going on sixty perhaps?'

Jan grinned, then pointed at a door with a glass pane in the middle of it, the letters 4C embossed at head height.

'This is the one.'

Mark lifted his head and checked the clock on the wall above the door. 'Ten minutes until his class starts.'

'Let's hope he has some quick answers, then,' said Jan, and pushed open the door.

'The class is in room 6E this morning,' a baritone voice bellowed across the expanse of desks.

As Mark's eyes adjusted to the bright sunlight streaming through the windows, compared with the muted tones of the corridor, he could make out a figure, head bowed as he pondered a newspaper held up to the window.

The newspaper fluttered closed.

'Oh. Who are you?'

'Detective Sergeant Mark Turpin, Thames Valley

Police. My colleague, Detective Constable Jan West.
Are you—'

'Wayne Brooks, yes.' The newspaper was tossed
aside onto a desk before the figure advanced towards
them. 'I suppose you're here about Jessica. Bloody
terrible news.'

Mark returned the firm handshake.

'Where were you last week?' said Jan. 'Our
colleagues left a message for you, but you haven't
returned their call.'

'I was going to phone after class this morning,' said
Brooks. 'I was in Wales, visiting my father.'

'Whereabouts in Wales does he live?'

'Near a small place called Tintern. Wye Valley. Very
pretty.' Brooks moved across the room towards a
blackboard and then began wiping the chalk scratchings
from its surface with methodical strokes using a yellow
duster.

Jan wandered across to where he stood. 'Did anyone
go with you?'

She watched with interest as the man's cheeks
coloured, and then his shoulders sagged.

'Yes.'

'Who?'

'Well, if you're asking the question, I'm presuming
you've already spoken to her. Bethany Myers.' He
shook his head, his gaze finding the floor. 'I knew the

moment our phones started showing all those missed calls that something was wrong. But Jessica—'

'What was she like, Jessica? As a pupil?'

'Studious. Hard-working.' He frowned. 'Except for the past three or four weeks. I don't know what was going on – I never had a chance to ask her about it, but she just seemed to lose interest.'

'Was that unusual?'

'For her, yes.'

'Did she show any signs of stress, other than her grades failing?'

'Not really, apart from seeming a little preoccupied sometimes during class. Daydreaming, I mean. I had to call out to her a couple of times in the past few weeks to get her attention. That wasn't like her.'

'Were you having an affair with Jessica?'

'What?' He took a step back. 'Good God, no.'

'But you're having an affair with Bethany Myers?'

A hunted expression crossed Brooks' face, his eyes darting to the door. 'Please, keep your voice down.'

'Do you know of anyone who might have cause to harm Jessica Marley, Mr Brooks?'

'No, I don't. She was a model student. Everyone liked her. I couldn't believe it when I heard what happened.'

Jan pursed her lips, then pulled out a business card. 'We'll be in touch again, but if you think of anything in the meantime that might assist with our investigation, call me.'

His hand shook as he took the card. 'Okay.'

Jan crossed the room to Turpin and then followed him towards the door as a cacophony of voices began to emanate from the stairwell.

'Detective?'

She turned, to see Brooks frozen next to the blackboard, her card between his fingers. 'What?'

'Please, don't tell my wife about this.'

'And her name is?'

'Well, if you've found me you've already spoken to her. Angela Spetcroft.'

CHAPTER TWENTY-SEVEN

Mark floored the accelerator as soon as they reached the dual carriageway and pointed the car in the direction of the Berkshire Downs, keen to reach Dominic Millar's racing stables while their uniformed colleagues were still conducting interviews.

Kennedy's frustration at the lack of progress was beginning to make for a fraught atmosphere in the incident room, and Mark was keen to report back with some results by the end of the day.

Next to him, Jan drummed her fingers on the sill of the passenger door, her jaw clenched.

'Still pissed off with Wayne Brooks?' he said.

'Yes. What on earth is he doing having an affair with Bethany Myers? She must be at least twenty years younger than him.'

'It makes you wonder how long it's been going on for.'

'And whether they'll break it off after what happened to Jessica,' said Jan. 'I mean, it's not going to take much for people to realise they were both in Wales, is it?'

'Does Brooks live anywhere near Harton Wick?'

'No – he and Angela have a house about a mile and a half from the college. Caroline said that when she left a message with his wife last week she mentioned he tends to walk to work. I think she has the car – they work different hours and she visits her mother on the way home most days.'

'They're a strange couple.'

Jan shuffled in her seat to face him. 'Do you think she knows about his affair? Angela, I mean.'

'Hard to say. I do wonder if Jessica knew though.'

'Do you think she threatened to tell Angela?'

'Possibly, but for what purpose?'

Jan bit her lip and stared out of the windscreen. 'Blackmail's the obvious one. But would Brooks take her threats seriously enough to kill her? Or would Bethany for that matter?'

'Bethany's young – probably not interested in settling down yet. I'm not sure about Brooks – he came across as being timid.'

'Maybe.' Jan sat forward and pointed at a signpost

coming up on the left-hand side of the road. 'This is the place.'

As Mark pulled into the yard for Millar's racing stables, he ran his gaze over the two patrol cars already parked outside a stable block, and braked to a halt next to them.

PS Tom Wilcox appeared through the front door of the low-set main house and raised his hand in greeting as they approached.

'We're using the kitchen and the office,' he said. 'Mr Millar has been very helpful; he only has four full-time staff and three part-timers, and he managed to rustle them all up to be interviewed this morning. We've got another three to go and we'll be done.'

'Anything of interest?' said Mark, as he followed Wilcox into the hallway.

'Not yet,' said Tom. 'Mr Millar is in the dining room through there, if you want to have a word with him. I'd best get back to the interviews.'

'Thanks.'

Compared with the darker decor and traditional furnishings of MacKenzie Adams' home, Mark was surprised to find that Dominic Millar's tastes were a stark contrast.

As he walked into the room Tom had pointed out, he ran his gaze over whitewashed walls adorned with framed photographs of racehorses and paintings of local landscapes, interspersed with various objects d'art that had been set upon strategically placed shelves.

A man turned from a large picture window at the far end of the room and held out his hand as they approached.

'Dominic Millar. I presume you're the detectives Sergeant Wilcox told me would be coming over at some point?'

Mark made the introductions, then gestured to the photographs. 'Are these of you?'

Millar's mouth twisted. 'Yes. Another life. I tend to use this room for meetings when I have clients here, so it serves me well to have the old career up on the wall. Take a seat.'

He gestured to the chairs nearest to them, waited until they'd sat down, and then pulled out a seat opposite. 'I'd offer coffee, but if my lot catch a whiff of that, you'll never get through the interviews in time for them to make the afternoon training session.'

'Thanks for getting everyone together.'

'No problem. I figured it was easier to do it in one go there rather than expect them to come to you. Gets it over and done with, doesn't it?'

'Have any of them mentioned to you if they knew Jessica Marley?'

'I think two of the younger lads might have known her in passing, but only because they drink down the Farriers.'

'And what about you, Mr Millar? Did you know Jessica?'

'No. I didn't drink in that pub. I don't drink much at all, to be honest, and I certainly don't go out of my way to socialise with other jockeys.' He waved a hand dismissively at the photographs. 'All of that's behind me now. Besides, it's never a good idea to drink where your staff do.'

'Fair enough. We need to ask – where were you between ten o'clock last Monday night and seven o'clock Tuesday morning?'

'Here. My brother and his wife came over for dinner and ended up staying rather than driving back to Norfolk. They'd been visiting friends in Hampshire that weekend and decided to call in on the way home. We had a late dinner and sat up talking until about midnight, and then I was up at five o'clock to oversee the lads in the yard.'

'You don't have a manager?'

Millar managed a smile. 'I don't make as much from this as Adams. Yet.'

'What's the story with the gallops? You both use them.'

'Yeah, we lease them from the farmer who owns all the land up at that end of the Downs – Morgan Drake. He's got a big place out near Hazelthorpe. Well, I say "farmer" – he owns land, but he made his money in some sort of investment firm up in London. I don't think he actually does any farming. Tends to lease out land for agistment, grazing rights, that sort of thing. Very much a hands-off approach, which suits us fine. At least we can get on and exercise the horses without him sticking his nose in.'

'Do you ever visit MacKenzie Adams' stables?'

'God, no. Not since my accident.'

Mark frowned. 'Were your injuries sustained there?'

'I used to ride for Adams. Years ago. I was riding one of his horses when this happened. Stupid bugger of a four-year-old gelding tripped over his own feet approaching a hurdle, threw me and then rolled on top of me. I'm lucky to be alive.' His gaze travelled to the photographs before he shrugged. 'That's what I tell myself on the bad days, anyway.'

'I suppose going over to the yard would bring up bad memories,' said Jan.

'It probably wouldn't have been so bad if he'd actually supported me more than he did,' said Millar. 'As it was, the moment he realised my recovery was going to take longer than the eight weeks we first thought, he got rid of me. I only managed to keep my head above water because I'd saved hard that year.'

'And all of this?' Mark gestured to the yard beyond the window.

'Inheritance,' said Millar. 'My father died four weeks after I left hospital. I had to do something with my life, so I figured I'd get back into racing the only way I knew how without actually being on a horse.'

'We heard Nigel White had a similar mishap when he was riding professionally. Has he shown any animosity towards you?'

'No, not really. He tends to avoid me if I do happen to see him up on the gallops.'

'Is that because you had family money to start up your own venture, and he didn't?'

Millar snorted a bitter laugh. 'Nigel's only got himself to blame. If he hadn't spent all his winnings on stupid things like cars during his racing days, and invested instead, he might have had more money to start over when he couldn't ride horses anymore.'

'Is business good?' said Mark.

Millar's shoulders relaxed. 'Yes, it is. It was hard, the first two years, but I had a good reputation as a rider – people know I'm trustworthy. Once word got around what I was doing with the training side of things, the owners started trickling in. And, do you know what? I enjoy it. I don't have to be out there in all weathers if I don't want to be.'

He smiled, then glanced up at a knock on the door.

Tom Wilcox appeared, and nodded to Mark. 'We're all done, guv, so we'll head off now. Thanks for your time, Mr Millar.'

'No problem at all, Sergeant. Thanks for getting that done expeditiously.'

Mark waited until Tom disappeared, and then rose from his seat and slid a card across the table. 'As PS Wilcox said, thank you. We'll be in touch if we have any further questions.'

'I hope you find whoever killed that poor girl,' said Millar. 'My sister's only a few years older than her, and I don't know what I'd do if something happened to her.'

CHAPTER TWENTY-EIGHT

Will Brennan shifted his weight as the black horse beneath him lashed out and kicked the side of the starting enclosure.

Steam rose from the animal's nostrils while Onyx tossed his head from side to side, stamped a front leg, and harrumphed.

The horse to his left whinnied in response, and the rider peered over the barrier to where Will sat with his gaze roaming the floodlit all-weather track ahead of them.

Out the corner of his eye he saw the man grinning, and sighed.

'What do you want, Charlie?'

'Didn't think we'd see you here, Brennan.' The jockey called across to the rider to Will's right. 'Ain't that right, Connor?'

Will didn't hear what the other jockey said in response. He gathered up the reins between fingers that were fast becoming numb. 'I didn't have a lot of choice.'

'I'll bet old MacKenzie is lapping this up.' Charlie laughed, a brash sound that set Will's nerves on edge. 'Did you see his face when he saw all those television cameras around the parade ring? Thought he'd died and gone to heaven, he did.'

Will swallowed, biting back the searing retort on his lips.

It wasn't the only insensitive comment he had been subjected to since arriving at Newbury.

Incredulous stares and murmured insults had accompanied his walk from the lorry that transported MacKenzie's two horses and riders to the racecourse from the yard, and the changing rooms were worse.

People wanted to know how he was feeling, why he was there, what the police were doing about it.

And some wanted him to hurt.

Paul hadn't been any help – he had been riding in the earlier race and had cleared off as soon as he had finished in a comfortable second place, saying he was hungry and wanted a burger from one of the fast food vans that were parked below the public stands.

Will rolled his shoulders, forcing himself to relax.

If he was taut and strung out, Onyx would sense it and then all hell would break loose.

Charlie was right, if rude – MacKenzie Adams had worked his way around the parade ring, a permanent look of sadness on his face that didn't quite reach his eyes.

He had shaken hands with fellow trainers, kissed the hands of several owners' wives and pointed out Will to anyone who would listen while Will kept his gaze lowered and fussed over Onyx, dread crawling through his veins.

'Bet he phoned them,' said Charlie.

'What?'

'MacKenzie. Cunning bastard. Bet he phoned the media to let them know you'd be racing tonight.'

Before Will could respond, the front gates swung open and Onyx surged forward.

Too late.

The horse to his right and the one who had started closest to the inner track soon took the lead, and Will cursed under his breath.

Cursed Charlie for distracting him from focusing on the race.

Cursed Adams for using him to further his own career ambitions with the media.

He hunkered down into the stirrups, cutting down the wind resistance and tucked in behind the two riders, conscious of Charlie and the others nipping at his and Onyx's heels.

The horse beneath him was enjoying the race, his

pace in keeping with the training sessions they had practised over and over, but Will was conscious of a heavy weight on his chest as they breezed around the first corner of the track.

Was Charlie right?

Had MacKenzie Adams alerted the media to Will riding this weekend despite Jessica's murder?

What was he telling them in the parade ground?

What would Jessica's parents think?

The final corner veered into view, and Will gritted his teeth.

It would be worse in the winners' enclosure.

Bright lights, microphones thrust in his face. The questions—

How do you feel?

It was only a sprint race. Five furlongs maximum, just to show what Onyx could do.

Demonstrate what his capabilities were.

What if?

But could he do it, after everything he had been working for?

The two horses in front cleared the corner, and he tightened his grip on the reins.

What would Jessica do?

Onyx stumbled at the sudden twitch at the bit and Will felt rather than heard Charlie's mount take advantage – a quickening of hooves, an excited huff of breath, and then his third place became fourth and they were over the line.

He reined in Onyx behind Charlie's horse, the animal somewhat mollified after the excitement of the race and easier to manage.

In front, he could peer between the colourful caps of the other jockeys.

There were no reporters lying in wait to ambush him, no camera flashes. Just regular members of the public lining the railings that led to the unsaddling area, smartphones aloft.

Will tucked in his chin, hunched his shoulders and focused on the tail of Charlie's horse, pulling down the peak of his cap to shadow his face from the floodlights above.

Muted conversation flowed between the riders as they dismounted, pulled saddles from the backs of their horses and handed the animals over to the stable hands who would care for them prior to the drive back to the yards spread around the country.

Will fell into place behind two other jockeys at the weighing scales, ignoring the banter and jibes that accompanied the relief of a race completed without injury.

His throat tightened at the realisation that Jessica was gone forever, that there would be no more excited phone calls to her after a race to tell her how he had ridden, and that she would never be at the end of the call to soothe his frustrations when he lost.

He nodded to the steward as he rose from the scales and headed towards the changing rooms to shower as the voice of the winning jockey brayed across the room.

The hot water soothed his mind, and he hurriedly towelled himself dry before dressing in jeans and a sweatshirt.

A shadow fell across him while he was pulling on his boots and he raised his head, wondering what derogatory comment would be flung in his direction this time.

Instead, an older jockey by the name of Patrick stood before him, his hand held out.

'I was sorry to hear about your loss, Will. And I'm sorry for what you've had to put up with tonight.'

Will shook his hand. 'Thanks.'

'There are other trainers out there, you know. Better ones. Keep that in mind over the next few weeks.'

Will gathered up his racing clothes after the other jockey wandered off and shoved them into a bag as the changing rooms emptied. He nodded to the steward who hovered at the door, and then made his way along the concrete path that wound between the racecourse buildings towards the designated parking area for the horse transport.

'Brennan.'

A figure moved from the shadows, towering over him.

'Mr Adams.'

MacKenzie placed a hand on his shoulder and steered him between the two cinderblock buildings, stopping when they reached a fire exit.

'Don't think I didn't see what you did there.'

'I'm sorry?'

'That horse should've won today. The competition out there tonight was shit. He should've come in lengths ahead. Instead, he came in fourth.'

'I don't know what was wrong with him,' said Will. 'He was playing up all the way around. I wondered if he was still spooked from the gallops last week.'

'The horse isn't the one who's spooked.' MacKenzie sneered. 'You didn't like the cameras being there, did you? What happened out there? Thought you'd lose so you didn't have to face them again in the winners' enclosure?'

'I—'

'You missed an opportunity, Brennan. They'd have wanted to speak to you, and we could have done with that publicity for the yard. That's worth more than any press interview, I can tell you now. We could've been all over the front pages tomorrow morning, not to mention the television news.'

Will swallowed, and dropped his gaze. 'Sorry, Mr Adams. I don't know if I'm ready for that. Jess has only been dead a week, and the police are still trying to find who killed her. I—'

'I told you.' MacKenzie's forefinger jabbed against Will's sternum. 'If you want the rides, you need to focus. If you work for me, you're representing the brand. That means if there's an opportunity to get the media focused on what I'm doing, you do it.'

He stepped away, glaring. 'Get yourself sorted out, Brennan, and fast. Otherwise Hitchens can ride Onyx instead. Christ, even Nigel could have done a better job than you out there tonight. We're leaving in twenty minutes.'

'Okay.'

Will watched as the racehorse trainer stalked back towards the concrete path, the man straightening his jacket before raising his hand in greeting to someone out of sight and hurrying after them.

He exhaled, leaned against the wall of the changing rooms and raised his eyes to the night sky.

Away from the glare of the enclosure's floodlights, away from the stares and the muttered comments, he could almost imagine she was watching him, cheering him on.

Will clenched his fists, digging his fingernails into his palms.

He would show them.

He would show all of them.

CHAPTER TWENTY-NINE

Mark chose to take a bus into the town centre the following morning, a blustery rain squall buffeting him as he jogged between the bus stop and the front door of the police station.

'Morning, Sarge,' said PS Wilcox, and pressed a button to release the security lock.

'Thanks, Tom. Quiet today?'

'Yes, for now.' The sergeant behind the front desk turned to him as he paused at the bottom of the stairs. 'Any new leads with the girl's murder?'

'Nothing yet.' Mark rested his hand on the newel post. 'Bloody frustrating. You know what it's like – headquarters will be expecting a result any day, but they won't give us more manpower.'

'Or can't,' said Wilcox. 'We're having to complement the weekend shifts with PCSOs for the next four months. That'll be an eye-opening experience for them.'

'It certainly will. Catch you later.' Mark threw a wave over his shoulder and jogged up the stairs two at a time, then pushed into the incident room in time to see the detective inspector emerging from his office.

'Are we all here? Good.' Kennedy put two fingers in his mouth, emitting a shrill whistle. 'Briefing, ladies and gentlemen. Two minutes. Do what you need to do.'

Mark hovered at his desk as the rest of the room dissolved into organised chaos.

Phone calls were tactfully ended, computer keyboards were attacked with gusto, and he reckoned the IT department would be getting several emails about the lack of photocopiers the way a queue was forming at the far end of the incident room.

He realised Jan hadn't appeared since his arrival, and cast his gaze over the heads of his colleagues, wondering where she had gone, and then spotted her balancing two steaming mugs of tea as she negotiated the throng.

Grinning, she handed one over, and then tugged a chocolate bar from the front of her blouse and held it out to him.

He blinked. 'I'm not even going to ask where you put that.'

'I've only got two hands. You can go hungry if you

want.' She laughed as he snatched the chocolate from her. 'Thought so.'

'Come on.'

He let her go on ahead so she could find a seat near the front of the crowd that was gathered around the whiteboard, and then took a sip of tea as Kennedy began the meeting.

'Right, let's crack on with it. First things first – we've still got search results to come in from forensics who worked with uniform to check the entrances to three fields and a woodland up that lane between the pub and the main road. Alex – chase that up, and let me know immediately if any tread marks are found that might be our killer's vehicle.'

'Will do, guv.'

'Okay,' said Kennedy. 'Interviews at Dominic Millar's stables. Tom, do you want to start us off?'

Wilcox took a step forward from his position next to the photocopier and held up a sheaf of paperwork. 'All the statements were entered into HOLMES2 last night but the gist of it is that although two or three of the staff there knew Jessica in passing, it was only because they drank at the Farriers and saw her from time to time. None of them socialised with her or Will.'

'Do all their movements check out for the timeframe we've got?'

'Yes, guv. We're doing a vehicle check on those who

have cars or motorbikes as a matter of course, and if anything crops up from that I'll let you know.'

'Thank you. Mark and Jan – I understand you spoke with Dominic Millar?'

'Yes, guv,' said Mark. 'His statement and his alibi check out – his brother was staying with him last Monday night and confirmed when I spoke with him that as far as he's aware, Dominic didn't leave the house until it was time to go to work in the yard at five o'clock on the Tuesday morning. Unlike MacKenzie Adams, he can't afford a yard manager so he oversees all the lads and horses himself.'

'All right, so we can discount him?'

'Not quite,' said Jan. She held up her phone. 'Sorry, but I was just doing a search for his name in relation to the accident that forced him into retirement. He seemed a bit reticent to talk about it yesterday, didn't he?'

'He did,' said Mark. 'What've you got?'

'Everything he told us is true,' she said, 'but he omitted to tell us that the race he was injured in was subsequently won by Will Brennan.' She dropped her phone to her lap. 'To all intents and purposes, the race that ended Dominic's career was the one that launched Will's.'

CHAPTER THIRTY

Jan pushed away the remains of a ham and cheese sandwich as her desk phone rang, and bit back a sigh.

She was starving, having worked through any semblance of a lunch break to research Dominic Millar's racing accident and his subsequent recovery in an attempt to find out if he'd ever crossed paths with Will Brennan again.

She had hit a dead end, and tried not to let her frustration show as she answered the call.

'It's Tom on the front desk. I've got Annie Hartman here with a hard drive. She says you were waiting for some CCTV images from the petrol station.'

'Fantastic.' Jan pushed back her chair and signalled to Turpin at the desk opposite. 'We'll be right there.'

'She did well to get that sorted out so quickly,' said

Turpin as he shrugged his jacket over his shoulders and followed her down the stairs.

'It's a small company,' said Jan. 'And I think Annie and Isaac want to do everything possible to catch Jessica's killer. She obviously meant a lot to them.'

She opened the door through to reception and saw Hartman silhouetted against the front window of the police station as she watched the traffic go past.

'Mrs Hartman? Thanks for coming in.'

'It's Ms. Please, call me Annie.' She shook hands with them both, and then reached into her bag and pulled out an envelope. 'I thought it'd make a lot more sense for me to hand this over in person rather than risk it going missing in the post. I would've brought it in sooner but head office only provided the files late last night.'

'This is great, thank you. Would you join us to watch the footage from that Thursday afternoon?' said Jan. 'It'd be a great help, in case we have any questions.'

'Of course. I don't have to be at the supermarket until five o'clock, so I've got all afternoon.'

'Come this way.'

Turpin buzzed his security pass and led the way upstairs to a room that was used as an observation suite for the interview rooms on the ground floor as well as a makeshift meeting space for non-investigative matters.

A musty atmosphere filled the space, and, as Jan

flipped the light switch, she noticed the thin layer of dust across the table in the middle.

While Turpin set up the computer and overhead screen, she turned to Annie.

'Have you heard anything in passing at work about Jessica?'

'No – apart from the customers who knew her quite well and have been passing on their condolences,' she said. She tugged her padded coat off and draped it over the back of a chair. 'I've started a collection tin to raise money for a charity of Jessica's family's choice when they feel up to making a decision about that, and a lot of customers have been dropping in cards as well. I still can't believe this happened to her. It's awful.'

'We're ready,' said Turpin, dropping into seat next to Jan. He reached forward and wiggled the mouse to wake up the computer, and then inserted the USB stick the supermarket manager handed to him. 'Which file, Annie?'

'You've got every day on there from the beginning of the month until last Friday. We figured you'd want to see if this person Jessica was worried about came back after she died.'

'That's good thinking, thank you. Which file is the one for the last Thursday Isaac and Jessica worked together?'

Annie pointed it out and then folded her hands in her lap as the CCTV footage began to play on the overhead screen. 'The IT man at head office had to splice them into twenty-minute clips, otherwise the files would've been too big. Is that all right?'

'Absolutely fine,' said Jan. 'We'll set it at a faster speed, and then if we want to highlight anything we can stop and go back at a slower rate.'

The camera from which the film had been extracted was set above and behind the two tills at the front of the petrol station so that she was looking at the backs of Isaac and Jessica's heads while they worked.

It was clear to see that the two enjoyed working together, with Jessica laughing and joking with her older colleague in between serving customers. A lump formed in Jan's throat as she watched the ease with which the young woman dealt with people, especially the elderly ones who seemed to want to spend time chatting with her.

'She was popular,' she said.

'She was,' said Annie, her voice cracking.

The next hour and a half went by with a grating monotony as they stared at the grainy black and white footage, and Jan began to wonder if Jessica had imagined the mystery man she thought had been watching her. She glanced at her watch, and then back to the screen as Turpin called out.

'Here we go.'

He stood and moved closer to the screen, his shadow

passing in front of it before he moved away and pointed at the image. 'What's in this refrigerator here?'

'Cold drinks, sandwiches, that sort of thing,' said Annie. 'The owners figured out that they could make extra money having those chiller cabinets close to the tills so people would be tempted while they were queueing. It works a treat, and saves us money by the staff not having to sort out issues with one of those rented coffee machines.'

On the screen, Isaac and Jessica were studiously serving, their usual friendly banter shortened due to the sudden influx of customers that snaked around the shelves nearest the tills and past the chiller cabinets.

She held her breath as a man's shape moved into view.

He lurked behind a shelf laden with oversized snack bags and loitered at the fringes of the queue without joining it, his face obscured by a display of car cleaning accessories.

'That's got to be him,' said Jan. 'Top right.'

'Shit.' Turpin crossed his arms and glared at the recording.

'Move,' said Jan. 'Come on.'

She held her breath as the figure hovered behind the queue, his feet clearly visible as he shuffled from side to side as if unsure what to do next.

'Yes!' She stabbed her finger on the "pause" button.

On screen, the man had taken a step forward,

perhaps to peer at Jessica around the elderly couple in front of him, perhaps to gauge how much longer he could observe her without being questioned, but the moment he moved, he'd revealed his face.

He'd worn a cap pulled down over his eyes; the sort made from thick cloth and chequered in subtle tones. In his haste to see what Jessica was doing, he'd forgotten about the camera above the till.

Jan had paused the recording at the exact moment recognition flashed across his face and he realised his mistake.

'Who the hell are you?' she whispered.

CHAPTER THIRTY-ONE

Annie Hartman had been unable to help Jan and Turpin ascertain who the man on the camera footage was, but promised to keep a look out for him in the event he returned to the petrol station.

After seeing Annie through reception and thanking her for her time, Jan hurried up the stairs to the incident room.

A murmur filled the space; a white noise that underlay the number of people who moved back and forth between desks, and the door to the corridor hissing shut as errands were made, lines of enquiry were exhausted, and favours negotiated in order that Kennedy could keep the staffing levels currently assigned to the investigation.

And, underneath that, a measure of desperation.

Now that the investigation was over a week old,

every move would be scrutinised by management and those in charge of the overtime budget.

She wished she could show the politicians the effect of budget cuts on her community; not only in her role as detective constable, but in the wider perception of the other mothers she met at school events, who glared at her as if her attendance should be attributed to more than the occasional sports day or parents' evening.

How could she even explain to them the passion she held for seeing justice done?

Thank God Scott understood and supported her, and the boys were of an age where they simply accepted the routine they all worked around.

She knew it couldn't last forever.

She'd seen colleagues' careers fall past the wayside as the pressures of family life and juggling long hours took their toll.

Jan bit her lip as she paused next to her desk and eyed the manila folders that had piled up in her tray in her absence.

In addition to the murder enquiry, she and Turpin were expected to close out enquiries about two assaults that had taken place in the town centre at the beginning of the month, a suspected domestic violence case, and a car theft.

She bit back a sigh and resolved to phone Scott to mind the boys tonight as soon as the afternoon briefing was over. Somehow, she'd make it up to them as soon as they had charged Jessica's killer.

She tossed the files back into the tray and walked towards the whiteboard.

While she'd been dealing with the formalities of signing out Annie, Turpin had taken screen captures from the CCTV recordings of the man's image and now stood at the front of the room, pinning the photographs to the board.

'Good work, you two,' said Kennedy. He tugged at his tie and dropped it onto a desk as he joined the detective sergeant.

'It would've been good if there had been more cameras beyond the forecourt as well,' said Jan. 'As it is, we don't know what he was driving, or where he went. He arrived and left the petrol station on foot.'

'But he was definitely interested in what our young Jessica was doing, wasn't he?' Kennedy pulled out a pair of reading glasses from his shirt pocket and moved closer to the images, running his gaze over each in turn. 'He's not waiting for anyone else. What happened after this was captured?'

'The queue began to disappear, and he left,' said Jan. 'Which makes me wonder whether he wasn't there to speak to Jessica – perhaps he went there to intimidate her.'

'I'm inclined to agree with you,' said Kennedy. He glanced over his shoulder as the rest of the team began to pull across chairs and form a semi-circle around them. 'All right, let's get this briefing done. There's going to be a lot to do tomorrow, and I want you lot rested. We've got a long way to go yet.'

Turpin wandered across to a space against the wall and leaned into it, Jan at his side while Kennedy brought the others up to date with the CCTV findings.

'Moving on,' he said. 'Witness statements from the pub – are they all done, Tom?'

The police sergeant nodded. 'They are, guv. All in HOLMES2 as well. Nothing untoward in what people have told us. The last two regulars to leave said that they were out the door by ten past eleven that night, and neither of them reported seeing anyone hanging around in the lane outside the pub.'

'Guv?' Caroline raised her hand. 'We've finally got the records from the company who leases the ATM to Collins, and there are a couple of transactions there I'd like to look into.'

'Oh?' Kennedy held out his hand for the report the detective constable held. 'Which ones?'

She joined him and pointed at the page. 'There's one here for three hundred and fifty pounds at five past nine, and then one hundred and fifty pounds at ten twenty-two.'

Kennedy handed the report back to Caroline. 'Can you and Alex take a look at Jessica's bank statements to see if either of those transactions show up? Mark and

Jan – get yourselves back to the Farriers Arms when it opens in the morning. Find out if Collins recognises the bloke in these pictures, and see what he might know about these two transactions in case neither of them match Jessica's statements.'

'Will do, guv,' said Jan.

CHAPTER THIRTY-TWO

Nigel White lowered the pint glass to the bar and glared at the caramel-coloured liquid that remained.

The Cornish ale probably tasted fine in the town where it was brewed, but it travelled poorly and a sickly aftertaste clung to his tongue.

'Noah,' he called out. 'Make it a Jack and coke for me.'

The landlord of the Farriers Arms looked up from his conversation with one of the other regulars further along the bar, then heaved his bulk away and reached up for a clean glass hanging above the beer pumps.

'When's the regular stuff back on?' Nigel slid the empty pint glass across the polished wooden surface. 'Can't drink that.'

'We've got a delivery on Thursday as usual,' said Noah. 'Last night was busy – it caught us by surprise.'

Nigel's heart lurched, his eyes locking with the man on the other side of the bar. 'Did I miss something?'

'No.' Noah passed him the drink, then leaned his forearm on the beer pumps and lowered his voice. 'People being nosy, that's all. Bastards. Never drank in here all the time me and Sonia have lived here, then Jess is killed and suddenly we're the most popular pub in the area.'

'Anyone I know?'

'Not by name, I don't think. Couple from up the road, Harton Wick way. They looked familiar, but, like I said – not regulars. I don't think they'd even been in for a meal.'

'Bastards,' Nigel agreed, and tipped his drink towards the publican before taking a sip. He smacked his lips before setting down the glass. 'Did you tell them what happened?'

'No, I bloody didn't. Gave them their food and made sure they left without bothering the real customers. Bet we won't see them again, either.' Noah winked, and then glanced over his shoulder as his name was called from the kitchen. 'Got to go – food order.'

'Oi, Nigel. What happened to your man at the races last night? I had ten quid on him to win.'

Nigel took another sip of his drink and then swivelled on his stool until he faced the pensioner who leered at him from a table off to the right of the bar.

'I've got no idea, I wasn't there, but I'd imagine he

was still upset about his girlfriend being found dead last week, wouldn't you, Sam?'

The man let out a squawk, his cheeks reddening. 'Adams shouldn't have put him on the horse if he knew he was going to lose.'

'He didn't lose, he came fourth.'

'Fourth's no good to me, is it? The missus has been nagging me about that lost money all bloody day.'

'Poor you.' Nigel turned around, ignoring the choked response over his shoulder.

MacKenzie had been furious when he had arrived back at the stables the night before. His mood had tempered the celebrations for Paul's win, and Will had skulked back to the cottage without a word once the horses had been stabled for the night.

The morning hadn't brought a respite from the atmosphere that hung around the place, which was why he and Paul had headed for the pub as soon as it had opened.

He glanced back at the sound of the front door swinging open, a stiff breeze clawing at his heels before it shut and Bethany Myers stalked towards the bar.

'Nigel.'

'Evening, Beth. All right?'

She gave him a weary smile as he pulled out the stool beside him for her and she sank onto it, looping her handbag strap over a hook under the bar.

'Noah – vodka tonic for Beth, when you're ready.'

Nigel waved a ten pound note at the landlord as he walked past carrying empty plates.

The man nodded before disappearing into the kitchen.

'You don't have to do that,' said Bethany.

'But I'd like to. Besides, I haven't seen you since… since Jess was found.' He fell silent as Noah returned, then picked up the conversation once she had her drink in her hand and the publican had moved to the far end of the bar.

'To Jessica,' he said, touching his glass to Bethany's.

'To Jess.' She took a sip, re-crossed her legs, and leaned closer. 'Have the police been to see you yet?'

She may as well have punched him in the stomach, such was the rush of air that left his lungs at her words.

Nigel peered over his shoulder.

Old Sam might have been staring at the crossword on the back of the free newspaper, but his ears were almost flapping in anticipation.

He wheeled around to face Bethany again. 'Keep your voice down in here,' he hissed. 'This ain't the time or the place.'

She frowned. 'I only asked. They interviewed me – here – when I got back from Wales on Sunday.'

'What did they ask you?' he said, beckoning her closer until their voices were no more than murmurs.

'Whether she was worried about anything.'

'What did you say?'

'That she seemed fine, but that the last shift we worked together, I thought she'd seen someone at the petrol station who'd frightened her.'

'What makes you say that?'

'I dunno. It seemed important at the time because Jess had mentioned it to me.'

'Who was it?'

'I don't know – she never told me.' Bethany shrugged before casting her gaze around the pub. 'I thought I'd ask around, find out if anyone else knew anything.'

'Leave it to the police, Beth. That's their job.'

'Yes, but people know me, don't they? I mean, bloody hell, some of the stuff I get told by the regulars when they've had too much to drink. I could end at least three marriages in this village.' She laughed, throwing her head back before reaching out for her drink and drowning half in three gulps.

Exasperated, Nigel straightened and eyed the drink in front of him, then took a deep breath.

'I'm only going to say this once, Beth, but keep your nose out of it. You don't want to end up like Jessica, do you?'

She froze, the glass held halfway to her lips. 'You what? Are you threatening me?'

He patted his hands in the air. 'Keep your voice down, girl.'

'What the hell—?'

'Just don't. Don't start asking questions.'

'Or else, what?'

She glared at him, and, when he didn't answer, she slammed her glass down on the bar and snatched up her bag before lowering her mouth to his ear.

'Don't threaten me again, Nigel. I know things about you as well. Remember – me and Jess were best friends.'

She straightened, a triumphant expression flashing across her features, and then spun on her heel and marched from the pub.

'Shit.' Nigel slurped the last of his drink, ignoring the stares from the regulars as he hurried past and pushed open the front door.

'Bethany!'

A figure on a moped pulled out into the lane, and he swore under his breath.

Running towards her, his gait unsteady after so many drinks, he waved his hands above his head in the hope she would spot him in her mirrors, but his efforts were in vain.

He stumbled to a standstill. 'Fuck.'

'Nigel – you having problems with the ladies again?'

Paul Hitchens wandered across the car park towards him, cigarette in hand.

'It's nothing. Thought you'd left.'

'Having a ciggie first. D'you want a lift back to the cottage? I'm going in a minute.'

'Might as well.' He peered once more into the darkness, the red tail light from Bethany's moped disappearing around the bend. 'There's nothing here for me anymore.'

CHAPTER THIRTY-THREE

Mark hunkered into the collar of his woollen coat while Jan reversed into the last narrow space in the car park of the Farriers Arms late the following morning.

A chill wind coursed from the Berkshire Downs, and he scowled at his phone when he saw the weather forecast for blustery showers later that day.

The scowl faded as a message popped up on the screen.

Got the wine. Looking forward to dinner later this week xx.

He grinned, then raised his gaze to see smoke from the pub's chimney blowing across the length of the roof. The promise of a warm fire sent him walking towards the front door while Jan locked the vehicle and hurried across to join him.

'Okay, let's see what Noah Collins has to say about these ATM transactions,' he said. 'There can't be many customers around here who withdraw that sort of money.'

He wrenched open the door and held it open for Jan before following her over the threshold.

Although the pub had only been open for twenty minutes, half a dozen middle-aged people sat on one of the tables nearest the window, their brightly coloured clothing identifying them as a fitness group of some sort.

The bitter aroma of freshly made coffee wafted on the air, and he glanced across to the bar as a woman emerged carrying a tray laden with cups and saucers.

'Be with you in a minute,' she called as she crossed the room to the group and began to serve.

Mark led the way over to the bar and leaned against an enormous supporting beam that bisected the arrangement of bar stools and rose from floor to ceiling. Notches and old bolts protruded from it.

'Old ship?' said Jan, running her hand over the painted surface.

'An original from the old forge, I think.' He broke off as the woman returned to the bar and smiled at them.

'Can I help you?'

Mark flicked open his warrant card and kept his voice low. 'Is Noah around?'

'Out this morning. Wednesdays are his days for

doing the banking and the cash 'n' carry for the kitchen. He'll be gone for at least three hours.'

Mark turned and eyed the ATM machine in the corner, and wondered exactly how much money Collins was banking. 'Sorry – you are?'

'Cheryl Matthews. I spoke to the police last week when they were in here. Are you still trying to find out who killed Jessica?'

'It's an ongoing enquiry, yes.'

Her jaw set hard. 'I hope you find the bastard.'

Mark raised his gaze to the low-beamed ceiling and squinted into the gloom of the corners. 'Does Noah have CCTV in here?'

'No,' said Cheryl. 'Those little cameras you can see in the corner are fake. He won't put real cameras in – says he can't afford it. The other things up there are for the burglar alarm system. Infra-red, something like that.'

'What about the ATM machine?'

'No, it's not like the ones the banks use. They just rely on us to keep an eye out for anyone acting suspicious.'

'And no cameras outside?'

The woman smiled. 'It's not that sort of pub. No – as far as I know, he and Sonia have never had any problems with locals or anyone else, so I guess they reckon they don't need to worry.'

'How are things here, since Jessica's death?' said

Jan. 'Have you noticed anything unusual or has it been quiet?'

Cheryl glanced over her shoulder to check on the group near the window, then turned back to them. 'It's been quieter. A few of the locals haven't been in since but they're the sort who only come in for a meal once a fortnight. The usual people have been in for drinks in the evening.' Her nose wrinkled. 'No offence, but the sooner you find who killed her, the better. Noah reduced all our hours last week.'

'Oh?' said Mark. 'Is he losing money with the downturn in trade, then?'

'There's no downturn, not really. I don't know why. First thing I knew about it was when I turned up for work last Wednesday night and he said I was to finish at nine o'clock instead of after closing.' Cheryl contemplated her nails. 'He's a good boss – I mean, he pays us a good hourly rate – so those two hours every shift means quite a chunk coming off my weekly wages.'

'And he hasn't given you a reason for that?'

'No.'

'I'm sure he's got your best interests at heart,' said Jan.

Cheryl rolled her eyes. 'Well, I'm sure he's pleased to be saving some money as well – I mean, by the time you count up everyone who works here, he must be saving a few quid every week now, right?'

'How was business here before Jessica died?' said Mark. 'Any signs of it struggling?'

The woman wrinkled her nose, and then leaned closer. 'No, actually it does pretty well here. Mind you, it helps that Noah and Sonia run a tight operation. It's better than the pub down at Hazelthorpe, you see. That place can get a bit rough, so anyone with money or who wants a quiet drink without fruit machines and football matches comes up here. I reckon they do all right. I just hope this whole business doesn't affect them. They don't deserve that.'

A door slammed shut at the back of the pub, and Cheryl bit her lip, guilt flashing across her face before she reached out for a cloth and began polishing the bar. 'I should probably get on.'

'One last thing.' Mark fished out a copy of the image captured from the CCTV camera in the garden centre. 'Do you recognise this man?'

Cheryl took the photograph and held it up to the bright lights under the bar, her brow furrowed. 'I don't know. He looks familiar, but I don't live in the village, so unless I'm working I don't really come over here. Sorry.'

'No problem.'

Mark thanked Cheryl for her time, then peered over her shoulder as a slight woman with short dark hair and wearing chef's whites appeared from the kitchen.

She jerked her chin at Cheryl. 'Don't forget there are

sauce bottles that need cleaning and refilling out there as soon as you've finished serving.'

'Sonia Collins?' Mark flipped open his warrant card and introduced Jan. 'We haven't had the chance to speak with you yet. Got a minute?'

'I'm in the middle of preparing for today's lunchtime session.'

'This won't take long.'

She sighed. 'All right, but out the back door. It's too dangerous to stand around in the kitchen, and you're already causing a distraction for the customers.'

Sonia turned on her heel without waiting for an answer, and strode past a stainless-steel commercial oven and two chip fryers, her shoes silent on the linoleum floor.

As Mark followed, he ran his gaze over the central worktop that gleamed under the strip lighting above, piles of plates in different sizes stacked ready for service that day. Two sinks had been built in under a window that overlooked a wood pile and a private yard, and off to his left a narrow doorway led through to where he assumed Sonia kept chest freezers and shelves stocked with food and ingredients.

She stopped at the back door and held it open for him, then beckoned to Jan. 'Don't hang about – we don't need flies in the kitchen.'

The door swished closed on an automatic hinge the

moment they were all outside, and then Sonia turned her attention to Mark.

'All right, what did you need to know? I already spoke to a pair of uniformed coppers last week. Is there any news?'

'I'm sorry, not that we're able to share at the present time,' said Mark. 'Did you know Jessica well?'

Sonia's shoulders dropped. 'I don't know if I knew her well, but she was a lot of fun to work with. I miss her. She was one of those people who you could show how to do something once, and that was it. She had a lot of intuition about the business.' She managed a smile. 'Unlike some of our other staff.'

'Cheryl mentioned that your husband has reduced her hours.'

'Just as a safety precaution, so that they get home early. Some of them don't like it, but that's not the point, is it?'

'Where were you at eleven-thirty last Monday night?'

'In there, cleaning up. Jessica always used the front door to leave, so I didn't see her go. The only way I knew she'd left was because Noah came into the kitchen to help me finish mopping up. We wanted to review the new menu before going upstairs as well, so that we could start ordering any special ingredients that we don't normally keep in stock.'

'When did you first hear about Jessica?' said Jan.

Sonia sniffed, and wiped at her eyes with her fingers. 'Sorry. I still can't believe she's gone. Um, I suppose it must've been just before we opened on the Tuesday and your lot came in to take statements – the bloke who delivers the oil had heard it from someone up at the stables and told us. I was shaking by the time he'd gone. I can't remember how many times I'd told Jessica it wasn't safe to walk home at night on her own, not along there.'

'You didn't offer her a lift?'

'Probably every other shift,' said Sonia. 'Her answer was always the same – she liked to walk because it helped her to wind down. I think she had trouble sleeping sometimes; insomnia or something like that. Anyway, she swore blind the walk helped.'

Mark heard a shout from inside, and Sonia peered through the glass panel of the back door.

'I'm sorry – I've got to get back,' she said. 'Looks like our group of walkers has decided to place an order.'

'Thanks for your time,' he said. 'Please, get in touch if you think of anything that might help us. Anything at all.'

'Will do. If you follow the path past the woodpile, you can reach the car park that way.'

Moments later, standing next to their vehicle, Mark ran his eyes over the outside of the pub.

'What do you think?'

Jan grimaced. 'All those people telling Jessica not to walk home. You'd have thought she'd have listened.'

CHAPTER THIRTY-FOUR

'What's the address for Bethany Myers?' said Turpin as Jan started the car.

'She's renting a room in a house in Hazelthorpe, on Crosshands Lane.'

'Let's go and see if she's in.'

Crosshands Lane turned out to be a narrow spur off the main road through Hazelthorpe and as Jan cast her eyes over the pebble-dashed frontage of number three, she couldn't help but wonder when the terraced house had last been painted.

Mould had collected under an overflow pipe next to the front door, while a pile of broken roof tiles had been stacked next to the step. Jan could smell the damp from the hallway carpet before the door was fully opened and Bethany Myers peered out through bleary eyes.

'It's early,' she said.

Turpin checked his watch. 'Half past one?'

'I had a late night.'

'Can we come in?'

'I suppose so.'

She pushed her dark hair away from her face and closed the door after them, then pointed towards the kitchen. 'Trust me, you don't want to see the state of the living room.'

Jan was taken aback at how young Bethany looked minus the layers of make-up she'd been wearing when they'd interviewed her at the pub the previous week. Without the dramatic eyeshadow and contouring, the woman appeared younger than her nineteen years, her features wan.

'How are you doing, Bethany?' she said as they were shown to two chairs beside a pine table cluttered with magazines, bills and other paraphernalia.

'Okay, I suppose.' Bethany pulled her chunky cardigan around her middle and frowned. 'Do you want a cup of tea or anything?'

'We're fine, thanks.' Turpin held out the photograph from the petrol station CCTV footage. 'Do you recognise this man?'

Bethany moved forward and took the photograph, then nodded. 'Yeah. I think so. It looks like Morgan Drake.'

'The same man who owns the gallops?'

'And this house, amongst others.' She handed back

the photograph. 'He's the local landholder. Y'know, the farm out the other side of the village. Bloody loaded, I reckon. He owns half the land around here, although I think he must have someone run the day-to-day stuff because I'm sure he still has a job in London.'

'Doing what? Do you know?'

Bethany's nose wrinkled. 'Investment banker, something like that. Where'd you get the photo from?'

'The petrol station where Jessica worked,' said Turpin.

Jan watched as confusion swept across the woman's features, followed by a slow realisation.

'Shit. Is he the one who was watching Jessica? Why would he do that?'

'That's what we're trying to find out,' said Turpin. He tapped the image with his forefinger. 'Any idea why Jessica would be nervous about Morgan Drake?'

'No, not that I can think of.'

'Does he drink in the Farriers Arms?' said Jan.

'Occasionally. I mean, very rarely.' Bethany leaned against the sink. 'If he does, he tends to come in late. I've always presumed that's because he has to commute from the City, though. The nearest train station is five miles away from here, so I assumed he stopped off for one on the way home if I saw him.'

'Did he socialise with anyone while he was there?' said Jan.

'I can't remember. I know I'd sometimes see him at

the far end of the bar chatting with Noah. But I guess that's to be expected.'

'What do you mean?' said Turpin.

'Well, Morgan owns the pub, doesn't he?'

'Does he?'

'Yeah – didn't Noah tell you?'

Jan caught Turpin's eye and then turned her attention back to Bethany. 'When were you going to tell us about you and Wayne Brooks?'

The young woman's jaw dropped open, and before she had a chance to recover, Jan pressed on.

'You deliberately withheld information from an ongoing murder investigation, Bethany. When we interviewed you last week, you made no mention of travelling to Wales and back with your form tutor. Why?'

Bethany bit her lip, and then threw up her hands. 'Why do you think? We didn't want his wife to find out. It's just a bit of fun, that's all.'

'Is that how Wayne views it?'

'Yes. I guess.'

'How long has it been going on?'

'What's that go to do—'

'Answer the question, Bethany,' said Turpin, his voice a low growl.

'A year. Just under.'

'Did Jessica know about it?'

'What? No – I don't think so.'

'What would happen if she did?'

'What do you mean?'

'How badly did you and Wayne Brooks want to hide your affair from his wife?' said Jan. 'How far would you go to keep it a secret?'

Bethany paled. 'Fucking hell – I didn't kill her! She was my best friend.'

'Do you know who did kill her?' said Turpin. 'Did you arrange for someone to kill Jessica while you and Wayne were safely out of the way in Wales?'

'God, no!'

Turpin folded the photograph of Morgan Drake back in his pocket and stood, glaring at Bethany.

'We'll see ourselves out. But make sure you report to the police station before you make any arrangements to leave the area while this investigation is ongoing. Is that understood?'

Jan watched as Bethany nodded once before dropping her chin, a single tear rolling over her cheek.

CHAPTER THIRTY-FIVE

Mark shoved his hands in his pockets and ran his eyes over the intricate detail of the Georgian farmhouse.

They had accessed the property via a long private driveway lined with beech trees that ebbed and swayed with the wind, their branches twisted and warped from seasons growing in such an exposed environment.

The views beyond the fields were impressive, but a melancholy seized Mark as he surveyed the landscape. Despite the obvious money spent on the place, a starkness clung to the farm buildings.

A cracked and split concrete driveway led to a farmyard with a corrugated steel-panelled barn taking up much of the right-hand side of the space that was in contrast with the deep multi-coloured gravel of the car park in front of the house.

To Mark's left, a brown pony with a black mane

peered over a fence separating the expansive gravel from a manège that contained a set of six low jumps set within the space at different angles. Blue plastic barrels propped up brightly coloured poles, and Mark offered up a silent thanks that neither of his daughters had expressed an interest in horse-riding.

He didn't think his salary could afford it.

'Ready, then?' said Jan, dropping the car keys into her handbag.

He nodded, then walked past a new silver four-by-four and a low-slung sports car to the front door, and pressed an intercom button on a panel set into the brickwork.

After a moment, a brusque voice answered.

'Yes?'

'Mr Morgan Drake?'

'Who is this?'

'Detective Sergeant Mark Turpin, and Detective Constable Jan West. May we have a word, please?'

A muffled curse crackled through the speaker. 'I'm very busy, detective. Couldn't you phone my office and make an appointment?'

'Actually, no,' said Mark. 'We're in the middle of a murder investigation, and time is of the essence. In the circumstances—'

'All right, all right.' A buzzing sound emanated from the door. 'Make sure you give it a good push to close it

– it tends to stick. Come down the hallway, second door on the left.'

With that, the intercom went silent.

Mark raised an eyebrow at Jan, then pushed against the door.

It swung open easily, and he stepped into a high-ceilinged hallway, his shoes echoing on black and white tiles that had been laid in a checkerboard pattern.

An intricately carved oak staircase began to his left, the wall beside it covered in various paintings depicting the bucolic life through the centuries.

He glanced over his shoulder as Jan slammed the front door shut and wiped her shoes on the mat, and then led the way through the hallway to the door Drake had described.

Rapping his knuckles twice against the hard surface, he pushed it open without waiting for a response, and found himself in a box-shaped room that had been lined from floor to ceiling with bookshelves. Running his gaze over the titles closest to the door, he was surprised to see that amongst the classics and business tomes, Drake also had a penchant for American action-adventure thrillers.

'I can't spare you long.'

Mark turned to see a man in his late fifties standing behind a large desk, his profile turned so that he appeared to have been staring out of the window before their arrival.

White hair closely cropped, his dark-brown eyes bored into Mark's as he stepped forward and shook hands. 'Time is money, detective. I know that'll sound harsh, but it's the truth.'

Mark didn't respond, and instead made his way around the room, peering at the spines of the books and taking in the soft leather sofas and expensive-looking furnishings.

Finally, having completed a circuit and standing next to Drake's desk, he smiled. 'I presume the farming life doesn't pay for all of this.'

Drake snorted and shook his head. 'You'd be right there. Take a seat, both of you.'

He gestured to one of the sofas, waited until Mark and Jan had sat, then sank into an armchair beside them and drummed his fingertips on his knee.

'All right. What do you want to know?'

'How long have you been the owner of this property, Mr Drake?'

'Since 2008. I invested wisely – unlike some of my colleagues in the financial industry – and bought this for a song when the previous owners' bank put it up for sale.'

'And do you still work in finance?'

'I'm sure you already know the answer to that, but yes, I do.' He stopped tapping his fingers and sighed. 'I enjoy it, to be honest. It provides a good contrast to all of this.'

'What do you farm here?' said Jan.

'Maize and barley, and we have a large flock of sheep on the other side of the Downs. We obviously cycle the crops every year – next year, for example, we'll plant wheat.'

'What area of finance do you work in?' said Mark.

'Mergers and acquisitions. My expertise is in finding businesses that are struggling, buying them cheap and then selling them on for a profit.'

'Will you do that here, with the farm?'

Drake smiled. 'No – I think my wife and daughter would have me shot if I so much as mentioned it.'

'And you own the Farriers Arms?'

'Yes.'

'But your name doesn't appear on the licence above the door to the pub, does it?'

'It doesn't, because it doesn't need to. Noah is licensed to sell alcohol on and off the premises, and he and Sonia are there seven days a week, unless they take a holiday. If I lived at the pub, then I'd probably have my name on the licence.'

'How often do you go to the pub?'

'Maybe a couple of times a month.'

'And what do you do when you go there?'

'I run through any marketing campaigns I want to run – things for Christmas, Mother's Day... Noah and Sonia are hands-on, so we tend to bounce a few ideas back and forth, and then I let them get on with it. Other times, Noah might want to change the ales to bring something more seasonal in or try something new – that sort of thing.'

'How long have Noah and Sonia Collins run the Farriers Arms for you?'

'Since 2018. They were already there when I bought it from the previous owner.'

'And it's freehold, I understand?'

'That's right – we have complete freedom to do what we want with the place when it comes to stocking ales and other drinks, unlike a leasehold or other tied public house. It gives us an edge on other pubs in the area.'

'What about staffing, Mr Drake?' said Jan. 'Who's responsible for that?'

'Again, I leave that to Noah and Sonia. They're a good judge of character, and I pay them to manage the place.'

'Whose idea was it to employ Jessica Marley?'

'As I said, that would have been left to Noah and Sonia.'

Mark pulled out the photograph from the CCTV camera at the petrol station, and handed it across. 'What was your interest in Jessica Marley, then?'

The man swallowed, and Mark noticed that his hand shook.

Drake placed the photograph on the arm of his chair,

then pulled a pair of reading glasses from his shirt pocket and peered at the image.

'Mr Drake?'

'Such a tragedy,' the farmer murmured.

'Why were you there?'

Drake removed his glasses and folded them, then tapped them against his knee.

'I wanted to ask her about a job.'

'A job?'

'Yes.' He waved his hand at the desk. 'The farm is getting busier, and I thought it would be a good idea to bring in a part-time manager. Jessica approached me with her résumé twelve months ago, but I didn't have anything suitable at the time.' His gaze fell to the photograph once more. 'It would've been the perfect role for her.'

'Were you aware she already had three jobs and a college course to complete?' said Jan.

He nodded. 'Oh, yes. But I was planning on paying her enough that she could stop working for everyone else. Delia – my wife – is brilliant at running the day-to-day office stuff, such as the bookkeeping, but I need someone who understands what an agricultural business requires. Jessica ticked all the boxes.'

'So, you went to the petrol station where she works to ask her about it?' said Mark. 'Why not interview her here?'

Drake shrugged. 'I was passing, that's all. It was a

spur of the moment thing. Then, when I got there, I realised how busy she was and that I should probably give her a call sometime instead. I didn't want her to get into trouble with her manager there if she spoke to me.'

'Where were you last Monday night from eight o'clock until seven o'clock the next morning?'

'Here. We had dinner guests – my wife's mother and her latest husband. They stayed overnight, and I cooked breakfast for them before they drove back to Harrow on Tuesday morning.'

'We'll need their details, please.'

Clearing his throat, Drake pushed himself out of his chair and crossed to the desk. Picking up a mobile phone, he recited a phone number for his mother-in-law. 'If that was all, Detective Turpin? Like I said, I have an enormous amount of paperwork to get through today.'

Mark stood, and handed over one of his business cards. 'We have no further questions at the moment, Mr Drake, but if you do think of anything that could assist our enquiries, I'd be grateful if you'd phone me immediately.'

'Absolutely.' Drake moved towards the desk and propped up Mark's card next to the desk phone. 'Will you see yourselves out?'

After he pulled the front door closed and stalked across the gravel towards the car, Mark glanced over his shoulder at the farmhouse, a prickle of unease at the back of his neck spreading across his shoulders.

A curtain in the top window twitched; a shadow momentarily moving across the room beyond the glass until it disappeared from view.

'Are you all right?' said Jan. She tossed the keys from hand to hand as she waited for him to catch up.

'I don't trust him. He's keeping something from us, but I can't work out what – or why.'

CHAPTER THIRTY-SIX

A steady stream of traffic was pouring through the village of Harton Wick by the time Jan pulled into the Farriers Arms' car park.

Despite a thirty-mile-an-hour speed zone along the lane, it was evident that many locals saw it as a rough guide rather than law, and for a fleeting moment she wondered what the drivers' reaction would be if she were using a liveried patrol car instead of the dusty silver four-door vehicle they'd been allocated that morning.

She stepped backwards as a sporty hatchback parked beside her, and joined Turpin at the door to the pub as a group of walkers stampeded past.

'Busy lunchtime,' he said, and nodded at the last space in the car park. 'I guess those walkers are just the start of the rush.'

'I wonder if it's always like this, or whether this is because of Jessica?'

His lips thinned. 'I'd hate to think it was because of her, but you know what people can be like. Come on.'

A hubbub of conversation and laughter greeted them as they entered the pub. All the tables were either full or had been reserved, and Jan spotted Cheryl weaving between a group at the bar, her hands and wrists balancing three plates of food.

Jan's stomach rumbled at the aromas that wafted on the air as Cheryl passed, and studiously ignored the menu written on the blackboard above the fireplace.

Turpin stopped Cheryl on her way back towards the kitchen. 'Where's Noah?'

'Changing a barrel. He'll be up in a minute. Sorry – got to go; there are another two plates waiting in the kitchen and Sonia won't thank me if the food goes out cold.'

She dashed away, disappearing through the door behind the bar from which a cacophony of clanging pots and pans emerged.

'This is bedlam,' said Jan, stepping to one side to let another group pass from the bar to an empty table at the far end of the pub. 'There's no way he's going to want to talk to us in the middle of service.'

Turpin's jaw clenched. 'This can't wait.'

He strode across the parquet flooring towards the

bar as a low door to the left of the bar opened, and Collins emerged, a plastic bucket in his hand.

The landlord began to pull on one of the beer pumps, sending a clear liquid sloshing into the bucket as he cast his gaze around the throng.

'Cheryl,' he called out. 'Get Martin out here to help you serve.'

A large balding man in his thirties appeared from the kitchen, wiping his hands on a tea towel before stuffing it beside a rack of wine lists, and started pouring drinks.

Gradually the crowd dissipated, and the noise subsided to the clatter of cutlery on plates, murmured conversations, and friendly banter among the locals who perched on stools next to the bar.

Collins glanced across to where Jan and Turpin stood.

'Be with you in a minute. Let me get this next barrel on first, otherwise there's going to be a revolt.'

Turpin nodded as the local men laughed and jeered. 'Is there somewhere we could wait?'

Collins jerked his thumb over his shoulder. 'Go upstairs – our living room is to the right of the stairs. Make yourselves comfortable.'

Jan led the way up a carpeted narrow staircase that brought them to a landing with several doors off it. Following Collins' directions, she turned into the living room and stopped, surprised to see sunlight streaming through floor-to -ceiling windows that overlooked the pub garden.

Wandering over, she eyed the wide grassed area, the lawn in need of cutting and picnic tables and benches that would need varnishing if they were to be used in the summer.

'Looks neglected,' said Turpin as he moved to her side.

'You can see why if they're as busy as this every lunchtime. I'm surprised they've even got time to think.'

'It goes hand in hand with the job.'

Jan turned at the sound of Collins' voice to see the landlord in the doorway, his hands on his hips.

'Can we make this quick, whatever it is you need to ask me? I daren't leave the bar for long.'

'Why didn't you tell us Morgan Drake owns the pub?'

Collins frowned. 'You didn't ask. I thought you'd have known. Everyone does around here.'

'Do you manage it for him?'

'Yes. We're tenants.'

'How long did you say you've been here for?'

'Since 2017.'

'And where were you prior to that?'

'Bishop's Stortford. It's where Sonia's family are from.'

'You're a long way from home.'

Collins' mouth quirked. 'So my mother-in-law tells me on a regular basis.'

'We heard that you've reduced the staff's hours, Mr Collins,' said Jan. 'Why is that?'

'For their own safety,' he said. He held up his hands. 'I've got no other choice until you find out who killed Jessica. I worry about them. Sonia and I sat down after you came in last week and we decided it was better if anyone working an evening shift finished at nine o'clock rather than leaving when we'd finished clearing up. At least that way there are plenty of people around when they're travelling home. Me and Sonia can manage the last two hours on our own for the time being. Hopefully it'll be a temporary measure, won't it?'

Turpin didn't rise to the bait, and instead thumbed through his notebook. 'What can you tell us about the last evening Jessica worked here? The night she died? Was it busy?'

'Yes, very much like what you're seeing down there now.'

'Is it always like that on a Monday?'

'Sometimes. Maybe twice a month – Sonia's got a good reputation for her food and we get people from all around here organising birthday meals and things like that. You should see this place on Mother's Day. We have to seat people on timed reservations, otherwise we'd never cope.'

'The ATM downstairs – what sort of profit do you make on it?'

'Nothing. It's provided as a service for customers, otherwise they'd have to drive into town if they wanted cash. Some of the older regulars don't like using their card to pay. It's not like the fruit machine or the cigarette machines in the old days when I used to make a bit of profit on them.'

'There were two large withdrawals from that machine on the night Jessica died. Three hundred and fifty pounds at five past nine, and then a hundred and fifty pounds at ten twenty-two. Any idea who made those?'

Collins scratched his chin. 'No, but at least that explains why I had a customer moaning on Tuesday that there was an error message on the machine saying it didn't have any cash left. I had to get the company over here at short notice to sort it out. What sort of person withdraws that sort of money from a pub ATM? I mean, if one of the regulars needed that sort of cash, they could borrow it off me – they know that.'

'That's what we'd like to know, Mr Collins.'

'Noah? The Heineken's gone.' Cheryl's voice carried up the staircase. 'And I've got no-one on the bar. Martin's back in the kitchen.'

Collins' shoulders slumped. 'Look, I'm sorry but that's another barrel that needs changing. I don't let the staff down in the cellar – they'll only screw it up. I have to go.'

'Final question,' said Turpin. 'Any problems or issues with Morgan Drake lately?'

The landlord's eyebrows rose. 'No. None at all. We've never had any issues with Morgan. He's a good boss. Leaves us to it. We meet every now and again to discuss strategies for marketing and things like that, but otherwise we rarely see him in here.'

'All right – thanks, Mr Collins. We'll see ourselves out.'

CHAPTER THIRTY-SEVEN

Bethany flicked her hair over her shoulder and tilted back her head, her lips apart as she applied another layer of mascara.

A collection of bottles, brushes and other paraphernalia cluttered the sink and vanity unit beside her while an upbeat playlist blasted from the music app on her phone propped up against a spare toilet roll above the mirror.

Remnants of steam curled around an ageing extractor fan that whirred from its position in the top left corner of the bathroom window, and she made a mental note to open the window for a few minutes once she was dressed.

The fan would never cope on its own.

Her skin pink from a hot bath, she relished the

chance to relax in the absence of her two housemates after finishing her shift.

Doug and Emma had been fun when they'd all moved in, but since the two of them had progressed from being friends to a fully-fledged romance, Bethany had had to fight down the resentment that she was in their way.

Instead, she focused on the fact that she only had another six months to go at college, and then she could leave.

She blinked as a well-known anthem began, the opening chorus providing a sudden kick to the chest as she remembered singing along to it with Jessica in the summer at a barbecue Noah and Sonia had held at the pub.

Re-capping the mascara, she snatched up the phone, silencing the music. She glared at the screen, then opened up her contacts list, her thumb hovering over Jessica's name.

'I'm sorry,' she whispered, and pressed "delete".

She padded across the landing to her bedroom at the back of the house and dressed in a long-sleeved T-shirt and jeans, tugging on a pair of thick woollen socks her grandmother had given her for Christmas last year. Wiggling her toes, she opened a food delivery app, ordered pizza for one (no pineapple) and then picked up one of the gossip magazines Emma had left behind.

A hammering on the front door sent her heart rate rocketing.

Checking her watch while she hurried downstairs, she tried to recall whether she was expecting any deliveries. The pizza wouldn't turn up for at least another thirty minutes, not this far out of town, and the clothes she had ordered online weren't due until tomorrow, so—

She groaned as she recognised the outline of the figure standing on the step, and wrenched open the door.

'I thought we agreed you wouldn't come here, Wayne.'

The college lecturer glanced over his shoulder to where his car was parked in front of the house, then back to her. 'We need to talk.'

'For f—' Bethany sighed, stepped back and waved him inside before slamming the door. 'What about?'

'The police came to see me.'

'So? They came to see me, too.' She ushered him through to the living room, and perched on the arm of the sofa as he paced the carpet.

He paused and ran a hand through his collar-length hair. Bethany caught the tell-tale smudges of dye at his temples, disappointment welling up inside. She'd had her suspicions, but—

'What did they ask you?'

'Same as you, probably. Did I know anyone who

might've wanted to harm Jessica, did she seem concerned by anything or anyone—'

'Did you mention me?'

'What do you think?'

'I don't know, that's why I'm asking you.' His nostrils flared and, in that moment, she wondered why on earth she'd bothered chasing after him in the first place.

'They wanted to know why I didn't tell them about you when they first spoke with me.'

'Why didn't you?'

'Because I didn't want your bloody wife to find out, did I? Jesus.' She rolled her eyes. 'I still have to pass my exams next year, and she invigilates them, doesn't she? She could make my life hell if she found out about us.'

'Mine, too,' said Wayne, his face glum.

'What did they ask you?' she said, folding her arms across her chest.

He flushed crimson. 'They wanted to know if I was having an affair with Jessica.'

Bethany laughed, hearing the bitterness pierce the air. 'Some chance. She had better taste.'

He stepped closer, holding out his hands. 'I'm sorry. Come here.'

'No,' she said, scowling and shuffling away from his grasp. 'I told you, you shouldn't have come here. You need to go.'

'Oh, come on.' He reached out, wrapping his hand

around her arm. 'Your housemates are away, aren't they?'

Arching an eyebrow, she snatched her arm from his grip and pointed at the door. 'Get out.'

'But—'

'Go!'

He hurried from the room, wrenching open the front door.

She followed him and kept her hand on the frame as he paused on the threshold.

'Will I see you again?' he said, his voice desperate.

'Sure.' She smiled. 'I've got a business economics class first thing on Friday morning with you, right?'

Her smile faded as his eyes hardened, and then he turned and stalked towards his car.

'Idiot,' she said under her breath.

The sound of another car approaching from her right caught her attention and she peered over the neighbour's low privet hedge in time to see a battered old hatchback pull up to the kerb beyond their gate.

Wayne gunned the engine to his mid-life-crisis sports car and roared away as the driver of the second car climbed out, and her heart sank as she recognised him.

'Now what?' she muttered.

She folded her arms across her chest and sneered as he walked up the path towards her.

'What do you want?'

CHAPTER THIRTY-EIGHT

Jan ground a generous portion of black peppercorns into the bolognese sauce and peered over her shoulder as Harry, the older of the twins by thirteen minutes and three seconds, slid past in his socks as if riding a skateboard.

'Will you stop doing that across the floor while I'm cooking?' she said. 'It's flipping dangerous.'

'Sorry, Mum.'

He wandered over to the hob and peered into the saucepan. 'Smells good.'

'So do you.' She kissed the top of his head, and realised with sadness that another couple of centimetres and she'd no longer be looking down on her son. They were both growing so fast. 'Is Luke out of the shower yet?'

'I think so.'

'Make sure he leaves the extractor fan on to get rid of the condensation and picks up the bath mat. I'm dishing up in five minutes.'

'Okay.'

'And bring down your football kit so I can wash it. Socks as well this time!'

The stomping of a nine-year-old running up the stairs reached her ears, and she wondered for the nth time how a boy could sound like a herd of elephants.

'Need a hand with anything?'

Strong arms wrapped around her, and then Scott leaned his chin on her shoulder.

'All under control, I think.'

'Glass of wine?'

'Perfect.'

Jan peered over her shoulder and smiled as her husband of fifteen years opened the refrigerator door and pulled out a bottle of white Rioja.

His hair was still wet from the shower – he'd seized the chance to have one while the boys were still squabbling over that night's football practice and demanding food like a pair of hungry sparrows. He padded around the kitchen in bare feet, content to relax in a T-shirt and jeans as he fetched plates from the cupboard and gathered cutlery.

Scott filled a glass, then placed it on the worktop next to her and smiled. 'I'll lay the table. Those two will never be down in time.'

'Can you make sure Luke's out of that shower for me?'

Her husband's voice carried up the stairs as he wandered out of the kitchen and into the dining area that divided the kitchen from the living room.

She leaned against the worktop and took a sip of wine as the water in the pan next to her began to simmer.

Turning down the heat, mindful that it could be some time before both boys were ready and not wanting to overcook the pasta, her thoughts turned to the case at hand.

Despite what everyone had said about Jessica being well-liked and not inclined to trouble, Jan couldn't help wondering if there was a hidden side to the teenager that they hadn't yet uncovered.

The lack of information or clues that might lead to her killer's motivation worried her – in a lot of murder cases, it transpired that the victim knew their attacker, but who within Jessica's tight-knit circle of friends had cause to harm her?

And why?

What were the circumstances that led that person to believe that there was no other course of action to take than to kill a young woman who had everything to live for?

Jan sighed, then took another sip of wine before placing the glass next to the chopping board and turning her attention to the pots on the stove.

A moment later, a waft of musk and whatever else was mixed in with the boys' latest choice of shower gel emanated from the stairs, and her younger son appeared in the doorway, a bundle of clothes in his arms.

'Did you pick up the bath mat?' she said.

'Yes. And I've left the fan running. Do you want me to put these in the washing machine?'

'Please. Have you got all of your brother's kit, too?'

'Yep.'

She smiled as Luke crouched by the machine next to the sink, shovelled the clothes inside, and added powder before peering at the dial and selecting the right programme. He might have been Harry's twin, but he couldn't be more different in personality.

Where Harry was content to wreak havoc on a daily basis, Luke was retrospective; thoughtful.

'How was homework tonight?'

He shrugged. 'All right, I s'pose. History.'

'Still studying the Romans?'

'Yes. They're talking about a field trip when it warms up. Somewhere down in Hampshire – to a villa.'

'That'd be good. Okay, off you go. I'm about to dish up.'

Luke grinned and scurried away, his voice soon audible over his brother's as they bickered about what to watch on television after dinner.

Jan turned down the heat on the stove, and then

closed her eyes as her mobile phone began to ring from its position next to her handbag in the hallway.

Wiping her hands on a tea towel, she hurried to answer it as Scott peered around the living room door.

'Do you want me to dish up?' he said.

She nodded as she saw Turpin's name displayed on the screen. 'Looks like I'm needed. Hello?'

'Sorry, Jan – I realise you're probably having dinner with Scott and the boys. How soon can you get over to MacKenzie Adams' yard?'

'What's happened?'

'Nigel White has been found dead.'

CHAPTER THIRTY-NINE

Mark scowled at the full moon blinking through a cloud-strewn sky, and then glared at the activities unfolding in the headlight beams from an ambulance and two patrol cars.

A fine drizzle created a mist in the gloom beyond the light that pooled from the open door to the cottage owned by MacKenzie Adams, turning an already miserable scene into one of desolation and despair.

Off to one side, in separate patrol cars, Paul Hitchens and Will Brennan sat on the back seats and provided their statements to a pair of police constables who took their time, noting every utterance the two men made.

The horse trainer had been and gone, his top lip curling at Mark as he'd informed MacKenzie that he wouldn't be allowed into the property until it had been processed by the CSI team and released by the police.

He'd taken off in his four-by-four ten minutes ago, shaking his head, and Mark realised as he reread the man's statement that his gruff demeanour served only to hide his shock at the death of a long-serving employee he had grown to depend on.

One of the ambulance staff pushed himself away from the side of the vehicle, walked around to the back and slammed shut the doors before returning to the driver's seat and starting the engine.

Mark sighed – Gillian had been running late through no fault of her own, and in the circumstances, they'd elected to wait for the Home Office pathologist to certify White's death, especially given the ongoing police investigation.

'What are the chances?' said Gillian as she paused beside him and pulled a paper mask away from her face. 'Brennan finding White, I mean.'

Mark wrinkled his nose. 'Have you done the paperwork?'

'Yes. They'll move him as soon as Jasper gives us the go-ahead.'

On cue, the bright flash from a photographer's camera strobed off the hallway walls of the cottage, blinding Mark for a moment.

He blinked to clear his vision, and then turned at the

sound of a vehicle splashing along the pot-holed lane towards them.

'That'll be West,' he said.

'I'll let you get on. It's been a harsh start to the winter, so we're busier than usual this week but I'll do my best to schedule the post mortem before the weekend.'

'Thanks, Gillian.'

She murmured a farewell before making her way towards her car, pausing to remove the rest of her protective clothing and shoving it in a biohazard bin provided by the CSI team.

Jan held up her hand to the pathologist and then hurried over to where he stood, her hair catching in the breeze and a harried expression on her face.

'Did you have dinner?'

She shook her head. 'We were dishing up when you phoned.'

'Sorry.'

'That's okay. Wouldn't miss this for the world, right?' The attempt at humour didn't reach her eyes as she peered at the open door to the property. 'What's the latest?'

Mark gestured to the two jockeys who were now being chaperoned into one patrol car. 'Brennan found him. They were both out on the gallops late, then at the stables clearing up afterwards before Adams sent him up here to find White. Apparently he was expected to take part in a telephone conference call with one of the owners.'

'Where are those two staying tonight?'

'MacKenzie Adams said there are camp beds stored in the canteen building down at the yard, so one of the uniforms is driving them down there. They'll have to make do until we can let them back here.'

'That's if they want to move back in, I suppose.' Jan jerked her chin at the CSI exiting the cottage. 'What happened to White?'

'It looks like he hanged himself from the stair bannister.'

'Looks like?'

Mark shrugged. 'There's a suicide note. We won't know more until Gillian's done the post mortem. Jasper's been busy with his team, so I'm just waiting until he's got a moment and he can show us.'

'And that moment has arrived,' said the tall CSI who approached them. He pulled down his mask and winked. 'Evening, Jan.'

'You're a bit happy, for someone working a crime scene,' she said.

'Overtime. What's not to like?' He held out a sheet of paper that had been placed into an evidence bag. 'We've managed to take some fingerprints off this, which we'll send through for analysis in due course. Did Gillian say when she'll do the PM?'

'As soon as possible,' said Mark.

'She reckons he didn't break his neck on the way down. It was strangulation that finished him off.' Jasper shivered. 'Nasty, when it doesn't go to plan for them.'

'*I'm sorry. It's my fault she's dead,*' said Mark, running his finger under the words scrawled across the page.

'Mystery solved, then,' said Jasper, and tugged away his mask.

'Was this found on his body?'

'Yes, in the right back pocket of his jeans – and we found some notes he'd jotted down in the margin of a newspaper upstairs. Just as well he wrote that suicide note in capital letters, because his normal handwriting is appalling.'

'We'll get the two samples sent off to our handwriting analyst, just to make sure,' said Jan.

'Okay. We found an envelope of cash in his bedside table as well. Four hundred quid. Your lot asked Brennan and Hitchens about it, but they say they don't know where he got it from. MacKenzie pays them by electronic transfer.'

'Fingerprints?'

'Off for analysis. We've finished here, and we've left everything bagged up where we found it before it gets passed to your lot to go into evidence, so if you want to take a look while I speak to the blokes from the coroner's office, you can. No need to suit up.'

'Thanks.' Mark passed the note to Jan. 'What do you think?'

'A bit convenient, isn't it?' she said, tilting the page until it caught the light from the ambulance as it passed behind them on its way to the dirt track down to the yard. 'Anyway, if he did kill her, what was his motive?'

'Come on, let's go and have a look around.'

He traipsed across the stony driveway to the cottage, standing to one side as two men from the coroner's office manhandled a stretcher into the hallway, and then following them inside.

'Jesus.'

Jan's words echoed his thoughts as he paused on the threshold and took in the broken figure of Nigel White dangling from a leather horse bridle that had been tied around the top balustrade.

The man's eyes bulged from their sockets while his head tilted towards his shoulder at an unnatural angle. Dark stains covered the inside legs of his jeans, a stench of stale urine cloying the enclosed space.

Mark stepped sideways as one of the men took the stairs and began to loosen the knot while his colleague took the weight of White's body. He gestured to Jan to follow him into the living room.

A dull glow emanated from the wood burning stove, any remnant heat driven away by the biting cold that was seeping into the room between the twisted and warped window frames and the front door.

He wondered how desperate for stardom he would have to be before succumbing to such decrepit living conditions, and then reminded himself that Hitchens and Brennan were fifteen years younger than him and fitter, and the cottage was at least warmer than the training areas and racecourses they frequented.

As for White, he had seemed resigned to living in the house all the while he worked for MacKenzie, and had given no indication when they had interviewed him at the yard on Saturday that his thoughts might turn to suicide.

'Which bedroom was his?' said Jan, as she ran her fingers over the back of the armchair, her top lip curling before she wiped her hand on the back of her trousers.

'The larger one at the back, according to Will.' Mark raised his eyebrows at a dull thud from the hallway. 'Sounds like we'll be able to take a look now.'

Casting his gaze aside from the two men manhandling White's body into a protective bag in the middle of the hallway, he climbed the stairs, keeping his hands in his pockets as he eyed the dark powder covering the bannister, evidence of Jasper and his colleagues' progress through the cottage.

He passed the first door, and called over his shoulder. 'That's Brennan's. Hitchens' room is behind us, next to the bathroom. This is White's, according to their statements.'

Pushing open the door, he took a moment before

entering the bedroom, letting his eyes wander over the spartan conditions.

An unmade single bed took up the length of the far wall, a green duvet cast to one side exposing a rumpled sheet and pillow. Beside it, a lamp sat on a low wooden square table next to which a well-thumbed paperback had been placed, a bookmark a quarter of the way through the pages. An overflowing ashtray perched on the edge closest to the bed, four butts curling amongst the grey-coloured dust.

To the left of where he stood, a wooden wardrobe teetered unsteadily on the uneven floorboards, one of the double doors open and exposing a selection of clothing that dangled from cheap plastic hangers.

'Anything?' said Jan over his shoulder.

He stepped inside and beckoned her to follow. 'Jasper's already passed a laptop to the uniforms downstairs to go into evidence. They found it under the mattress.'

'Odd place to keep a laptop. What about a mobile phone?'

'Nothing yet.'

'You'd have thought he'd have had that in his jeans pocket, or at least left it lying around here.' Jan's forehead creased as she moved to the wardrobe and peered inside. 'Did they try to access the laptop?'

'Didn't have to – it was already switched on when

they found it, just in sleep mode. No password necessary.'

She paused in her examination of White's clothing choices. 'What sort of man puts his laptop under the mattress if it's still switched on? I mean, I can understand it from a security point of view if he didn't want the other two using it, but—'

'Exactly my thought.'

'What was on it?'

'The usual apps that come with a laptop out of the box these days. He'd left it open on a website about poker tips.'

'Cards?'

'Yes.'

Jan paused next to the bedside table, then turned to face him, her expression earnest. 'Maybe he was hiding the laptop because he was interrupted. Maybe whoever interrupted him wasn't meant to know about the gambling.'

'It was only poker tips. That doesn't make him a gambler per se.'

'No, but if someone like MacKenzie Adams saw that, he'd think the worst, wouldn't he? The last thing a racehorse trainer would want is a member of staff with a gambling problem. Who knows where that might lead?'

Mark grunted under his breath, conceding the point. 'Motive?'

She shook her head. 'I don't know. Seems extreme, doesn't it?'

'And if that was the case, what's the connection to Jessica? She'd only recently started working for Adams, according to everyone we've spoken to.'

'He was a bit dismissive of her, wasn't he? White, I mean.'

'I got the impression when we spoke to him that he thought she was a waste of space, not a threat.'

Jan blew out her cheeks and raised her hands. 'Well, I don't know then.'

Battening down his frustration at the turn of events, Mark led the way out of the room and back down the stairs to the hallway where the cold milky gaze of Nigel White stared up at him from the body bag before it was zipped closed.

He had a feeling it would be some time before he forgot the dead man's accusatory eyes.

CHAPTER FORTY

Showered, dressed, and blinking back tiredness after only six hours' sleep since leaving MacKenzie Adams' stables in the early hours, Mark stumbled into the incident room as the scheduled morning briefing was due to start.

Jan held up a cup of coffee in salute as he chucked his backpack under his desk, stifling a yawn before picking up her desk phone and redirecting a call through to another investigation team.

She replaced the phone and snapped her fingers at him as he began to log in. 'Don't get comfortable – the guv wants us out straight away to interview Adams. Caroline and Alex are already on their way over there to re-interview Brennan and Hitchens when they get back from exercising the horses this morning.'

'What about the briefing?'

'He says he'll do it when we get back.'

'All right. Ready when you are.'

In reply, she pushed back her chair and held up a set of car keys. 'Best we get you a coffee on the way. I'll stop at the petrol station down the road.'

Fifteen minutes later, slightly less groggy and clutching a steaming takeout cup containing the sort of coffee only a desperate man would drink, Mark squinted against the bright sunlight streaming through the windscreen while Jan powered the car away from the urban sprawl towards the Berkshire Downs.

'Any more thoughts about Nigel White?' he said.

'Yes, hence the bags under my eyes this morning. I still don't see him as a threat to Jessica, but until the handwriting expert raises any doubts, or we receive evidence to the contrary, what option does his death leave us with but to accept he was guilty of killing her?'

'I want to be sure, too,' he said, grimacing as he sampled the coffee and then vowing to throw the rest in the nearest waste bin. 'I was surprised at Adams' reaction last night. Compared with the way he acted when Jessica was found on the gallops last week, he seemed genuinely shocked by White's death.'

'Where do you think the cash came from?'

'No idea – let's hope the fingerprint results tell us something.'

Jan swung the car through the open gates and into the horse trainer's yard a few minutes later, and parked next to an off-white vehicle Mark recognised from the police station pool car park.

Off to the right, nearer to the stable block, a bright-red van with the livery of a local blacksmith emblazoned down the side had been parked haphazardly next to a pair of stable lads who watched the detectives' arrival with interest.

Alex McClellan emerged from the low-slung building used as a canteen and raised his hand in greeting as they walked towards the farmhouse.

'How's it going?' said Mark, pausing at the front door.

'We'd just finished the interviews when you pulled up. Thought you'd better know – Adams is in a foul mood this morning.'

'I suppose too much publicity can be a bad thing,' said Jan, an edge of smugness in her voice. 'Poor dear.'

'What did the two jockeys have to say for themselves?' said Mark.

'They've both reiterated their statements taken by uniform last night,' said Alex. 'They were out until late afternoon exercising horses that are going to be racing this Thursday. Sounds like Brennan's going to be riding in a race next Tuesday for Adams.' He shrugged. 'Anyway, they stayed down here in the yard until nearly six o'clock, polishing tack and the like. Adams came to find them, and asked if either of them had seen White around because he was late for a telephone conference call with an owner. When they said no, Adams told Brennan to go up to the cottage to find him. When he got there, he phoned back to the farmhouse to tell him he'd found White hanging from the stair balustrade.'

'Wait,' said Jan. 'He said he phoned the farmhouse first? Why didn't he dial triple nine?'

'He told us he could tell there was nothing he could do for White, and panicked,' said Alex. 'The emergency call was made by Adams – Caroline got a copy of the recording emailed to her phone while I was finishing the interview with Hitchens.'

'Where is Adams now?' said Mark.

Alex pointed over his shoulder. 'We left him in his office. He said he was busy, but that you should head on in when you got here.'

'All right, thanks. We'll see you later.'

Mark sensed the horse trainer's reluctance to talk as he walked into the man's office and waited near the door to be summoned.

Adams had his back to the room and his hands clasped behind his back as he stared out at the row of stables and the yard busy with horses being shod by the local farrier. His shoulders heaved as a loud sigh escaped his lips, and then he glanced over his shoulder.

'I've known White for over a decade,' he said. 'I never would have guessed him to be a murderer.'

'Do you mind if we have a word?' said Mark. 'I'd

like to ask a few questions as part of our ongoing investigation.'

'Into Nigel's suicide, or the girl's death?'

'Both.'

Adams pointed to the two seats opposite his desk, then dropped into his leather chair and held his head in his hands for a moment. 'What a nightmare.'

Mark said nothing, and waited while Jan retrieved her notebook from her handbag and then crossed her legs, settling in for the conversation ahead.

'He was a brilliant jockey, you know,' said Adams eventually. He raised his head, a faint smile crossing his features. 'And he was one of the few who understood the business side of things.'

'Is that how he ended up working for you?'

'Yes. I told the policeman that when they were taking my statement last night. He had a nasty fall a few years ago, and couldn't risk racing again for fear of breaking his spine. Having him working here in the yard instead was a natural progression – for both of us.' Adams shook his head, the smile fading. 'He was one of the few people I trusted.'

'What was his relationship with Jessica Marley like?'

'There was no relationship as far as I know. Jessica only started working here three, four weeks ago now, and Nigel was the one who gave her jobs to do around the yard. I realised she was only after a bit of work experience to put on her résumé, and she wasn't expecting to get paid much so it worked out fine for both of us.'

'Are you aware of any altercations between the two of them?'

'No, but then I left the day-to-day running of the yard to Nigel. I certainly didn't hear about any arguments, and she never came to me to complain about him. I'd have been surprised if she did – like I said, I've known him for years, and I trusted him.'

'What happened yesterday?' said Mark. 'Was he working down here in the yard all afternoon?'

'Until three o'clock, yes. Then he wandered in here – he looked worried, and said he had to dash back up to the cottage. I said it wasn't a problem, and that I'd see him later for a conference call with one of the owners.'

'What did he say he had to go there for?'

'I think he said he'd forgotten something. I was in the middle of something, so I didn't really hear what he said.'

'When did you think something might be wrong?'

'I was busy with paperwork – half my time is spent filling out forms for The British Horseracing Authority and various racecourses – so I didn't look at my watch again until I heard the horses coming back into the yard from the training session.'

'What time was that?'

'Just after five o'clock – that lane out there turns

into a race circuit with commuters from a quarter past and I like to know they're all back here safely before rush hour.'

'Go on.'

'I realised then that I hadn't seen White in the yard – with that window facing the stables, it gives me a good view of everything going on out there, and I try to look away from the computer screen every twenty minutes. My optician tells me it's supposed to help with eye strain.' His mouth twisted at the memory. 'I wandered off down the hallway and called to Brennan, but he hadn't seen Nigel up at the gallops either, so I told him to go up to the cottage and make sure he was all right. Next thing I know, my mobile phone's ringing and it's Brennan telling me that he's found Nigel… and that he was dead.'

Adams shuddered, his face paling at the memory.

'Why did Will phone you, not the police – or an ambulance?'

'I don't know. Because I'm his boss, I suppose. Anyway, I dialled 999, told your lot what had happened and then drove up to the cottage with Paul. We found Brennan sitting on the bottom stair tread, staring into space.'

'Did any of you touch anything?'

'No – I've seen enough television shows.'

'Did either of you remove anything from the property?'

'I told Brennan to grab a change of clothes for him and Hitchens, and told him they could use the bunks in the canteen down here. I figured you wouldn't want either of them in the cottage last night. I couldn't imagine the pair of them wanting to stay there, anyway.'

'And you say you removed nothing apart from their clothes?'

'That's right.' Adams glared at him. 'What are you insinuating, Detective Turpin?'

Mark smiled. 'Nothing at all, Mr Adams. Just wanted to make sure I understood you correctly.'

CHAPTER FORTY-ONE

A fog of frustration hung in the air as Ewan Kennedy strode to the front of the incident room and faced the investigation team.

Paperwork lay strewn across desks, reports lay open with pages well-thumbed and creased, and desk phones blinked with alerts that messages were waiting.

Fatigue was setting in as was the realisation that ten days had passed since Jessica Marley's body had been found on the gallops, and they were no further forward in their work despite Nigel White's suicide note.

Until such time as the handwriting expert confirmed the words belonged to MacKenzie Adams' stable hand, Jan guessed her DI would be reluctant to consider the case closed or assign his team to other tasks.

'Right, everyone.' Kennedy's voice carried across

the assembled group of officers. 'Alex – I hear you've managed to interview the two bus drivers at last?'

'Yes, guv.'

'Get up here and let us have an update then.'

Mark put down his coffee cup and moved so he had a better view of Alex and could hear what the detective constable had to say.

Alex cleared his throat as he joined the DI. 'Can you all hear me at the back? Good. All right – we got two names from the bus company, and, thanks to Tom's work chasing this up, they were able to attend here for interview with their union representative late yesterday afternoon. Leonard Smith drove the last bus between here and Harton Wick on Monday night, passing the location where we now know the streetlight to have been broken. He says he saw no-one around at that time, and that he dropped off his last passenger at eleven fifty-five up at the crossroads on the main road before turning into the village. We've had a look at the CCTV from his vehicle, and can confirm the light was working when Leonard went past.'

Alex flipped through the notes in his hand. 'The second driver was Michael Brockman. He drove the last bus coming the other way through Hazelthorpe. He passed Smith's bus in Hazelthorpe at ten past twelve and reached Harton Wick at twelve twenty-five, according to the CCTV footage from his bus. He states that he had to put his lights on full beam because one of the streetlights was out.'

The incident room exploded with voices, and Mark peered around to catch Jan's attention. She stuck up her thumb, then turned back to Kennedy, who raised his hands.

'Pipe down, everyone. Thanks, Alex. Anything else from the second driver, Michael Brockman?'

Alex shook his head. 'We've passed the CCTV recording over to digital forensics, guv, but it's pretty grainy. We all had a look at it, but couldn't see anyone parked near the streetlight when the bus passed and there was no-one lurking around the pub or further up the lane. I'm guessing whoever smashed the light hid somewhere close by.'

Kennedy scratched his jaw. 'Which still means that somehow they had to coerce Jessica to their vehicle, wherever that was parked.'

'Or carry her,' said Mark.

'What about the blood spatter found on those stones nearby? Have we got a match?'

'Yes, guv,' said Alex. 'The lab says it's definitely Jessica's.'

'We let the CCTV recording run for the rest of the route up the lane to the crossroads and a couple of miles after that,' said Caroline, 'but there were no abandoned vehicles in plain sight. We made a note of all the vehicles the bus did pass, and they've checked out as belonging to residents who live along that stretch of road. Any further than the crossroads where the main road is, and I don't think Jessica's killer would've got away with carrying her. Too far, and too risky.'

'Guv? Noah and Sonia Collins have told us that Jessica left the Farriers Arms at eleven-thirty,' said Jan. 'So, where did she go after that? I mean, if we're proposing that her killer broke the streetlight sometime between eleven fifty-five and twelve twenty-five in order to give themselves some cover, then where was Jessica during that time?'

A series of murmurs rumbled through the incident room, and then Wilcox raised his voice.

'If we follow up with her mobile phone provider, we could trace her number and see where her phone was at the time,' he said. 'If it was switched on, we might be able to narrow it down.'

'Check with Noah Collins as well,' said Kennedy. 'Ask him if he or Sonia saw anyone talking to Jessica outside the pub after she left, or whether they heard any vehicles idling nearby.'

'Will do, guv.'

'Next – what the bloody hell is going on at those stables? Turpin – you first.'

'Guv.' Mark walked to the front of the room and then faced his colleagues, an expression of consternation flitting across his face. 'We spoke with Adams, who confirmed that it was Brennan who found

White's body and phoned him from the cottage. Adams drove up there with Paul Hitchens after dialling triple nine, told Brennan to grab a change of clothing for both of them, and says nothing else was touched.'

'But Adams couldn't know for sure what Will Brennan was up to between leaving the stables to go and find White and when he turned up with Hitchens,' said Kennedy. 'How long was Brennan on his own for?'

'Adams reckoned on about fifteen minutes,' said Mark. 'It's only a five-minute drive cross-country from the yard to the cottage. Allowing five minutes to get there, discover White and phone Adams, who then phoned it in before heading up there himself, the timeframe works.'

'Alex – what did Brennan tell you?' said Kennedy.

'The same as he told the officers who interviewed him last night,' said the detective constable. 'He didn't deviate from the original statement at all. When we asked him if he'd removed anything from the cottage, specifically from White's room, he said he hadn't, and that he'd only gone upstairs after Adams turned up and told him to go and get some spare clothes. He said when he first got there, the front door was unlocked – and confirmed that wasn't unusual if one of them was home – and that he was too shocked to do anything apart from calling Adams when he discovered the body.'

'Does anyone have any evidence other than the suicide note to suggest White killed Jessica?'

A murmur of negative responses rippled through the room.

'What about motive? Any ideas?'

Kennedy paced the floor in front of the whiteboard as Alex returned to his desk, resting his hands on hips as he waited for someone to enlighten him.

Jan held her breath. Kennedy was a good boss, but impatience at the lack of progress showed in the way his shoulders stiffened at the sound of silence and the knowledge his officers could do no more with the information they had to date. In her experience, it was better to stay quiet than hazard an unsubstantiated guess.

'All right, if we have no ideas about motive, why now?' said Kennedy eventually. 'Jessica was killed over a week ago, so why has White killed himself now? Why not last week?'

'Maybe he thought he'd got away with it, guv,' said Caroline. 'Maybe, until recently, he had nothing to fear. Perhaps someone said something to him that made him panic.'

'Adams did say, when we spoke to him yesterday, that White had told him that he had to return to the cottage. He said he'd looked worried,' said Turpin.

'About what?' said Kennedy.

'He didn't know,' said Jan. 'He was up to his eyeballs in paperwork, apparently, and wasn't paying much attention. He just told White to remember they had a conference call with an owner later on. It was when he didn't show up for that, that Adams sent Brennan to find him.'

'The laptop that Jasper's lot found underneath White's mattress,' said Turpin. 'It wasn't switched off, it had gone into sleep mode. What if he was using it when he first went back to the cottage, and then got interrupted? Perhaps a knock at the door, or movement downstairs. The way it was shoved under the mattress suggests he was hiding it from someone in a hurry, rather than keeping it out of sight from any would-be passing burglar that might go up to the cottage while they were all at work.'

'What of it?' said Kennedy.

'We wondered if he might've hidden it from someone like Brennan or Adams – someone from the stables who he didn't want to know he'd been on the gaming sites that had been left open.'

Kennedy turned to Alex, who was sitting at his desk with White's laptop open beside him. 'Have you managed to access his account with that gaming site?'

'Yes, guv.' The detective constable spun the computer around to face the DI as he crossed the room to join him.

Her interest piqued, Jan reached Alex at the same time as Turpin.

'What have you found so far?' said Kennedy, resting a hand on the desk as he peered at the screen.

'It's the sort of site where you've got the option to

load up your credit card details or you can buy credit to spend on an as-and-when-needed basis,' said Alex. 'White seems to have preferred the first method, so once we have copies of his bank statements available, I'll do a cross-check between those and this account.'

'Was he getting in over his head with the repayments?' said Turpin.

'No,' said Alex. 'That's the thing. He wasn't getting behind at all. In fact, he paid a few hundred pounds up front every week or so, and didn't spend over that. He budgeted well, but he wasn't a good player.'

Jan moved closer and peered at the screen. 'Bloody hell. MacKenzie Adams can't be paying him that much to work for him, can he? How's he affording this sort of a habit?'

'That's the thing,' said Alex. 'It's not a habit. You're seeing his overall spend for the past twelve months there. I've been taking a look at what White was up to on these gaming sites, and it doesn't look like he was really gambling at all – the spending pattern is too sporadic.'

'Well, what was he doing then?' said Turpin.

Alex pushed the laptop away and spun his chair around to face them. 'It looks almost like he was doing research.'

CHAPTER FORTY-TWO

Mark pulled a navy polo shirt over his head, and then froze.

A sharp bark from Hamish confirmed his suspicions – the doorbell had rung.

He ran a hand over wet hair, peered in the mirror above the bathroom sink, and sighed.

'It'll have to do.'

Heart racing, he fastened his belt with trembling fingers as he launched himself down the stairs, steam from the bathroom chasing his bare feet.

He forced himself to take a breath, battling down a sudden flurry of nerves and choked out a laugh.

'I'm worse than a bloody teenager.'

Mark opened the door, letting in a cold wind that nipped at his toes.

'I'm so sorry, I'm early,' said Lucy, her forehead creased.

'No, you're not. I'm still running late,' said Mark. 'Come on in.'

'Here, wine – as promised.'

'Thank you.' He closed the door behind her, placed the bottle bag on a small table near the stairs beside his car keys, then helped her out of her coat. 'And I'm sorry I couldn't pick you up. One of those days.'

'That's okay, I don't—'

Hamish launched himself from the living room, a bundle of fur-covered joy. His paws clawed at Lucy's jeans, and she pushed her long curls from her face while she pretended to fight him off with her other hand.

'Good boy,' she said.

'Good boy, but get down,' said Mark. 'Come on, Hamish. Enough.'

The dog wagged his tail, dashed a circle around Lucy's heels and then trotted along the hall to the kitchen, his tail in the air.

Mark laughed. 'I'm sure if he had thumbs, he'd be opening a couple of beers for us right now.'

'We'd better go and check he isn't,' said Lucy. 'Oh, here – it's late, but I remembered I hadn't given you a housewarming present.'

She reached into a canvas tote bag and withdrew a tissue-wrapped rectangle.

Mark turned it in his hands. 'You didn't have to do

that, thank you.'

'You haven't seen it yet.' She grinned. 'Open it, then.'

Buoyed by her enthusiasm, he tore open the wrapping to discover a charcoal sketch she'd made of the old narrowboat he'd rented over the summer, a miniature Hamish scampering along the towpath beside it. She'd made the frame from driftwood, and as Mark ran his thumb over the uneven surface, tracing the whorls, he blinked.

'This is lovely, thank you.'

'I figured it'd be a nice reminder of a new start,' she said.

'It is.'

Mark swallowed. Lucy's kindness and intuition had been something he'd enjoyed about her company when they'd been moored next to each other on the river, and he realised how much he missed living there.

'So, are you going to give me the grand tour?' she said, smiling.

He snorted. 'Now, that isn't going to take long.'

'You're talking to someone who still lives on a boat, mister. Humour me.'

He laughed, before leading her up the stairs. He hurried forward, pulling the bathroom door shut, and then turned to her on the landing.

'You're right – you were early. Don't go in there.'

She laughed, a pretty sound that made him smile as

he brushed past her and gestured towards the main bedroom. 'That's me in there, and I'm using one of the spare rooms for storage at the moment until I decide what to do with everything. I'm using this middle bedroom as a sort of office.'

He leaned forward to switch on a desk lamp, then stepped to one side to let her pass.

Two full bookcases lined the wall to the right of the door, and he'd set up his desk and a two-drawer filing cabinet to the left so his chair faced the landing. A dog bed, squashed and well used, took up the floor space next to the radiator.

Mark placed the framed sketch next to his laptop.

'This is nice. It feels like you spend a lot of time in here.'

'Probably more than I should.'

Her brow creased as she saw the photograph of Anna and Louise beside the desk lamp. 'I was sorry to hear about your divorce. Thanks for telling me.'

He shrugged. 'In hindsight, I think it was inevitable. We did the best we could.'

Lucy stepped over to the window and peered outside.

Dusk was settling over the landscape beyond the garden; a purple and blue hue that hung over the trees, the twilight sky bustling with clouds that raced towards the horizon.

'If you stand on tiptoe you'll be able to see the river

between the trees,' said Mark.

Lucy did as he suggested, her eyebrows raised. 'Oh, yes.'

He moved closer, his heart tilting as he inhaled her perfume. 'I can see your boat from here.'

'Can you?'

'Almost. Through there, down to the right a bit. See it?'

'I think so.' She turned and reached out for his hand, then kissed him. 'I'll sleep better at night knowing you're keeping a lookout for me.'

'Good.' He smiled. 'Hungry?'

'Starving.'

Lucy sat at the dining table and regaled Mark with news from her latest art exhibition while he dished out generous portions of the roast dinner he'd been preparing since returning from work. He enjoyed the excuse to cook something more substantial than the meals for one he'd been living on, and her easy conversation helped ease away the stresses of the current investigation.

Later, as she set down her cutlery and picked up her wine, Lucy smiled over the rim of her glass. 'That was fantastic, thank you.'

'You're welcome. I'm glad you enjoyed it. I thought you might be busy with your exhibition at the moment, so I made extra for you to take home.'

'Really?'

'That's what those two empty takeaway containers are for over by the sink.'

Dimples punctured her cheeks. 'I thought those were there because you only cooked dinner on special occasions.'

'That, too.'

They laughed, and then Lucy set her wineglass down, turning the stem between her fingers.

'What do you want in life, Mark?'

'Pardon?'

She sighed. 'I mean, the divorce and everything. Does that mean you're going to stay? Here in the Vale, I mean?'

He pushed back his chair, picked up the wine bottle from the worktop, and wandered back to where she sat. He topped up her glass before setting the bottle on the table.

'It means I'm staying.'

'I'm glad to hear it.'

'Me too.'

'Your voice is starting to sound better. It doesn't sound so rasping.'

'It's getting there.'

She reached out for his hand. 'I worried that it hurt you, every time you spoke when we first met.'

Mark shrugged. 'Sometimes. But it's more like a very sore throat. And, only when I get tired.'

'Has the case come to court yet?'

'About the drugs bust? Not yet.'

'I suppose those things take time, don't they? I mean, if—'

A loud whine from under the table interrupted her, and a moment later two brown eyes peered out from under a shaggy fringe next to Mark.

'How's Hamish settling in?'

'Better than I thought. I wondered if he might miss the freedom he had living rough on the towpath, but he seems happy to have left it behind.'

'Maybe he's older than we thought. I imagine he's going to have a better winter living here with you.'

'Did he sleep rough last winter?'

Lucy squeezed his hand and picked up her wine glass as Mark began to clear away the plates. 'I don't know. I hope not. He didn't stay at mine, but he never looked like he'd lost weight. A couple of mornings he turned up with a bit of frost in his fur but I put that down to him being out early.'

Mark looked down at the dog who was now lifting a paw, one ear up, the other flat.

'I think he knew he was onto a good thing when I turned up.' He picked off a small piece of meat that clung to a leftover bone and held it out to Hamish.

The dog didn't hesitate, licking Mark's fingers before running back to where Lucy sat.

She laughed. 'Scrounger. Some things don't change, do they?'

CHAPTER FORTY-THREE

The next morning, Jan dropped off her twin boys at their primary school in the leafy northern suburbs of the town with clear instructions to wait in the school yard after the final lesson until their dad appeared, and then accelerated away.

Berating herself for the hurried goodbye, she vowed under her breath that she would make it up to them by treating them to an afternoon at Oxford's ice rink as soon as the current investigation was over.

By the time she was steering the car through the security gate to the police station, guilt had transformed into determination to find out if Nigel White had been telling the truth about his role in Jessica's murder.

She locked the vehicle and made her way across the car park. The bustle and roar of rush-hour traffic on Marcham Road filled the air, accompanied by the blast of truck horns from the A34 as drivers jostled to exit the busy dual carriageway.

An early morning rain shower had passed, leaving shallow puddles that she sidestepped to avoid before swiping her security card across the panel next to the back door.

She heard Alex's voice at the top of the stairs and paused at the first-floor landing as he and Caroline passed.

'Where are you two off to?'

'Oxford. Gillian's doing the post mortem,' said Caroline. 'We were in first, so the guv is sending us.'

'Anything you need me to do while you're out?'

Caroline stopped halfway down the next flight of stairs, her hand on the banister. 'Actually, yes. Would you mind making a start on Nigel White's bank statements? They came through this morning.'

'Blimey, that was quick.'

'The benefits of him banking with a building society, and not with one of the big institutions. I've logged them into HOLMES2, but knowing what the guv is like at the moment, he'll probably want a progress report at this afternoon's briefing. Alex has already been through Jessica's statements – there's nothing untoward there.'

'No problem. Leave it with me.'

'Thanks, Jan.'

Caroline threw a wave over her shoulder and hurried after her colleague.

Fifteen minutes later, Jan had a steaming mug of tea in one hand and a sheaf of warm paper in the other having printed off all the bank statements Caroline had obtained.

Given that the investigation now hinged on Gillian's post mortem and the expertise of the handwriting analyst, Jan found herself trying to corroborate White's suicide with the information they had managed to glean about the man's background.

She flicked through the old new stories and photographs that had been logged into HOLMES2 as she blew across the surface of the hot tea, but it was as MacKenzie Adams had told them – once his riding career had come to an end, White had seemed content to work in the yard. There was even an article in which he had appeared in a magazine about country living six years ago where he had extolled the way Adams ran his business.

Jan frowned as she looked at the photo of the man smiling out at her from the computer screen, unable to correlate it with the surly man she had interviewed last week.

What had changed in the relationship between White and his employer?

Or, was it something else entirely that was worrying the man?

Such as being found guilty of killing Jessica Marley?

She locked the computer screen, pushed the empty mug out of the way, and set to work on the details provided by White's building society.

Deciding that it would be prudent to begin her review of the statements at the beginning of the current month, she flipped the older ones aside and ran her gaze down the list of transactions.

It appeared that MacKenzie Adams preferred to pay his full-time employees on a fortnightly basis and she wondered if this was a way to help with his cash flow rather than theirs.

White appeared to use his debit card on a regular basis rather than make cash withdrawals, so when she reached the previous Monday's transactions, her heart rate increased.

She looked up as Turpin entered the incident room with a bounce in his step and whistling under his breath.

'Someone got lucky last night, then.'

The whistling stopped. 'I don't know what you're talking about.'

'Bullshit. Who is she?'

He laughed, draped his suit jacket over the back of his chair and rolled up his sleeves before pointing to the bank statements she'd laid out across her desk. 'Lucy. She came over for dinner, that's all.'

'The hippie from the narrowboat?'

'She's an artist, I'll have you know. Got the bank statements, then?'

'Yes – they emailed them over late yesterday afternoon. Caroline's logged them into the system but she's busy with Alex at the post mortem this morning so I said I'd take a look.'

'How's it going?'

'I was just about to check something when you turned up, actually. Take a look at this.'

She passed him the statements and pointed at two large cash withdrawals made the previous week. 'He had a habit of using his debit card to pay for everything, except when he was at the Farriers Arms. These two here, and similar large amounts the previous four months around the same date.'

'He could have been paying his bar tab.'

'I wondered that, but then why wouldn't he use his debit card?'

Turpin scratched his chin, then leaned forward and signed into HOLMES2.

'What are you doing?' she said.

'Checking those amounts against the ATM withdrawals the night Jessica was killed. We've already ascertained they weren't made by Jessica – Alex updated the system last night after he finished going through her statements.'

She held her breath as the DS clicked his way

through the data in the system, and then exhaled as he tapped the screen.

'Bingo,' he said. 'Same date, same amounts. It was White who made those two large withdrawals from the ATM in the pub. But, why?'

'And he had four hundred quid cash in his bedside table.' Dread seeped through her veins, sending goosebumps shivering over her arms. 'Sarge? What if he was trying to bribe Jessica with that money?'

Fury flashed in his eyes. 'For sex, you mean?'

'It's just a thought. What if he propositioned her after taking out that first lot of money, and when she turned him down he thought that by offering her more, she'd change her mind? What if he killed her because she refused him again?'

'Get onto Noah at the pub, and tell him we need to speak to him urgently.'

Jan was already reaching for her mobile phone, dialling the number for the Farriers Arms as her colleague barked into his desk phone and tried to wangle the use of a pool car from Tom Wilcox on the front desk.

After four rings, a harried Sonia Collins picked up the phone.

'It's DC Jan West. We need to speak to Noah about our ongoing investigation – is he there?'

'He can't come to the phone at the moment,' said Sonia. 'I'm sorry, but we're going to have to call you back later – we've got thirty in for lunch, and we're on our own.'

'I thought Bethany worked on Fridays?'

'She hasn't turned up, and she's not answering her phone. No-one's seen her since she left here on Wednesday night.'

Jan tapped Turpin on the shoulder before fleeing down the stairs towards the car park, her phone held to her ear.

'We're on our way.'

CHAPTER FORTY-FOUR

'Any luck?'

Mark glanced over to the passenger seat as Jan redialled Bethany's mobile number, and then forced himself to concentrate on the narrow winding lane that led from the pub in Harton Wick to the girl's home.

'She's not answering.'

'Why is she on her own, anyway? I thought she shared a rental property with someone else.'

'Sonia said they're away on holiday at the moment – the Canadian Rockies or something. They won't be back until next week.'

'Christ.'

He gritted his teeth as the back wheels slewed across muddy streaks from a tractor's tyres, and then pressed his foot to the floor as the road straightened out. 'Keep trying. We're nearly there.'

Jan's phone trilled.

'Hello? Sonia? We're pulling up outside her house. Have you heard from her? All right – phone me if she turns up.'

By the time Mark locked the car, Jan was already pounding her fist against the frosted windowpane of the front door and ringing the bell.

Mark moved to the front window and shielded the glass from the sun's glare as he peered inside.

The living room was a shambles – remnants of a Chinese takeaway and an empty pizza box were stacked on top of a low table in front of a sofa, and four beer cans had tipped onto their sides next to an open magazine of indeterminate content.

'The television's on,' he said to Jan as he returned to the front door. 'The sound isn't up loud, though – I can hardly hear it.'

Jan's mouth twisted as she raised her fist to knock again.

Before she could do so, the door swung open and Bethany Myers glared out at them.

'Keep the bloody noise down,' she said. 'Next door's baby'll wake up otherwise, and then I'll never hear the end of it.'

On cue, a child's wail reached a crescendo from a top-floor window of the neighbouring property, and Bethany's shoulders slumped.

'Too late.'

'Can we come in?' said Mark.

The young woman shrugged, and turned away. 'S'pose so.'

'Are you all right?' said Jan, closing the door.

They followed Bethany into the living room, where she stopped, her hands on her hips, and stared at them with bloodshot eyes, her face stark without the careful application of make-up. 'What's it to do with you?'

'Why aren't you at work? Sonia's worried about you,' said Mark.

Bethany snorted. 'No, she'll be worried she'll make a mistake and won't have anyone to blame.'

'Why didn't you answer your phone?' said Jan. 'I've been trying to call you for the past half an hour.'

'I didn't hear it. I was upstairs, asleep.'

Mark raised an eyebrow. 'Bethany, people are worried about you. *We're* worried about you—'

'You can't do anything.'

The teenager flounced across to the sofa, pulled her feet up underneath as she sat, and adjusted the thick woollen cardigan she wore.

He locked eyes with Jan for a moment, then wandered across to the armchair opposite Bethany, perching on the arm.

'If someone is threatening or has harmed you, we can help,' he said. 'Don't be scared.'

A tear rolled down the young woman's cheek, before

she wiped it away and sniffed. 'He said it was all my fault, that I'd been stupid.'

'Who are we talking about, Bethany?' said Jan. She eased onto the sofa next to her, keeping her voice even.

'Nigel.'

Mark blinked. 'Nigel White?'

'Yes.'

'When?' said Jan.

'He came around here on Wednesday afternoon – after I'd finished my shift at the Farriers. In a right mood, he was.'

'What happened?'

Mark moved away, content to let his colleague take the lead with the questioning. It was evident that the teenager was uncomfortable talking to him, so he crossed to the window and extracted his notebook.

Bethany continued to stare straight ahead. 'I'd just said goodbye to a friend who popped in when I saw his car turn up. I asked him what he wanted. I couldn't understand why he came here. We… we'd had a row, y' see.'

'About what?' Mark moved closer, his interest piqued.

'I was only trying to help. I went to the Farriers on Tuesday night. I figured people might talk to me more than you. They know me better, right?' She looked at each of them, her eyes desperate. 'I just wanted some answers. Why Jessica was killed. Nigel got all funny then – telling me I need to learn to keep my mouth shut.' She choked out a sob, then took the paper tissue that Jan retrieved from her bag and handed out.

'Did he threaten you?' said Mark.

'I've never seen him like that before. He was... so intense. I-I told him he should be careful about threatening me, 'cause I knew stuff about him.'

'Like what?'

'Nothing – I was bluffing, all right? Anyway, I left the pub and came back here.'

'So, why did Nigel come here on Wednesday?'

'He apologised first, saying he didn't mean to frighten me, but then he asked what I meant when I said I knew stuff about him. I tried to tell him I didn't mean it, that I was joking when I said that, but he grabbed me by arm and shook me really hard. Jesus, I was so scared...'

She broke off as another sob wracked her slight frame, and Mark gave her a moment to compose herself before continuing his questioning.

'What happened next, Bethany?'

'He said there were some things I shouldn't stick my nose into. I – I asked him why, but he wouldn't tell me. He just said that I'd regret it if I didn't stop asking questions about Jess. I managed to get away from him, and locked myself in the bathroom until I heard the front door slam shut.'

'Have you told anyone what happened?' said Mark.

The girl's eyes opened wide. 'Of course not. I don't want this to happen again, do I? Not after what happened to Jessica. What if it was him who killed her? That's why I couldn't go into work today – they would have asked all sorts of questions, wouldn't they?'

'What did you do when you realised he'd gone?' said Mark.

'Not much. I think I was in shock, to be honest. I made sure the doors were locked, and stayed in here all night.'

'What did he mean about you asking questions?' said Jan. 'What sort of questions?'

Bethany held up her hands. 'Like I said, all I did was pop into the Farriers on Tuesday night. It was my night off, so I thought I'd see what I could find out.' She looked from Jan to Mark, then back. 'I was going to tell you if anyone told me something that could help you find out who killed Jessica, that's all.'

'And did you find out anything?' said Mark.

'No. Nothing.' She shrugged, dabbing at her eyes with a tissue. 'At least I tried, anyway.'

'Bethany, where were you between the hours of three o'clock and seven o'clock on Wednesday night?' said Mark.

'Here. Why?' Bewilderment flashed in her eyes. 'What's going on?'

'Nigel White was found dead on Wednesday evening.'

The teenager's mouth dropped open. 'He's dead?'

'Hasn't anyone texted you to tell you?' said Jan.

'No…' Bethany pushed herself off the sofa, staggered, and then held up a hand as Jan moved towards her. 'H-how did he die?'

'It looks like he hanged himself,' said Mark.

Bethany raised a shaking hand to her mouth. 'I think I'm going to be sick.'

She brushed past him, her footsteps thundering up the stairs before he heard a door slam shut, followed by the unmistakable sounds of retching.

Jan moved to the window, and sighed. 'What the bloody hell is going on around here?'

'I don't know,' said Mark, running a hand over his hair. 'And White's dead, so we can't ask him.'

CHAPTER FORTY-FIVE

Ewan Kennedy lowered the report in his hand as Jan knocked on his office door, and beckoned.

'Good timing.' He waited until she and Turpin had taken their seats, and then raised an eyebrow. 'Well, what have you two been up to? I was about to send out a search party.'

'We were planning to speak to Noah Collins about some withdrawals Nigel White made from the ATM in the Farriers Arms on the night Jessica was murdered,' said Turpin, 'but when Jan phoned to see if he was around, Sonia answered the phone and told us Bethany was missing – she hadn't turned up for work today.'

'We tried to phone her, but there was no response,' said Jan. 'When we got to her house, she was pretty shaken up. She said Nigel White had visited her when she got home from work on Wednesday afternoon – and that ties in with the timing MacKenzie Adams provided. He told us that White left the yard at three o'clock on Wednesday, saying he had to return to the cottage.'

Kennedy rubbed a hand over his chin. 'Any idea what he wanted with Bethany?'

'She said he told her she had to stop asking questions of her own about Jessica's death,' said Turpin. 'She seemed shocked when we told her that White had hanged himself.'

The DI dropped the report he had been reading to his desk and shoved it towards them, then leaned back in his chair.

'I hate to be the bearer of more bad news, but that's Gillian's preliminary findings from the post mortem this morning. She reckons White didn't kill himself.'

'What?' Jan leaned forward as Turpin began to flick through the pages, his brow furrowed.

'You can take that and read it at your leisure, but the short version is that she found marks on White's neck that suggest to her that he was strangled first, then strung up to make it look like he hanged himself. She's included some photographs on page five, so you can see what she means.'

'Jesus,' said Turpin. 'Anything from the forensics team to support this?'

'We're still waiting on the handwriting analysis,' said Kennedy, 'and, according to Jasper, it'll be a few days yet before the specialist laboratory finish processing all the samples taken from the property. I take it the cottage isn't the cleanest residence…'

'It's a pigsty,' said Jan. 'They'll have a hell of a job.'

'Why use the bridle to hang him with?' said Turpin, passing the report back to the DI. 'Do you think the killer was sending a message to someone by using that?'

Jan frowned. 'Like Jessica being left to die on the gallops, you mean?'

'Yes.'

'Who's the message for?' said Kennedy. 'MacKenzie Adams?'

'Or Will Brennan,' said Turpin.

'Maybe.' The DI stood, and ushered them out to the incident room before walking across to the whiteboard.

He stood for a moment, his eyes roaming the vast quantities of information that had been collated, and then called across to where Caroline and Alex sat. He waited until they joined them, and then tapped the first of the photographs stuck to the board.

'I want Gillian's findings kept from the media and public,' he said. 'At present, and as time passes, our killer is going to assume he's got away with it, and that his ruse to shift the blame for Jessica's death to White has worked. In the meantime – Alex, I want you and Caroline to start making some careful enquiries into these large sums of money that White was withdrawing from the ATM. Work with Jasper's lot to find any evidence of gambling – betting slips, online gambling accounts, the lot. We know he was using one website, so see what else you can turn up. What about Jessica's movements after leaving the pub on Monday night, Jan – anything from Noah and Sonia Collins?'

'Sonia said she wasn't aware of Jessica loitering around the pub after she left. She reckoned if she was waiting for someone, she would've waited inside, in the warm. And she confirmed she didn't hear any car engines outside, either.'

'Maybe she did meet up with Nigel, then,' said Caroline.

'Except we can't ask him, 'cause he's dead,' said Alex. 'So, we're still in the dark about where Jessica was for at least half an hour prior to that streetlight being knocked out.'

Kennedy moved to the photograph of Jessica. 'Jan, Mark – it's late in the day, so get yourself over to her parents' house first thing tomorrow. Find out if Jessica ever mentioned Nigel White to them, and in what context. Did he ever threaten her? We know now that he could be aggressive after what he said to Bethany, but we need to find out what connects the three of them. Ask them again if Jessica mentioned anything that was worrying her since she started working at MacKenzie Adams' yard.'

Kennedy picked up a red marker pen, contemplated the whiteboard for a moment and then found a clear space in the top right-hand corner.

'Right – suspects. Will Brennan. Gets cold feet about the engagement, and kills his girlfriend. Finds out White threatened her, and kills him. Probability?'

'Low,' said Turpin. 'The two motives don't tie in – if the deaths occurred the other way around, then maybe, but not like this. And if Brennan was out exercising the horses when White went back to the cottage on Wednesday afternoon, he didn't have time to go there and kill him.'

'All right. Bethany Myers. Pissed off that her ex-boyfriend is getting engaged to someone else, and clobbers Jessica. She takes umbrage at being beaten up by White, and kills him.'

'If she had the means to convince Jessica to go to the gallops that night, then possibly,' said Jan. 'But White? No – she's a slip of a girl. She'd never overpower him. There's no way she'd have been able to strangle him and then hoist him up to simulate a hanging. She's not strong enough.'

'Unless she had help,' said Turpin.

Kennedy added a note, and then glanced over his shoulder at them. 'Who else?'

'What about Morgan Drake?' said Caroline, then shrugged as they turned to look at her. 'It's just a thought.'

'Let's have it, then,' said the DI.

'The CCTV footage from the petrol station showing

Drake hovering to speak to Jessica and acting all furtive.'

'What do we know about him?' said Kennedy, writing Caroline's suggestion on the board.

'He gives the impression of being landed gentry – big house, impressive outbuildings, obligatory horses in the paddock,' said Jan, checking her notes. 'But he continues to work in the finance industry – he said he invests wisely, which might explain how he came to own the pub as well.'

'And, because Noah and Sonia Collins run the Farriers Arms on a day-to-day basis for him, it's their names on the licence above the door, not his,' said Turpin.

'True. Okay, well, perhaps he has more to hide from us than just the fact that Noah and Sonia Collins run the Farriers Arms on his behalf,' said Kennedy. 'Look into what you can about his finances, and then we'll make a decision with regard to how we proceed.'

'Will do, guv.'

'Right.' The DI re-capped the pen. 'Let's see what you lot manage to come up with over the next twenty-four hours.'

Jan moved back to her desk, sifted through a dozen post-it notes that had been stuck over her computer screen and keyboard, and then dropped into her chair with a loud sigh.

'Penny for your thoughts,' said Turpin, peering over his screen at her.

She shrugged. 'I was just going through in my head what I might say to Trevor and Wendy Marley tomorrow morning. They're going to be expecting some answers by now, aren't they?'

'I'm sure they'll appreciate us taking the time to give them an update, whatever we tell them. At least we can show them we're still working to find out who killed their daughter.' Turpin glanced up as an administrative assistant passed beside them and lowered his voice. 'Kennedy was right about the media, though – and I think we should tread carefully with what we tell the Marleys about White. I'm not sure now is the right time to tell them he might have been murdered as well.'

Jan's shoulders sagged. 'I know. I just felt really shitty turning up and lying to them. It's as if we're adding to their grief when they find out the truth, isn't it? It's not as if we even have something positive to tell them. We've got nothing.'

'It wouldn't serve any purpose telling them the truth about White now. It'd only take one reporter to ask if they had any information concerning the case under the pretence of telling them it'll help.' He screwed up two notes that had been left for him and pitched them into the wastepaper basket beside the desk. 'You'll be fine tomorrow, Jan. You're good at what you do, and this isn't an easy one.'

'I suppose you're right.' She frowned. 'I can't work out the connection between the two of them, though.'

'Well, I think you're right about Bethany not being able to do that on her own. If she's the one, then she needed help.'

'Especially as she doesn't have a full driving licence. I checked with the DVLA before we left the station – she's only got a licence for the moped, and I can't see her getting Jessica on the back of that, can you?'

'Not really. Even if Jessica went willingly, how the hell would Bethany have ridden it to the middle of the gallops and then attacked her?'

'And you don't think Will is responsible?'

'I don't. I mean, it's sheer bad luck he found both of them, but…' Turpin sighed. 'No. I don't think it's him.'

'Has to be Drake, then,' said Jan.

'Motive?'

His colleague shrugged. 'I'm not sure, yet. Jealousy, perhaps?'

'I could understand that about Jessica, but why White?'

'Maybe Drake heard White saying something bad about Jessica after she died, and took umbrage. There's got to be a connection between Drake and White, hasn't there?'

Turpin raked his hand through his hair. 'You know, we haven't once considered the fact that Jessica might not have been the nice person everyone has described. She might have done something to provoke her killer, not expecting her actions to have such terrible consequences.'

'Well, it makes you wonder why she started working at Adams' yard four weeks ago now, and why Drake felt compelled to try to speak to her while she was working at the petrol station.'

'Don't you believe what he told us about offering her a better job?'

'I'm not sure what to believe right now.'

CHAPTER FORTY-SIX

Jan peered through the rain-soaked windscreen at the Marleys' home, and shivered.

Despite Turpin's assurances the previous evening that a milder day was forecast, she had pulled on a thick sweater over her blouse before leaving the house that morning, and her breath fogged in front of her face when she removed the key from the ignition and left the warmth of the car.

She fell into step beside her colleague, thankful that he kept a golfing umbrella on the back seat as they hurried across the road.

Bouquets of flowers were placed alongside the open gate, and while Jan glanced at the cards that fluttered from string tied around the wooden front fence, she saw a smattering of messages from well-wishers further afield than the local Oxfordshire area.

Jessica's death had struck a nerve.

The garden bore the evidence of a grieving family – the lawn was unkempt and windblown leaves fluttered at the base of the wall under the front window.

Jan reached the front step and closed her eyes for a moment, then rang the bell.

Wendy Marley opened the door a few moments later, her face devoid of make-up and an exhausted look in her eyes. 'Have you caught him? The man who killed my daughter?'

'Mrs Marley, could we come in, please?' said Jan. 'We'd like to ask a few more questions.'

The woman's face fell, and she stepped aside. 'That's a no, then.'

'We're doing everything we can,' said Turpin.

Wendy Marley didn't answer, and instead led the way through to the living room after shutting the front door. She gestured to the armchairs that Jan and Turpin had sat in over a week ago, and then called to the dog that was whining from its position on a bed under the window and lifted it onto her lap.

'Is your husband in?' said Jan.

'No – he had to go into town.' Wendy tugged a tissue from the pocket of her trousers, and dabbed at her eyes. 'The coroner released Jessica's body yesterday, so Trevor's gone to get a death certificate. The registry office is only open until twelve today.'

Jan waited a few moments while the teenager's mother composed herself, and then caught Turpin's eye.

He nodded.

'Wendy, we wondered if we might take a look at Jessica's bedroom?'

'Why? There were some police officers here last week doing that.'

'There have been some developments in our investigation, and we'd like to see it through fresh eyes, as it were.'

'Is this about the man who killed himself?'

Turpin leaned forward and rested his elbows on his knees. 'We don't know if the two deaths are connected at the moment, Mrs Marley. It is an angle of the investigation, but one we have to either corroborate or rule out.'

'What are you looking for?'

Jan side-stepped the question. 'Did Jessica enjoy her work at the Farriers Arms?'

'She loved it.' A faint smile crossed Wendy's lips. 'It's lively there, and of course it's where she met Will. Noah and Sonia trusted her – they were always telling me they couldn't cope without her…. Oh.'

The teenager's mother broke off as a tear rolled down her cheek, and Jan swallowed.

She hated traumatising the woman and asking her to talk about her daughter, but they desperately needed answers. Questioning a bereaved relative was essential, but required care.

She knew she would feel wrung out by the time they left the house.

'Did Jessica mention anything about a job offer from Morgan Drake?' she said.

Wendy sniffed, and shook her head. 'No, but it wouldn't surprise me if he did.'

'Why's that?'

'Well, with him owning the Farriers, I'm sure she'd have spoken to him at some point – it's the same with MacKenzie Adams. If Jess saw an opportunity to get some experience on her résumé that she thought might help her future prospects after college, she wasn't shy in asking about work.'

'What about her job at the racing stables?' she said. 'Had Jessica mentioned Nigel White to you?'

Wendy's gaze wandered to the window as she stroked the dog's ears. 'Maybe a couple of times, but only in those last three weeks when she was working one day a week up at MacKenzie Adams' yard. He was her supervisor, you see – once she got the job, she didn't have much to do with MacKenzie.'

'Did she tell you whether she was experiencing any issues with him about anything?'

'No, not really. She might've said something about him being a bit short with her.' Wendy sighed, and turned her attention to them both. 'I'm sorry. I'm not being a lot of help, am I?'

'Anything you tell us is a help,' said Jan. 'Do you know why he might have spoken to her in that way?'

'I think he saw her as a waste of time. She did say that he'd said to her that she should watch herself around Adams, and that if she had any problems, she should talk to him.' The woman sat upright. 'Did he kill her? Adams?'

'We're still working through a lot of information at this time,' said Turpin. 'And while I think of it, we have to ask that you and your husband don't talk to your friends or family about any of this, or the media if they approach you.'

'We're at a critical point in our enquiries,' said Jan, 'and any speculation at this time could be damaging.'

'I won't be talking to them – any of them,' said Wendy. 'I know what social media can be like. I used to warn Jessica to stay away from it. As for the press... No, don't worry – we won't be speaking to them.'

She moved the dog from her lap, and it ran across the room to its bed before lying down. 'Did you say you wanted to take a look at her bedroom?'

'Please, Mrs Marley. If you wouldn't mind.'

'Go up the stairs – it's towards the back of the house. Second door. It's shut.' Wendy closed her eyes. 'I can't bear to go in there yet.'

Jan rose from the armchair and pursed her lips at the

woman's grief. 'We won't be long, and we'll be very careful with her things.'

'Thank you.'

Two minutes later, she stood in the centre of Jessica's bedroom, her heart aching for the childless mother downstairs.

A faint scent of citrus perfume clung to the air, a blonde hair clutching at the seam of the pillow on the bed, and a clutter of textbooks and notebooks covered a desk in the corner that also served as the teenager's dressing table.

She wandered across to it, her eyes falling upon the photographs that had been placed in silver frames on each side of a mirror. In one, Jessica stood between her parents, arms around their shoulders, a huge grin on her face as they'd posed for the camera. The other photograph was of Jessica, Bethany Myers and two other girls outside the college grounds, all of them pulling faces for the camera.

While Turpin began to work his way through Jessica's bedside table and wardrobe, Jan busied herself with the contents of two drawers under the desk.

Wendy Marley was right – uniform had searched the teenager's bedroom last week, but with Nigel White's death and a new context to the investigation, it had to be done again.

She checked the bedroom door was shut, and then

glanced over her shoulder. 'Do you think Jessica was blackmailing someone, and Nigel found out?'

'It's a possibility, I suppose,' came Turpin's muffled voice as he peered into the wardrobe. 'Why, though?'

'Well, her mum and dad told us that she was planning to take a year out to travel. I mean, okay, she was working to save for it, but what if she found out something about someone and decided that was a quicker way to boost her funds?'

'I'm not ruling out anything at the moment, Jan.'

She mumbled an agreement under her breath, and then closed the drawer and dropped to her hands and knees, peering under the bed.

The sheets had been pulled away from the mattress by the police search team that had attended the family home the previous week, and the carpet under the bed only yielded a hair grip and a one pound coin.

She frowned, spotting a bulge in the lining of the divan near the foot of the bed and stretched out her hand.

Her fingers touched tape, the sort used by electricians, and she scratched at the edges with her nail. One end broke loose, then the other before a large flat object fell to the floor.

'Got you.'

She stretched further, got a better grip on the large hardback notebook and then pulled it towards her.

Rising to her feet, she began to flick through the heavy pages, and then blinked in wonder.

'Sarge?'

'Hmm?'

'Come over here.'

'What've you got?' said Turpin, wandering over.

'A sketchbook. Wendy and Trevor never said Jessica was an artist, did they?' She turned the page, running her eyes over the pencilled outlines of buildings, flowers, and sweeping landscapes. Here and there, the teenager had captured people in their day-to-day lives – a rough sketch of Noah Collins polishing glasses at the bar of the Farriers Arms as he gazed into space, students gathered in a break-out area outside the college, and strangers sitting at tables in a café.

'These are good,' said Turpin. 'I wonder why she wasn't studying art at college?'

'Maybe this was her way of relaxing, and she didn't want to turn it into something she had to do…' She broke off, frowned, and then emitted a gasp. She flipped back two pages, and pointed at the drawing. 'Look. This one of Noah, polishing the glasses. Look at the background.'

He took the sketchbook and held it closer to his face, frowning. 'What about it?'

'The clock on the wall. It says half past twelve, right?'

'Yes.' He glanced sideways. 'What about it?'

'She's drawn the wall calendar underneath it as well. When we were speaking to Noah the other day, I saw he has a habit of crossing out the days.'

'So she drew this on a Monday.'

'Exactly. But what if she drew it at half past *midnight*, not at lunchtime?'

'There are people at the bar.'

Jan smiled. 'Right, I know. They're all drawn in profile, too – so she was sat off to one side of them, out of sight perhaps, or they weren't taking any notice of her. Recognise him?'

'That's White.' Turpin lowered the sketchbook, frowning.

'We've been looking for some notes, a diary, anything that she might've written down to record what might've been bothering her – a reason for the college grades to slip recently,' said Jan, taking the drawings from him and holding it up. 'What if she *drew* what she saw instead? Who would think of looking for a sketchbook if she then made sure she never took it to the pub after this particular night?'

She flipped through the pages. 'I think she drew this five months ago, realised what she had, and then got into the habit of coming home from work every Monday night when these people were in the pub and drew what she could remember. Look, this one shows the calendar date two months later, but it's half eleven and she's shown someone talking to Noah at the bar. Whoever it is has got his face turned away from her though. This is daytime, I think – she's hinted at light coming through the window off to the right of the bar, see?'

'Noah looks angry.'

'He does, doesn't he? This next one, one month later. That's got to be White at the bar again, and this time she's showing the time as one o'clock. Noah looks tired.'

Turpin took back the sketchbook and paced the carpet.

Jan managed a smile, knowing he had caught up with the thoughts going around in her head. 'The pub is the key to all of this, isn't it?'

He held up the notebook to Jan. 'The fact she was keeping her sketchbook here in her room, and not in her bag, I think she knew she was in danger.'

'Yes. But she did it anyway.'

'The question is – why? What did she see going on there?'

CHAPTER FORTY-SEVEN

Jan walked through the door to the incident room an hour later, having telephoned Ewan Kennedy on the way back from the Marleys' home.

He hovered at the open door to his office as she shrugged off her coat and fished her notebook from her bag, along with the sketchbook retrieved from Jessica's bedroom.

Turpin wandered over to where the DI stood, the two men conversing in low voices for a moment, before Kennedy nodded and then raised his voice.

'Briefing, everyone.'

'Everything okay?' she said to Turpin as he pulled across a chair for her near the front of the room.

'Yes. Apparently Caroline and Alex have had some results, too. We're getting closer, Jan.'

They fell silent as Kennedy started the meeting.

'We have a lot to go through,' he said, 'so we're going to work through all the information you've been gathering as carefully as possible. If any of you hear something during this briefing that gives you cause for concern, or you want clarification, then speak up. Got that?'

A murmur of agreement filled the room, falling to silence after a few seconds.

Jan tensed as she waited, wondering if her colleagues' discoveries about Nigel White's finances would put paid to what she and Turpin had found.

Alex walked over to where Kennedy stood at the DI's signal, and cleared his throat.

'Just to clarify for anyone who didn't attend yesterday's briefing, we were tasked with finding out if White had an active gambling habit. We've established that he only has the one bank saved to his laptop – the one with the building society – and he appears to use that for the gambling site we're aware of, plus the day-to-day stuff. Most of that is covered by what he's been earning from MacKenzie Adams.' He paused. 'However, we've gone through the apps on his phone that Jasper's lot found in the cottage, and he does have a further account with an internet-only bank.'

'How was he funding it?' said Kennedy.

'Cash payments, paid into a post office in north Abingdon,' said Alex. 'They're not regular, but they're large. A couple of thousand at a time. And, we've managed to find a link to that account with two gambling apps on his phone.'

'What about call logs?' said Turpin.

'They'd all been cleared,' said Caroline. 'I've passed it on to digital forensics so they can try to access anything we can't see, but it could be weeks before we hear from them.'

A collective groan filled the room before Kennedy held up his hand. 'Have you managed to trace where the cash is coming from?'

Alex shoved his hands in his trouser pockets, his eyes downcast. 'Not yet.'

'Well, that's good work so far.' The DI pointed to two uniformed officers at the periphery of the gathered team. 'I want you both to assist Alex and Caroline in tracing where that cash came from, all right?'

'Guv.'

'Right, next – has anyone heard from Jasper's handwriting expert yet?'

Tom Wilcox raised his hand. 'He says he should have something for us by late Monday, guv.'

'Make sure he does. Mark – do you want to get up here and give us an update about your morning?'

Turpin picked up the glass of water beside him, took a gulp and then crossed the room to where Jan sat, and took the sketchbook from her with a wink.

'Okay, so we spoke to Wendy Marley, who said that Jessica had never mentioned to her any issues about being threatened or feeling frightened. She allowed us to search Jessica's room, and Jan found this.' He paused, pulled on some protective gloves and then pulled the sketchbook from its protective wrapping. He opened it up to the drawings they'd found, and then continued to talk as he circled the room, allowing each team member to peer at the teenager's work. 'Notice how in these drawings, Jessica has always captured the date and time. We think she must have done these when she got back from working at the Farriers Arms every Monday night. You can recognise Noah Collins and Nigel White, but I don't recognise anyone else – especially this tall bloke who's standing next to White in this one here.'

'We think that scene took place during the day,' said Jan. 'The timing is out of place compared with the others, but Jessica must have thought it was important enough to draw because of whoever that man is.'

'And perhaps Jessica's killer found out she was keeping a record of whatever is going on here in the pub, and decided to put an end to it,' said Turpin.

'Maybe this unidentified person in Jessica's drawings was the man who was paying White,' said Alex, as Turpin returned to the front of the room and shoved the sketchbook back into the protective bag.

'Get that into evidence, Mark,' said Kennedy. 'It's reasonable to assume, based on what you've all found, that White was working for someone else on the side. Our job now is to establish whether that person is responsible for White's death and faking his suicide note.'

'Guv, what if the killer didn't place the note on White's body?' said Jan.

A hushed silence filled the room, the change in tone almost deafening to her ears. A blush crept across her cheeks, but she maintained eye contact with Kennedy.

He blinked, and then gestured for her to join him at the front of the room.

'Speak up, so everyone at the back can hear you,' he said. 'Go on.'

'Well, we assumed at first that White wrote that note and tucked it into his back pocket before hanging himself,' she said, her voice gaining in confidence as she settled into her explanation. 'Now that's changed because we know from Gillian's report that somebody else strangled him, and Alex and Caroline have worked out that someone was paying White in cash for something. But what if the person who wrote the suicide note wasn't the same person who killed Nigel White? What if the killer didn't know anything about the note?'

Kennedy exhaled. 'So, White receives a note from someone who says, "I'm sorry, it's my fault she's dead", he pockets it, and then at some point opens the door to whoever killed him.'

'Exactly, guv. Maybe we're interpreting the message the wrong way.'

'Well if neither White nor his killer wrote the note, who did?' said Caroline.

'Guv?' said Turpin, his tone urgent. 'We need to formally interview Morgan Drake now and find out if he has any connection to White, and whether he knows what's going on in those drawings. He owns the Farriers Arms, after all. We can't put it off any longer. We know he tried to speak to Jessica at the petrol station, and we're not convinced it was about a job offer.'

'Maybe he's the killer,' said Alex. 'It's his pub, like you say. Maybe he wanted to keep whatever is going on in there a secret.'

Kennedy crossed his arms, and stared at the floor. When he spoke, his voice was a growl.

'Bring him in for questioning. And make sure he's got legal representation. He's going to need it.'

CHAPTER FORTY-EIGHT

Morgan Drake had elected to drive himself to the police station upon finding out he was required for formal questioning, his sleek sports car following a liveried patrol vehicle through the gates into the parking area at the rear of the Abingdon complex.

Two floors above, Jan let the plastic Venetian blinds snap back into place across the window. 'Did you see what he's wearing?'

'Jeans, and what looks like a very expensive tweed jacket over a white shirt.'

'I've seen that jacket before. Back in a minute.'

He waited, checking his watch, while his colleague rushed back to her desk. A familiar tightness clutched his chest, a sense that he was close, so close, to finding out what had happened to Jessica, and yet—

'Okay, I'm ready. Are you all right? You were miles away there.'

'Just going through what I want to ask him, wondering if there's anything we've missed,' he said.

'Well, I don't think you've got anything to worry about. Kennedy seems happy with the way you want to run the interview.' Jan jerked her thumb over her shoulder. 'We should head downstairs. His solicitor arrived fifteen minutes ago, so they'll be ready for us.'

Mark buttoned up his jacket as he followed her between the desks and out into the corridor. 'Who's representing him?'

'Bernard Peters.'

'Have you dealt with him before?'

She nodded, switching her phone to silent before leading the way downstairs. 'A while ago. A bit abrupt, but fair. There are worse.'

'Everything ready in the interview room?'

'Tom has set up a laptop with the footage we requested, plus I've brought Jessica's sketchbook in case we need it for reference. I think that's all we need, isn't it?'

'I hope so – it's all we've got.'

He didn't hear Jan's response over the squeaky hinges of the door at the bottom of the stairs, but it sounded noncommittal.

Mark didn't blame her – the whole investigation left him feeling like he was running blind, and he hated the fact they hadn't had a significant breakthrough since Jessica's body had been discovered.

They waited while the custody suite sergeant took a telephone call. Eventually, he ended it and then jerked his thumb over his shoulder.

'Room three,' he said. 'Drake and his solicitor were shown in ten minutes ago.'

'Thanks, Tom,' said Mark.

When he entered the room behind Jan, he found Drake sitting next to his solicitor, head bowed as he listened to murmured instructions from the man.

Both looked up as Mark shut the door and crossed to the table, and he noticed how the solicitor's jaw clenched before he dropped his gaze and pulled a fountain pen from his jacket pocket.

Once satisfied the recording equipment was working, Jan provided Drake with a formal caution and introduced the parties present, then asked the financier to confirm his full name and address.

'Morgan Owen Drake. The Paddocks, Hazelthorpe, Oxfordshire.'

'Thank you, Mr Drake,' said Mark. 'How long have you lived there?'

'Since 2017.'

'And where did you live before that?'

'Surrey.'

'For the record, could you tell us what you do for a living?'

'I'm a financial consultant, working for a large mergers and acquisitions firm in the City.'

'Do you have any other business interests or investments?'

Mark watched as the man settled back in his seat and dropped his hands into his lap.

'Yes. I own the Farriers Arms in Harton Wick, and I own another pub just outside Chelmsford. I also own three houses.'

'Where were you between the hours of nine-thirty Monday night and seven o'clock on the morning Jessica's body was found?' said Jan.

'I told you – I was at home with my wife and daughter. My mother-in-law and her latest husband were having dinner with us. After they left, we went to bed. I cooked breakfast for them the next morning,' said Drake. 'I've already provided a statement to that effect. You can ask my wife.'

'And she'll confirm those timings, will she?'

'Of course she will.'

Mark reached out and opened one of the manila folders beside Jan's elbow, thrusting a photograph across the table at Drake.

'Did you kill Nigel White?'

The solicitor recoiled at the sight of the dead man.

Mark had selected a photograph taken by Jasper's team before the body had been lowered to the ground, and Drake's face turned grey before he cleared his throat.

'I didn't. Of course I didn't.'

'It was meant to look like suicide, Mr Drake. Except it turns out that someone strangled Nigel first, then strung him up to make it look like he killed himself. You're a big man. I reckon you could've hefted him up there on your own without much trouble – or did you have help from someone?'

'It wasn't me!'

'Detective,' said the solicitor, straightening in his seat, 'unless you have some evidence to suggest my client was somehow involved in these deaths, you've provided nothing except speculative and spurious claims.'

'Speculative? All right then, perhaps your client can explain why he went to the petrol station to talk to Jessica, but then changed his mind?'

'I told you before – I wanted to talk to her about a job offer,' said Drake. 'I was passing by, and thought I'd mention it to her.'

'A bit bold, planning to talk to her about a new job in front of her colleagues,' said Jan. 'Why would you do that?'

Drake leaned back in his seat. 'I realised my error in judgement – that's why I left.'

'And did you speak to her about this job offer at all?' said Mark.

'No. I didn't get a chance, because someone killed her.'

'Why not just speak to her at the Farriers Arms if you wanted to offer her a job?' said Jan. 'After all, you knew she worked there.'

The financier gave a half-hearted shrug. 'I didn't know when I was going to be next in there.'

'It's only a few miles from your house,' said Mark.

Drake said nothing.

Jan reached under the manila folders and extracted an evidence bag, pulling on gloves before opening it and extracting Jessica's sketchbook. 'For the purposes of the recording, I'm showing Mr Drake the sketchbook found in Jessica Marley's bedroom.'

She flipped through the pages that had been flagged with scenes from the pub, pointing each one out to Drake and his solicitor.

'Notice the date and time in each of these,' she said. 'It's after last orders, and always on a Monday night. Noah is here, White appears at the bar here – who are the other men in the drawings, Mr Drake?'

He leaned forward and peered at the fine lines that swept the pages. 'I don't know. I've never seen them before.'

'Are you sure?'

'Yes.'

'The jacket you're wearing today, is that a favourite?'

'Pardon?'

Jan smiled. 'Your jacket, Mr Drake. You seem fond of wearing it.'

Mark held his breath as his colleague flipped through the sketchbook before pausing at the drawing Jessica had made during daylight hours of White and an unknown man at the bar.

She tapped her finger on the figure of the mysterious man. Jessica had drawn him wearing a jacket with the tell-tale pattern of a dark tweed, which he was wearing with jeans.

'This is you, isn't it, Mr Drake?'

He frowned. 'I don't think so.'

'Why were you talking to Nigel White three weeks before Jessica was murdered? Were you threatening him? Were you asking him to kill Jessica for you?'

Drake gave a slight shake of his head, and folded his hands on the table.

'What's going on, Morgan?' Mark softened his voice, the hairs on the back of his neck standing on end.

Jan pulled the sketchbook away, placing it back in the evidence bag and removing her gloves while Drake sat with his eyes downcast, his jaw working.

'You were the one who wrote the note that was found in White's pocket the night he was killed,' said Mark, unable to keep the adrenalin from surging through his body. 'Weren't you? "I'm sorry. It's my fault she's dead." What did you do, Morgan? Why is it your fault?'

Drake let out a shaking breath, then leaned back and stared at the pitted ceiling tiles for a moment. He blinked, and then met Mark's gaze.

'Because Jessica was trying to help me,' he said. 'They both were. And now, they're dead.'

CHAPTER FORTY-NINE

A silence descended on interview room three, the only sound an electronic hum from the recording equipment.

'I'd like a word with my client in private,' said Bernard Peters, recovering from Drake's statement and holding a hand up to silence the financier.

'It's okay. I want to tell them. I should've come to them in the first place.' Drake ran his hands over his face before dropping them into his lap with a sigh. 'What a bloody mess.'

'We're listening,' said Mark. Aware that the man could change his mind if left to mull over his thoughts too long, he wanted him to keep talking – now.

'It was why I wanted to offer Jessica a job working with me,' Drake said. 'I realised we were pushing our luck. White tried to get her a job at the yard, but Adams only offered her a few hours on a Saturday morning – it wasn't enough, not with her plans to travel once she'd finished her studies. She refused to give up her job at the pub.'

'Start at the beginning, Morgan,' said Jan. 'What's going on at the pub? Why did you want her to stop working there?'

Drake rubbed his hands together, hunched on his chair. 'I've had my suspicions about the way Noah and Sonia have been running the Farriers Arms for some time. It might be their name above the door, Detective West, but it's my reputation on the line if they're caught doing something they shouldn't be doing.'

'So, you thought you'd carry out your own investigation, is that it?'

The man nodded, and picked at a loose thread on his shirt cuff. 'Yes.'

'What were your suspicions?' said Jan.

'At first, I thought they might be siphoning off profit from the business – you know, a little bit here and there from the till, or something like that.' He choked out a laugh. 'God, I wish it had been.'

'When did you start investigating?'

'About six months ago, but I could only go there on the way home from work – it was obvious after a few weeks that nothing was going on. Jessica wandered over to where I was sitting one night, and asked if she could have a word in private, but away from the pub. I think she latched on that I was spending more time in the

Farriers than usual. We met the next day in town when she was between classes, and she asked outright what I was doing.' He sighed. 'I don't know, I just knew I could trust her, so I said I had some concerns about Noah and Sonia, and that's when she told me.'

'Told you what?' said Mark.

'About the illegal poker tournaments they run in the pub on Monday nights.'

'Poker?'

'Yes.'

'How much money are we talking about?'

'Thousands. Every week. And that's on top of what they're charging people to play.'

'How many players are there?' said Jan.

'About half a dozen. Noah keeps a tight operation – invite only.'

'And so you decided to take advantage of Jessica and put her in danger,' said Mark.

'No – that's not what happened at all. She offered to help me. She was scared – Noah and Sonia had told her they trusted her, and they knew she'd want the extra hours to pay for her trip, so they told her to work late on Mondays so she could run the bar while Noah played poker. She wanted to quit, but was worried what they'd do to her if she did.' His face crumpled. 'She knew too much.'

'How did Nigel White get involved?' said Jan.

'He did some odd jobs over at my house about four

months ago, rebuilding the fencing around the paddock, things like that. He mentioned in passing that he didn't want to cause trouble, but that he felt something had changed in the last year at the Farriers, and wanted to raise his concerns with me. The stable lads love the pub – they're always in there, and it used to be the case that there'd be an occasional lock-in. If they weren't racing the next day, most of them would stay.' He held up his hands. 'I know that's not legal, but—'

'Go on,' said Mark, waving away his explanation.

'When I told him I thought there was an illegal poker syndicate being run from there, he offered to help. He wasn't like the lads who ride out with the horses, you see – he didn't have to be up as early the next day, even though he did sometimes out of habit, so he could stay late. He said he just wanted the pub back to how it used to be. He said that Noah and Sonia were starting to alienate the locals and not making them feel welcome anymore. It was terrible for the business, and I realised if I didn't do something about it, they'd run the actual pub side of things into the ground. Nigel told me he'd played a bit of poker in his time, and I agreed to finance him.'

'How did he manage to convince Noah to let him into the syndicate?' said Mark.

'He and Jessica started a rumour in the pub that he'd inherited some money. Not as much as Dominic Millar, but enough that he wanted to have some fun and a bit of a splurge with it. Jessica made sure Noah was within earshot when they were discussing it, and made a big deal about the fact Nigel didn't want Adams to find out, because he still wanted to keep his job there. It only took a week before Noah approached him one Monday night – this was about two and a half months ago – and asked if he'd like to join the syndicate.'

'Did you provide him with the funds to take part?'

'Yes. He wouldn't have been able to play otherwise. Plus, he needed to learn how to play properly, so I funded that as well.'

'We found some online gaming sites on his laptop.'

'It was the safest way for him to learn,' said Drake. 'I needed him to be good enough to be invited to play the higher stakes' games at the Farriers Arms.'

'What went wrong?' said Jan.

'Oh, God.' Drake ran a hand over his head, and then leaned forward on his elbows. 'When we found out that Jessica had been killed, Nigel was inconsolable. He blamed himself for her death. He was convinced it was his fault that she'd overheard him talking with Collins about raising the stakes on the poker games to make them more lucrative, and that she didn't realise it was a ruse to gather more evidence. If Noah had offered higher stakes, I thought I could get a friend from the City to contact them and start taking names.' A sardonic smile twisted his mouth. 'White was allowed to play, but it was evident the other players only tolerated him. Wrong class, you see.'

'So, what happened when Jessica overheard White talking to Noah?'

The financier sniffed. 'She was only a few years older than my daughter.'

'What happened, Morgan?' said Mark, his patience snapping.

'Jessica confronted him outside the pub when he stepped out the back for a cigarette between games. He said they had a blazing row, but he eventually told her what he'd been doing. He managed to calm her down, and get her back into the pub. About ten minutes later, Noah announced he was closing down the game for the night. He said he'd received an anonymous tip-off that there was a police patrol in the area and he didn't want to risk an ad hoc visit. I think Nigel realised soon afterwards that it was all a ruse and that he and Jessica had been overheard – either by Noah, or by Sonia. He said he was planning on coming to see me Tuesday morning to tell me to come to the police, to tell you what was going on because it had gone too far.'

'So, White left the pub at what—'

'About twelve-fifteen, along with all the other players.'

'Where was Jessica at that time?'

'She offered to stay behind, to help clear up. No-one saw her again after that.'

'What about this note, then? The one that was found in Nigel's pocket?'

'I still owed him four hundred pounds from the poker tournament the previous week, and I wanted to talk to him, to tell him how sorry I was about Jess. When I got to the cottage on Wednesday afternoon, he wasn't there so I left a note with the cash in an envelope with his name on it and posted it through the letterbox. I wanted to let him know it was all my fault, that I should never have put them in such a dangerous position.'

'Morgan, are you accusing Noah and Sonia Collins of murdering both Jessica Marley and Nigel White?'

The financier leaned back in his seat and glanced at his solicitor, then back to Mark.

'Yes, detective. That's exactly what I'm doing.'

'Why didn't you raise your concerns with us before now? Such as when Jessica was killed? Before Nigel White was murdered?'

'I was scared,' said Drake, his voice shaking. 'I couldn't risk making an accusation without knowing I was right – I have a young daughter. What are the chances that they'd harm her if I'd come to you? You've seen what they're capable of doing.'

CHAPTER FIFTY

Kennedy turned his ballpoint pen between his fingers as Jan provided a précis of the interview with Morgan Drake, his face twisted in consternation.

When she had finished, he dropped the pen to his desk and eyed her, then Turpin before speaking.

'Does he have any idea how they've managed to get away with it for so long?'

'It's a closed group,' said Jan. 'Noah limits it to about six players, and he doesn't start the first match until close to midnight – if there are any locals who leave after last orders, it can take a while for them to drift away.'

'What about the players?'

'White told Drake that they stayed away until about fifteen minutes before the first game was due to start. Noah never let anyone turn up early and hang around, because otherwise the locals would expect a lock-in. Once White was invited to play, he had to hang around outside the back of the pub until Sonia gave him the all-clear.'

'Notwithstanding the late time-keeping, how certain is Drake that these poker games are illegal?'

'Each player is charged a participation fee of a couple hundred quid, and the stakes are higher than allowed under the 2005 Gambling Act,' said Jan. 'Drake said that Jessica reckoned there were some nights where people were taking home nearly twelve thousand pounds.'

'We checked after talking with him, and there's no record of Noah and Sonia Collins applying for a gaming licence from the council either,' said Turpin.

'If he wasn't smart enough to tell us in the beginning about his suspicions, why the bloody hell didn't he think of reporting it to the Gaming Commission?'

'He tried,' said Jan, 'but they're understaffed and don't have the resources to investigate every incident that's reported to them. He phoned up to give them an anonymous tip, but nothing happened. He says that's why he decided to gather enough evidence together to bring it to the police so he'd be taken seriously.'

'F—' Kennedy banged his fist on the desk, then shoved his chair backwards, making Jan jump in her seat. 'And now we have a dead teenager and another murder to deal with, all because he decided to play vigilante…'

'Guv, even if he did report it to us, what would have happened?' said Turpin. 'We would've sent uniform around there with the licensing authority to warn them, perhaps give them a fine. With the sort of money that we're led to believe has been changing hands, chances are they wouldn't have stopped. They'd have found somewhere else to set up.'

'Or simply carried on at the Farriers and changed their game schedule to one that wasn't routine,' said Jan. 'Given what we've learned from Drake, I don't think Noah and Sonia would have stopped. They're earning too much from it.'

'Which in turn gives them plenty of motive,' said Turpin.

Kennedy rubbed the back of his neck as he paced behind the desk. 'Do you think he's right? Do you think they're capable of killing two people to protect their sideline?'

Jan glanced at her colleague, then back to the DI. 'Yes, guv. I do. I think all along we've been thinking we're looking for one killer, when in fact we might have two.'

'And they have the means,' said Turpin. 'Drake has stated that White told him that Noah sent everyone home early that night – everyone except Jessica, because he thought they'd been overheard while arguing outside. Noah could've lulled Jessica into thinking they'd got away with it under the pretence of telling them he'd received an anonymous tip-off about a passing police patrol car, sent her home after clearing up as usual, and then followed her.'

'Why take her up to the gallops though?'

'The land belongs to Morgan Drake,' said Jan. 'Not only would it send him a message – if they suspected he was sniffing around – but it also served to make sure Nigel White kept his mouth shut in future. Perhaps they told the other players, too, in order to guarantee their silence.'

'Apart from Morgan Drake's statement, what evidence do we have to support these accusations?' said Kennedy. 'Was he able to identify anyone in those drawings?'

'No,' said Turpin.

'We have no other suspects, guv,' said Jan. 'And out of everything we've investigated these past two weeks, this is the closest we've come to understanding the motive behind the two murders.'

The DI drummed his fingers on the desk for a moment. 'All right. Based on what we've got to hand, I agree we need to bring in Noah and Sonia Collins for questioning. I don't want arrests made until we can corroborate what they have to say for themselves in relation to what Drake is accusing them of. For all we know, he could be our killer and he's deflecting the blame. Where is he at the moment?'

'On his way home, guv,' said Jan. 'We didn't have anything to charge him with…'

'Apart from stupidity—'

She shrugged. 'We've asked him to make himself available for further questioning, and told him to stay away from the Farriers Arms until we've concluded our enquiries.'

'Guv? Despite any misgivings we might have about his motive in telling us about Noah and Sonia Collins, he seemed genuinely concerned for his family, particularly his daughter,' said Turpin. 'Any chance we could have uniform keep an eye on the house? Perhaps as part of a local patrol or something so as not to draw attention to the fact he's under our watch?'

'Do you think Noah or his wife would try to harm them?' said Kennedy.

'If we don't get to them before they hear about him talking to us, then possibly. If he's telling the truth, then they've already killed two people to keep their scheme a secret. He's the only one who's made the connection between the two murders and the pub, and if he hadn't mentioned the illegal poker games, we might never have found out. On the other hand, if he is the killer, then we don't want him disappearing while we're talking to Noah and Sonia.'

'Okay, then do it first thing in the morning before

the pub opens. Have Alex speak to someone in the control room upstairs to coordinate the patrols, and flag his car details on the Automatic Number Plate Recognition system in case he does decide to run away. Who are you taking with you to pick up Noah and Sonia Collins?'

Jan pushed her chair back and straightened her jacket. 'The biggest two constables we can find, guv. Noah Collins is built like a rugby player.'

CHAPTER FIFTY-ONE

A fine mist clung to hedgerows and overhanging tree branches as Turpin guided the pool car along the narrow lane into Harton Wick.

Half past six, a countryside quietened by a darkness contemplating dawn, and only the sound of tyres on tarmac breaking the silence.

Metres ahead, brake lights flared when a second unmarked police vehicle approached the speed limit signs into the village, and Turpin changed gears as he followed suit.

Cold air seeped through the door seal beside Jan, and she reached forward to adjust the heat settings before shuffling in her seat, her jaw set.

On either side of the road leading to the Farriers Arms, she cast her eyes at the sleepy properties with closed curtains and an air of blissful ignorance of what had been taking place less than quarter of a mile away.

She turned her attention back to the road as Turpin braked, and blinked at the sight of a council-owned van and two men in high-visibility jackets in conversation on the verge.

'What are they doing?' she said.

In response, her colleague jerked his chin at the ladder one of the men had dragged from the back of the van, before manoeuvring around the vehicle. 'Fixing the broken streetlight by the look of it. They must've heard that forensics had finished.'

Jan swallowed, battening down the surge of sadness that rose in her chest.

Less than two weeks since Jessica's murder, and already the circumstances leading to her death were being erased as if it had never happened.

Turpin glanced across at her, braking as he followed the patrol car into the Farriers Arms car park and blocked in the old four-by-four owned by Noah Collins. 'Life goes on, Jan. You know that.'

'I know. It's just – well, if we hadn't brought Morgan Drake in for questioning, we might never have known why she died, would we?'

'But here we are.' He tugged the key from the ignition and opened his door. 'Let me and the others go in ahead, all right? Just in case.'

'Stab vest?'

'If you're happier wearing it, put it on.'

She reached behind his seat, and wrapped her fingers around the bulky armoured material, then stepped out of the car and lifted it over her head.

The two uniformed constables they'd hand-picked from those available on roster walked across to where she and Turpin stood, and the older one jerked his thumb over his shoulder at the pub.

'Is there a back door to the accommodation?' he said.

'There's a side door,' said Jan. She peered at the upstairs windows, but there was no movement; no twitch of curtains to suggest their early morning arrival had been noticed by the two occupants. 'It faces the car park along there. The back door leads into the kitchen.'

'All right. Well, we're ready when you are.'

'I'll wait by the front door in case anyone tries to come out that way,' she said. 'What about the kitchen exit?'

'We'll have to risk it,' said Turpin. 'We've blocked in their four-by-four, so they're not going to get far if they try to make a run for it.'

'Okay.'

'See you in a minute.' He waved over his shoulder as he walked away with the two constables.

Exhaling, Jan watched around the corner of the pub

as he hammered on the side door and announced their arrival.

The sound of movement in the room above her head caught her attention, and she looked up to see Sonia Collins peeking through a gap in the curtains at the vehicles below, her eyes wide.

'Got you,' Jan said under her breath.

The curtains fell back into place, and she heard raised voices before footsteps hammered across the centuries-old floorboards.

Moments later, the side door was jerked open, and Noah Collins' indignant voice carried to where she stood.

'What the bloody hell's going on? It's half past six in the morning.'

Turpin's calm voice followed, explaining to the publican that he was required to come to the police station for questioning, and then reciting the formal caution.

She didn't catch Noah's response, but the context was one of bewilderment followed by anger as the two constables led him to the waiting patrol car and drove away.

A second patrol car slewed into the car park before she could turn her attention back to the pub, the passenger climbing out and hurrying across to her while Sonia's indignant tones carried from the confines of the bar.

'Sorry for the delay, ma'am,' said the female police constable, raising an eyebrow as Sonia's voice reached a crescendo. 'We were stuck behind a string of racehorses, until Rick remembered a shortcut.'

Jan shook her head. 'No problem. You all right to take her in?'

'Will do. Have you already got the husband?'

'He was in the car that just left.'

They turned as Turpin appeared at the side door, his hand on Sonia Collins' arm.

The woman's expression was one of pure fury as he passed her over to the police constable.

'How did it go?'

He grinned and watched the second patrol car leave the car park. 'She was worse than him. Right, I've got the keys to the place, so I'll lock up and then we'll head back.'

'Wait.'

'What's wrong?'

'If Drake is lying – if Noah and Sonia aren't our killers – then we don't want to tip off the real killer, do we?' she said.

'Right… so—'

'We need the pub to open and trade as normal today,' she said.

'What have you got in mind?'

She held up her mobile phone. 'Let me make a

phone call. You head back and do the interviews – I'll hold the fort here.'

He frowned. 'Are you sure?'

'Yes.' She winked. 'Trust me.'

CHAPTER FIFTY-TWO

Noah Collins' mouth twisted into a sneer as Mark entered the interview room behind Alex, turned to his solicitor and murmured under his breath.

William Hawsey, a man in his early fifties with a sanguine complexion, turned to both detectives as they sat opposite. 'My client demands to know why he's been brought here. He has a business to run.'

'Hold your horses,' said Mark. 'We're not discussing anything until we've started properly.'

Alex recited the formal caution, and then sat back in his seat, pen poised over his notebook.

'For the purposes of the recording,' said Mark, 'we have Detective Sergeant Mark Turpin, Detective Constable Alex McClellan, Mr Noah Collins, and—'

'William Hawsey; Hawsey and Wainwright Solicitors.'

'Thank you.' He folded his hands. 'Mr Collins, perhaps you could start by confirming your place of work?'

Noah rolled his eyes, then sighed. 'I'm the licensee of the Farriers Arms pub in Harton Wick.'

'How long have you been there?'

'Since 2017.'

'And you run the Farriers Arms on behalf of its owner, Morgan Drake, is that correct?'

'Yes.'

'How often does Mr Drake visit the pub?'

Noah shrugged. 'Once or twice a month. Maybe less sometimes.'

'What do you discuss when he visits?'

'Ideas for marketing, any issues we might have – things like that.'

'Do you need his permission to change anything in the day-to-day running of the business?'

'No. He pays me to do that.'

'So, you're in charge of everything that goes on under that roof?'

Eyes narrowing, Noah raised his hands and picked at a ragged thumbnail while he eyed Mark. 'That's right.'

'Right.' Mark opened the folder on the table under his elbow and pulled out copies of Jessica's drawings. 'Ever seen these before?'

A vein began to pulse in Noah's neck. 'No.'

'Jessica Marley drew these. We found her

sketchbook at her mum and dad's. She was a very gifted artist – lots of landscape drawings, things like Waylands Smithy, Donnington Castle. You get the idea. Mind you, she only started drawing these particular ones four months ago. Look – you're in this one.'

Mark spun around the sketch and jabbed his forefinger at the figure behind the bar.

Noah's solicitor frowned, his ruddy cheeks darkening as he scrawled a frantic note to himself, and then glanced sideways at his client.

The publican remained silent, his jaw clenched.

'Now, I recognise you and I reckon this bloke here is Nigel White – but who's he talking to, Noah?'

'I've got no idea.'

'No? All right. What about the man in this sketch? I presume that's a woman he's talking to – we can't see her face, but you can tell from the hair, can't you?'

'I don't know.' Noah folded his arms, affecting a bored tone. 'Is there a point to this, Detective Turpin?'

'Funny you should ask.' Mark turned all of the pictures around to face Noah and his solicitor, then pointed at each in turn. 'Notice how every drawing Jessica made included the date and time. Now, I'm no expert, Mr Collins – after all, you're the licensee – but aren't you meant to stop serving by eleven o'clock at the Farriers Arms? It seems to me these people are drinking well after midnight. On a Monday, too, which is unusual in itself. Can you provide us with documentary evidence to support successful applications for a Temporary Event Notice for these dates under the Licensing Act 2003?'

'I'd have to check the filing cabinet in the office,' said Noah.

'Good to know.' Mark turned to his colleague. 'Alex, would you mind passing on that message to DC West and the search team at the Farriers Arms?'

The publican's face turned white at the sight of Alex shoving his chair back. 'Wait.'

Mark cocked an eyebrow at him.

Noah's solicitor rested a hand on his client's arm, then turned to the two detectives. 'What my client will state is that his wife, Sonia, is responsible for all paperwork for the premises. If there is any indication of oversight in relation to licences, then you'll need to speak to her.'

'Oh, don't worry – we will.' Mark waited until Alex retook his seat before focusing on the man in front of him once more. 'Was it her idea to kill Jessica, or yours?'

'Detective, that is preposterous,' said Hawsey, his face reddening further. 'Unless you have evidence to suggest—'

'Did you, Noah?' Mark leaned forward. 'Did you make her stay late that night on the pretence of clearing up after you stopped the poker match early? Did you do that because you heard her discussing the matches with Nigel White?'

'No comment.' Noah glared, rubbing a thumb over clasped hands that bobbed up and down on the table.

'What did you use to kill her with? That big hammer you keep in the cellar to knock taps and spiles into the barrels? Our forensic team are analysing that for traces of her blood, you know. What about one of those meat tenderisers that Sonia keeps in the kitchen? We've got those too, by the way.'

He could hear the publican's teeth grinding from where he sat, but still the man said nothing.

'She wasn't dead,' said Mark.

'What?'

Mark picked up each of Jessica's drawings in turn, placing them into the manila folder before slapping it shut. He pushed back his chair, and eyed the man before him.

'She wasn't dead, Noah. You hit her over the head, but it wasn't enough to kill her straight away. You could've taken her to the hospital, or phoned for help. Instead, you took her to the gallops and left her to die.'

CHAPTER FIFTY-THREE

Mark leaned against the wall of the corridor, exchanged files with Caroline, and read through the interview questions he'd devised with Kennedy's input that morning.

'How did it go, Sarge?' she said.

'He's not admitting to anything,' said Alex. He shoved his hands in his pockets and assumed a similar posture to Mark's as he waited for him to finish reading. 'And he's trying to blame his wife for the "oversight" with regard to the licensing for the games.'

Caroline wrinkled her nose. 'Doesn't matter who applied for it. They'd have never been granted one for the sort of money that was exchanging hands there. What did he have to say about killing Jessica and Nigel?'

'Not much,' said Mark. 'But I think we hit a nerve

when I told him Jessica was still breathing when he dumped her body on the gallops.'

'Do you think he meant to kill her?'

He slapped the folder shut and tapped it against his leg. 'I don't know. I'd have said maybe, but then he – or his wife – went on to kill Nigel and tried to make it look like a suicide. That doesn't convey remorse, does it? Are you ready, Alex?'

'Yes, Sarge.'

'Come on then. Let's see what Mrs Collins has to say for herself.'

Sonia Collins had chosen a solicitor from a firm in Banbury, a woman who peered over reading glasses as the two detectives sat, and handed over her card, introducing herself as Michelle Yates.

'Thank you, Ms Yates,' said Mark once the formal caution had been recited. Tucking the card under the folder, he drummed his fingers on the surface while eyeing her client.

'How long have you been married to Noah, Sonia?'

'Six years.'

'Happy?'

'Of course.'

'Business doing well?'

'Yes.'

'Right. So, at what point did you decide you needed some extra income and start up the illegal poker matches?'

Sonia blinked, green eyes boring into his with a ferocity he hadn't seen in her husband. 'I don't know what you're—'

'Enough of the bullshit, Sonia.' Mark pulled out the drawings from the folder, sifting through them until he found one from three months ago. He shoved it across the table so it landed between the two women. 'That's you, isn't it? Standing under the clock, talking to the man with his back to us. Who is he?'

'I don't know – we're always busy serving in the evenings. He could be anyone.'

'Look at the time, Sonia. Since when does the Farriers Arms serve food at one in the morning?'

Another blink.

'What are the names of the players? Who turned up for these events?'

She shrugged.

'Your husband said you're responsible for the licensing arrangements in the pub. Seems to me you like to take charge. Did you kill Jessica Marley as well?'

'No.'

'Who did? Who attacked her in the lane between the pub and her parents' house, and then took her body up to the gallops?'

'I don't know.'

Mark shrugged. 'We have a forensic team at the Farriers Arms at the moment—'

'Do you have a warrant?' said the solicitor. 'I don't believe my client has granted permission—'

'The last time I looked, your client wasn't the owner,' said Mark. 'Morgan Drake is giving us his full cooperation.'

Sonia snorted, and crossed her arms over her chest. 'He would, wouldn't he? Can't help sticking his nose in.'

'Care to elaborate?' said Mark, then smiled as she glared at him. 'All right – Nigel White. Why did you kill him?'

A tic began to twitch under her left eye.

'You lured him to his house, where you strangled him, then strung him up to make it look like he killed himself. Or was that Noah's work?'

Sonia turned and murmured to her solicitor.

The woman inclined her head for a moment, then raised her gaze to Mark. 'My client would like assurances that anything she tells you won't be repeated to her husband. She's afraid of him.'

Ignoring his heart rate ratcheting up, Mark took a deep breath before answering. 'We'll do our best, but we reserve the right to use any information you give us in order to form further questions for Noah Collins.'

'I TAKE it from the expression on your face that it's not going well?' Kennedy tossed his pen onto the desk, where it bounced off the surface and landed on his computer keyboard. 'Did you and Alex get anything useful from them?'

'Sonia has indicated she's scared of her husband.' Mark ran a hand over his head. 'I'm still inclined to think she's the one wearing the trousers in that relationship, though. When we put our questions to her, she looked bored for the most part. If she was innocent, I'd have expected more emotion from her.'

'Well, the forensics team arrived at the pub half an hour ago.' Kennedy paused to check his watch. 'It's an hour until opening time for the lunch session. What do you want to do?'

'Jan is there at the moment, and Bethany Myers agreed to come in and run the bar so we can keep up appearances with the locals. I'd like to see what the search team finds before we question Noah and Sonia Collins again – neither of them is going to admit to killing Jessica and Nigel if we don't find something to corroborate Morgan Drake's information. Jessica's sketches are nowhere near enough – the CPS won't touch it.'

Kennedy retrieved his pen and scrawled a note. 'I'll approve the additional time to hold them both today. You're right, though – we'll need something more before I can get a magistrate to agree to a further extension for questioning.'

Mark chewed his lip, then glanced down as his mobile phone vibrated.

He smiled as he read the text message from Jan and turned his attention back to Kennedy.

'Guv – just a thought, but it's quite apparent from what we've heard so far that the poker tournament went ahead last week. None of the participants appears to have baulked at the fact there have been two murders, which goes to show the sort of people we're dealing with.'

'Not to mention the sort of money involved.'

'Exactly. So, we might be able to take advantage of that, right?'

CHAPTER FIFTY-FOUR

Jan peered through the net curtains at the window of the flat above the Farriers Arms, her figure silhouetted by the pale light from a streetlamp in the lane beyond.

She turned away from the view and yawned, Turpin following suit before taking a sip from the can of energy drink he'd bought from the bar downstairs half an hour ago.

Bethany was managing the pub into the late hours after refusing to go home.

'I know this place as well as Noah and Sonia,' she'd said. 'You can't do this without me.'

Jan smiled at the memory. The teenager had been right, of course.

Bethany had arranged with Jan that if anyone turned up expecting food, she would tell them that Noah and

Sonia had been called away for a family emergency and were expected back later that evening.

To the regulars and drop-in customers who had come to the pub during the course of the day, it appeared that it was business as usual at the Farriers Arms.

It was a different matter upstairs.

While Bethany ran the downstairs operations, Jan had remained in the flat above, able to act as soon as Mark phoned her after concluding the interviews that morning.

The living quarters above the bar had been taken over by a team of uniformed officers and forensic investigators who had arrived mid-morning, ferried from their vehicles to the pub by minibus after parking at Morgan Drake's property so their presence remained unseen.

The lunchtime shift had been a quiet one for the teenager, with only one regular turning up – the man with the Jack Russell terrier – and a couple visiting family in the area who had wrinkled their noses at the prospect of no food, and left soon after.

With the pub closed as usual for three hours during the afternoon, Bethany stayed on and watched with growing shock as the team worked through each of the rooms and a steady collection of evidence in relation to the poker games was set aside as evidence.

Now, Jan could hear the murmur of voices through

the floorboards, the clink of glasses, and laughter joining in the general hubbub of a country pub winding down for the night.

A bell rang out for a second time, followed by Bethany's voice calling time on the day's trade.

'How long do you think it'll take her to empty the place?' said Turpin.

'She said there are only a couple of stragglers when I spoke to her a moment ago. One's a retired engineer who lives in the Hazelthorpe direction, and the other is an older bloke who lost his wife a few months ago. She said they tend to drink up and go as soon as the bell rings.'

On cue, she heard the front door to the pub close, and crossed to the window in time to see the two men stride across the car park to the lane, turn right, and disappear from view.

Adrenalin surged as she watched the lane for signs of activity and strained her ears for the sound of approaching vehicles.

'Best sit down, in case they arrive early,' said Turpin. He took another sip of the sugary drink.

'I don't know how you can drink that stuff. I've banned my boys from going near it.'

'Coffee wasn't working.'

'Your teeth will fall out.'

He grinned, and she choked out a laugh.

'God, I always turn into my mother when I'm worried.'

'I haven't met her, but yes – you do tend to mollycoddle when under pressure.'

'Mollycoddle? Which century were you born in?'

He winked in response, then reached out for the earpiece that snaked over his shoulder and picked up a radio from its position on the low table in front of him.

'That was Force Control,' he said. 'They've confirmed there are unmarked patrol cars either side of village, which will move into place and form roadblocks once all players have arrived.'

'Okay. Hang on.' Jan left the room and walked to the top of the stairs. 'How're you doing down there, Bethany?'

'I'm all right. Don't worry. I've switched off most of the lights – I figured Noah would do the same so the place looks closed. I've locked the front door, too. Anyone coming here this time of night would probably use the side entrance.'

'Good idea.'

'First car is here.' Turpin's voice carried from his position at the window, and she hurried back to a room in darkness.

She swore as her leg caught the edge of the table, and then joined him by the window after checking the time.

'Eleven forty-five. He's keen.'

'Business as usual, then.'

'Lucky for us. Do you recognise the driver?'

'No. Not enough lighting out there for a start.'

They fell silent, and she listened while the figure drew closer and the sound of a man coughing floated up to where they stood.

Bethany's hunch proved correct – the figure disappeared around to the side of the pub, and moments later Jan heard the door open.

'Evening,' said Bethany, a forced cheer to her voice.

Turpin swore under his breath as the response was lost to them.

'They've been out all day – a family emergency or something,' said Bethany. 'Noah phoned to ask me to stay on. They're only twenty minutes or so away, and he didn't want to cancel.'

The till drawer pinged open, coins rattled, and then a chair scraped across the parquet flooring.

'First player's settled in, then,' said Jan.

'Good. If he hasn't suspected anything, his presence will serve to convince the others to hang around.' He turned at the sound of a car engine, followed by a second vehicle. 'Here we go.'

One by one, they watched as vehicles pulled in and drove as far back in the car park as they could before the drivers made their way to the side door of the pub. Murmured greetings were made as each player joined the others in the bar, and the sound of conversation grew louder.

'All right. Let's get uniform to block off the road, and then we'll make the arrests,' said Turpin. He picked up the radio, relayed his instructions, and then signed off and strode to the door.

'Sarge – wait.' Jan spun around, her heart racing. 'We've only got five cars. Five players. Morgan Drake said that both Jessica and Nigel told him there were usually half a dozen players. We're missing someone.'

He paused, his hand on the doorframe. 'Shit, you're right.'

Jan crossed the room, snatched the radio from him and murmured into the microphone. 'Cancel that last command. Maintain your positions. Repeat, maintain your positions. One player hasn't arrived yet. We're missing a car.'

She handed back the radio, and exhaled. 'Christ, that was close.'

'Good call, Jan.'

In the glow from the light at the bottom of the stairs, she could see the colour had drained from her colleague's face.

'I might be wrong.'

'Even so, we'll give it ten minutes,' he said.

They didn't need that long.

Within two minutes, the engine noise from a sixth vehicle ebbed into the car park as its driver eased into a space beside an expensive-looking sports hatchback, switched off the headlights and opened the door.

Jan's sharp intake of breath was echoed by the grunt of surprise from her colleague.

'Shit,' said Turpin. 'That's Annie Hartman, isn't it? Jessica's manager at the supermarket.'

CHAPTER FIFTY-FIVE

'How the hell did we miss that?'

DI Kennedy paced in front of the whiteboard, his tone incredulous. 'How is she funding a gambling habit?'

'We've been onto the supermarket's head office as soon as they opened,' said Jan. 'It turns out they've had their own suspicions for a few months about funds going missing from the petrol station and store that Annie manages. An internal investigation was launched eight weeks ago, and the bloke I spoke to said they're concentrating on the cash transactions in particular. Most people use a debit card these days to pay, and they think Annie has been able to siphon off the cash because it would be harder to trace. As manager, she has the ability to override the stock records in the main database to adjust the balances, and she was in charge of ordering new stock – so no-one suspected anything.'

'What changed?' said Kennedy.

'The head office received an anonymous tip-off three months ago,' said Turpin. 'They might never have found out otherwise.'

'Any suggestions as to where this tip-off might have come from?'

'Might have been Jessica. We'll cover that in the interview.'

'Make sure you do. Speaking of which, get yourselves downstairs. You've got a busy morning ahead of you.'

Ten minutes later, Jan and Turpin entered interview room two.

Annie Hartman sat alongside a duty solicitor who had been appointed for her, and kept her gaze lowered to the pockmarked surface of the table while Jan began the recording and recited the formal caution.

The woman in front of her seemed broken, her body language unchanged since uniformed officers had swept into the Farriers Arms the night before and made the arrests.

Perhaps a night in one of the cells in the station's large custody suite had given her a taste of what her future held.

Turpin made the introductions, and turned his attention to Annie.

'How long have you been participating in illegal poker games, Ms Hartman?'

Annie wiped at a stray tear that streaked down her cheek. 'About five months.'

'How did you get involved?'

'I went to the Farriers Arms at Easter for a party. It was Jessica's idea – she was working that night because they needed extra staff to work, and she invited me and Isaac. He couldn't make it because his wife had bought tickets to a gig in Oxford, but I decided I'd go along. I don't get out much.'

'What happened?'

'It got late – I wasn't drinking. I had to drive back home and then open the store the next day. It must've been just before last orders when I overheard Noah Collins talking to someone about an event happening on Monday night. I was surprised – there were no posters up in the pub. Being at the party made me realise I'd been missing out. I was enjoying myself for the first time in ages. My husband left me two years ago, and I guess I became a recluse. I'd forgotten how much I relied on him to boost my confidence.'

Jan rested her pen against her notebook and raised an eyebrow, wondering if Annie was hoping for sympathy.

After a moment, the woman shrugged, then continued. 'Noah introduced me to the man, and said that it was a private party. That I probably couldn't afford it, and that's why he wasn't advertising it – he didn't want to make people feel bad if they couldn't join in. I told him I'd done all right out of the divorce, and that I'd had a good time that night so would he mind if I came along.'

'What did you do when you found out what the private party really was?' said Turpin.

A flash of excitement flittered across Annie's face. 'I thought it was great. When my husband was still around, we'd spent a couple of holidays in Las Vegas. I knew how to play poker, and Sonia said she thought it was good that they finally had a woman playing.'

'Did Sonia ever play?'

'No. She never joined in.'

'How much did you have to pay to play each time?'

'Two hundred and fifty pounds. But that included food and any drinks we wanted.' Annie straightened, her tone eager as if to justify the expense.

'Did you know your employee, Jessica Marley, would be there?'

'No, but it didn't matter. The first time I went, Noah made me sign a confidentiality agreement.'

Mark paused, and wrote in his notebook.

'So you went along to the first tournament,' said Jan. 'What happened next?'

'I had a good time,' said Annie, her chin jutting. 'A really good time. I won a bit, lost a bit – and it was exciting. They were serious players, just like some of the tournaments I'd watched in Las Vegas. Noah spoke to me afterwards and said that I'd have to keep quiet, and I agreed. I didn't have a problem with it – it was harmless. I asked him to let me know when he next organised a match, and he told me then that it was a weekly occurrence.' She dropped her gaze. 'I just didn't realise how addictive it would be.'

'So you started stealing from your employers,' said Turpin.

Annie widened, and then she cleared her throat. 'Yes.'

Jan managed to avoid rolling her eyes as the woman burst into tears, and Michelle Yates held up her hand.

'I'd like to give my client a moment before we continue the interview, please,' she said.

'Interview paused at nine thirty-three,' said Turpin, and jabbed his finger on the "stop" button.

CHAPTER FIFTY-SIX

When Mark walked into the interview room next door, it was obvious from the dark circles under Noah Collins' eyes that he hadn't got much rest in the cells since he was first interviewed on Sunday night.

Fingernails bitten to the quick, he scratched at the collar of his shirt and trousers that had been assigned to him by the custody suite sergeant, and shuffled on the plastic chair.

Beside him, William Hawsey rolled back his jacket sleeve, then wrote the time at the top of a new page of his legal pad and crossed his legs before giving Noah's forearm a light tap with the end of his pen.

The publican straightened, brushed the sides of his thinning hair with his hand, and attempted to look complacent.

Mark was buying none of it. 'Interview commenced

at nine forty-five. Present are Noah Collins, William Hawsey of Hawsey and Wainwright Solicitors, DS Mark Turpin and DC Jan West. Mr Collins – we currently have six people in custody, all of whom arrived at your pub after closing time last night wondering what had happened to their regular poker tournament. Do you have anything you'd like to tell us?'

'No.'

'Annie Hartman was the last person to turn up. We've just spoken with her, and she says you invited her to join in with the poker games after Easter this year. Were you aware of her financial situation?'

'None of my business.'

'Except that by inviting her to those games, you made it your business.'

Noah smiled. 'It's not my business if someone has a habit they can't afford.'

'Did you give any of the participants the option to stop?'

'Why should I? It's their money.'

'Annie is currently under investigation by her employers for embezzlement.'

To Mark's surprise, Noah slapped the table with his hand and barked with laughter.

'The stupid bitch,' he said. 'She told me she had money left over from her divorce. Life and soul of the party, she was.'

'Annie also told us that you made her sign a

confidentiality agreement and made threats to her about what would happen if she broke that agreement. Did Jessica have to sign the same document? Did you kill her after you overheard her talking to Nigel White about reporting the tournament to the police?'

'Is that what Annie told you?' Noah choked out a bitter laugh before shaking his head. 'She probably wishes that *was* what happened.'

Mark frowned, glanced at Jan – who wore a similar perplexed expression he was sure matched his own – and then rested his hands on the table. 'Well, what *did* happen to Jessica then?'

Noah glanced at his solicitor, who leaned forward.

'Anything my client tells you should be taken into consideration by you when contemplating his actions,' said Hawsey. 'He is a hard-working member of his local community, despite any mistakes or errors of judgement on his part.'

Mark ignored him, and glared at Noah. 'Get on with it.'

'First thing we heard about it was when Annie phoned the pub ten minutes after Jess left at twelve-thirty. In a right state, she was.' Noah gave a slight shake of his head.

'Why did you end the tournament early?'

'Because I overheard Jessica arguing with Nigel – he was telling her to keep her voice down, but I heard enough. She was going to report the poker tournaments to someone – I presume you lot – and I was worried we might get raided.'

'What did Annie want when she called?'

'What a fucking mess. I couldn't help her – I'd had a few drinks while the match was on, so Sonia had to go.'

'Go where?'

'Up the lane. I don't know whether Annie suspected Jessica was the reason I closed the game for the night or what, but when I called time on the night, she was winning. Handsomely, I reckon, by the look on her face when I wrapped things up at twelve-fifteen and kicked everyone out. They were still playing the first game, and I took a lot of flak for that.'

Mark bit back the surprised retort that attempted to pass his lips, and instead tried to keep up with Noah's revelation. 'Are you suggesting that Annie Hartman killed Jessica Marley?'

'Well, she tried to. That was the problem, see. She didn't hit her hard enough, despite using a bloody wheel jack. You've seen Annie – she's not a big woman, and I don't care how pissed off she was. She wasn't going to be able to lift Jessica into the back of her car on her own. She needed help.' He shrugged. 'So Sonia helped. She and Annie put Jess in the car, covered her up and dumped her.'

Fighting down the anger that surged through him,

Mark ignored the stunned expression on the solicitor's face at the turn of events. 'Why the gallops?'

'I don't know. Ask Sonia. When she came home later that night – early morning, I suppose – and she told me, I said to her it was a stupid idea. I think that's when she realised she'd made a mistake.'

'You mean helping Annie?'

'No – leaving Jessica in the middle of the bloody field.'

Stunned at the man's lack of remorse, Mark pressed on. 'Why did Nigel White tell Bethany to keep her nose out of it? He frightened her.'

Noah leaned his elbows on the table. 'Someone had to tell her to keep her mouth shut. If she hadn't thought she was going to get away with coming into the pub that night and asking questions about Jessica's death, she'd have been left alone. It was all Nigel's fault we were in this mess in the first place, and I thought he had a vested interest in protecting our poker syndicate, so I told him to have a word with her. Didn't expect him to lose his temper like he did, though. Turns out the guilt got too much for him.'

'Except Nigel didn't kill himself from remorse, did he?' Jan slipped a photograph from the folder and turned it to face Noah and his solicitor. 'This was taken at the post mortem. See the markings around his neck? That's caused by someone strangling Nigel. That person then hanged him to make it look as if it was suicide.'

Noah's jaw clenched.

'Why kill Nigel White?' said Mark.

Hawsey placed a hand on his client's arm, but Noah shook it off.

'It was pretty obvious by then that he wouldn't be able to keep quiet for much longer. He'd already been in the pub asking Sonia if we knew anything about Jessica's death. Maybe it was the guilt at being overheard arguing with her. It was both their fault, after all.'

'Did Sonia kill him, too?'

'Don't be daft. She wouldn't be able to lift him.'

'Did you kill Nigel White?'

Noah ground his teeth together, the sound grating with the ticking clock on the wall for a moment. Then he shrugged.

'He's got no family. He didn't have much of a life working for MacKenzie Adams.' Noah shrugged. 'No-one's going to miss him, are they?'

CHAPTER FIFTY-SEVEN

'How are you getting on with the others we picked up last night?' said Mark as he and Jan passed Caroline in the corridor outside the interview rooms.

'Singing like birds,' she said, and winked. 'One of the blokes we spoke to earlier is a retired judge, and has been most helpful in return for what he and his solicitor are calling an understanding with regard to privacy. Alex is doing the paperwork after the last interview with a…' she paused, checking her notes, '…here we go – a Mr Montague Stanley. Turns out he knows Morgan Drake through a mutual contact in the City, called in to the pub one night on the way back from dinner at the Drake residence and got talking to Noah. Next thing you know, he's back at the Farriers Arms every Monday night.'

'Have any of them given any indication as to an involvement with either of the murders?' said Mark.

'No – Alex had a chat with Kennedy an hour ago, and the DI reckons we've only got enough on them to charge them with participating in the illegal poker games – if that.' She wrinkled her nose. 'Are you two having better luck?'

'Oh, it's just one revelation after another,' said Jan. 'I can't wait to hear what Mrs Collins has to say for herself.'

With that, Mark opened the door into the interview room where Sonia and her solicitor sat.

The change in body language between the two women since last night was telling; Michelle Yates kept her gaze on her notebook, flicking through the pages, feigning busyness, whereas her client sat beside her with her arms across her chest, a defiant glare in her eyes as the two detectives sat down and began recording.

'Tell me about Annie Hartman,' said Mark.

'She works at the supermarket in town. Manages it, I think.'

'Would you say she knew Jessica Marley quite well, then?'

'I suppose so.' The glare remained.

'Did Annie ever give you any indication that she could be violent?'

'No.'

'Did you ever see her arguing with Jessica?'

'No.'

'And yet Annie Hartman waited up the lane from the Farriers Arms when your husband closed down the poker tournament early, decided to smash a streetlight because she knew the lane wouldn't be in darkness by the time Jessica walked past, and then killed her.'

'Did she?' Sonia's hands fell to her lap and she turned to Yates, her mouth open. 'Why would she do that?'

'More to the point, Mrs Collins, why would you then agree to help her to move Jessica Marley's body to the gallops?'

Sonia's eyes snapped back to his. 'I didn't.'

'We have a statement from your husband who says that after Annie hit Jessica with a wheel jack from the boot of her car, she realised she couldn't lift her body on her own. So, she phoned the pub and asked one of you to go and help her.' Mark paused. 'You went. Between you, you lifted Jessica into the back of Annie's car. Why didn't Annie drive her to the hospital?'

The familiar blankness clouded Sonia's eyes, and she held up her hands. 'What was the point? She was dead.'

'She wasn't dead, Sonia,' said Jan. 'She had a life-threatening head injury. Why didn't you tell Annie to drive her to the hospital?'

'Annie wasn't capable of driving,' said Sonia, sneering. 'She was bawling her eyes out, saying she didn't mean to kill her. I knew we had to move before any of the residents along that stretch of lane wondered why a car engine was idling outside their houses at that time of night, so I drove to the gallops.'

'Why there?'

'Why not? It was far enough away from the pub to avoid us being suspected, and it was on land that belonged to Morgan Drake. It's all his fault Jessica was poking her nose in anyway. Him and Nigel White. Wish I could've been there to see *his* face when he found out. Besides, all the stable lads fancied her. You all suspected that lot at MacKenzie Adams' yard, didn't you?'

'Is that why you tried to remove her underwear?' said Jan. 'To make it look like a sexual attack?'

'That was Annie's idea. She was huffing and puffing by the time we'd carried her that far and was worried our footprints might show up in the grass in the morning. She said if we did that, the police wouldn't look for a woman. She was right, wasn't she?'

Astounded by the woman's tone, Mark ran a hand over his jaw. 'Again, why didn't you take her to hospital? Why dump her on the gallops? She died out there, Sonia – from the head injury, from exposure. She didn't stand a chance. She might've lived if you'd acted differently.'

'Maybe, maybe not. She'd changed, though. Since Will came back down south. Used to look down her nose at me and Noah, like her job with us wasn't good enough anymore. Of course, he was talking about his racing career, and how he was going to become one of MacKenzie Adams' star jockeys and she reckoned she'd be hitting the high times with him.'

Sonia crossed her arms once more.

'Good bloody riddance, if you ask me. Annie did us all a favour.'

CHAPTER FIFTY-EIGHT

An exhausted investigation team sat in front of the whiteboard late that afternoon, a melancholy atmosphere settling on the detectives, uniformed officers and administrative staff who had worked together to hunt down Jessica Marley's killer.

Detective Inspector Ewan Kennedy handed a clipboard to Tracy, murmured some final instructions under his breath, and then turned to face them.

Mark perched on a desk off to one side of the chairs next to Jan and put his phone away as Kennedy's voice rang out.

'I'd like to begin by thanking each and every one of you for your tenacity and effort in bringing this investigation to a successful conclusion,' said the DI. 'I can confirm that we've heard back from the Crown

Prosecution Service and we will be bringing charges against Noah and Sonia Collins, Annie Hartman, and the five remaining players in the illegal poker tournaments held at the Farriers Arms.'

He wandered closer to the whiteboard and rapped his knuckles against a photograph of the country pub. 'An hour ago, Jasper Smith phoned from the car park to confirm that the wheel jack used by Annie to hit Jessica with was located in the boot of her vehicle. Some attempt had been made to wipe it clean, but traces of blood were found and have been collected for further analysis.'

'Why didn't she get rid of it?' said Wilcox, his voice incredulous.

'When we asked her, she said she was in shock, and then a couple of days after Jessica's body was found and she thought about the wheel jack, she worried that if she did get rid of it, she'd need another one for the car in case she broke down. She said she didn't want to raise suspicion by going into a car accessories store and buying a replacement,' said Mark, and nodded at the murmured comments that followed. 'I know. Callous.'

'What about Jessica's belongings?' said Tracy. 'Only her phone was found at the side of the road, wasn't it? What about her bag and everything else?'

'When the search team reached the pub garden, they discovered the remains of a fire that had been lit in one corner,' said Jan. 'Remnants of a leather handbag were found, together with an ornate metal clasp.'

'When I showed it to her parents,' said Wilcox, 'her mother confirmed it matched a bag Jessica had had.'

'And so far, neither Noah nor Sonia are taking responsibility for trying to burn the evidence,' said Jan.

Kennedy let the hubbub die down, and took a sip of his coffee before speaking again. 'We have had some news – MacKenzie Adams has contacted me to say he will pay for Nigel's funeral, given that the man had no family. And he tells me that Will Brennan has handed in his notice – he's going to race for Dominic Millar in the New Year.'

'I don't blame him,' said Mark. 'Not after the way Adams has treated him during all of this.'

Caroline let out a huge yawn, raising a laugh from her colleagues. 'Sorry, guv.'

'A timely reminder that you've all been working some long hours on this,' said the DI. 'And on that note, you're all dismissed. You can head home once you've finalised any reports that need to be on my desk.'

Mark eased himself to his feet as the noise in the incident room rose by several decibels, then wandered back to his desk.

His phoned chirped, and he pulled it out of his pocket, glanced at the screen, then at his watch.

'What's up, Sarge – late for another hot date?' Jan looked up at him from her computer screen, her pen twiddling between her fingers as she waited for the printer to churn out the paperwork requested by Kennedy and others. 'You've been checking that phone non-stop since we got back from the interview suite.'

He grinned. 'With my daughters – it's their parent/teacher night at school, and I don't want to get caught in traffic. Louise is meant to be choosing her exam subjects for the next two years, and she doesn't want to do that until she's heard what the teachers think.'

He lowered his gaze and typed in a reply to his ex-wife.

'Sarge?'

'Hmm?'

'If you need to go, then go.' Jan jerked her thumb over her shoulder towards the door. 'Go on – you heard Kennedy. Early finish.'

'What about the statements?'

'I've nearly finished. I'll be out of here in half an hour, max.'

'Are you sure?'

'Go.'

'Thanks.' He tugged his jacket off the back of his chair, and switched off his computer.

'You didn't say how Anna is doing at school,' said Jan. 'Everything all right with her?'

He winked. 'Apparently, she's already telling her

classmates she's going to be a detective like her dad when she grows up.'

'What does Debbie think of that?'

'I think she'll be having words.'

THE END

ABOUT THE AUTHOR

Rachel Amphlett is a USA Today bestselling author of crime fiction and spy thrillers, many of which have been translated worldwide.

Her novels are available in eBook, print, and audiobook formats from libraries and retailers as well as her website shop.

A keen traveller, Rachel has both Australian and British citizenship.

Find out more about Rachel's books at: www.rachelamphlett.com.

Made in the USA
Middletown, DE
01 October 2021

49478193R00234